The *Cagliostro* Chronicles III:
Into the Heart of Evil

By Ralph L. Angelo Jr

Dedication-This one is for all the fans of this series that have made it so popular. I hope you enjoy it.-Ralph

Contents

Chapter 1

The big, stocky man slowly backed out of the cavernous hangar, waving his hands over his shoulders, as if beckoning someone to follow.

"That's it, ease it out, slowly. Rothschild, watch the right wing section, you're a few degrees off of even and flat. That's it, you got it now."

Dan Sledge continued to back onto the big airfield at Johnson Aerospace, and following him out of the tremendous and specially built hangar was the star cruiser *Cagliostro*. Its white surface was spotless and gleaming once again. It reflected the bright desert sunlight almost like a mirror.

"She's magnificent, isn't she?" a new voice intruded from over Dan's left shoulder. The big Jovian didn't need to look to know who it was. He grinned his big lopsided grin and answered, "Always was, Boss. But after six months of refits and reconfigurations she may be better than ever."

Mark Johnson slapped his friend on the shoulder and smiled. "Most of those suggested refits and reconfigurations were your ideas, Danny. Good job."

Dan Sledge nodded at Johnson. "It was just some stuff that seemed to make sense, Mark. We trimmed some storage space we never used, added another hundred an' fifty bunks. So now we got a full complement o' security people with us at all times instead of just a handful. After everything we went through on Chakix securin' that place this'll be a welcome addition."

1

Mark nodded in agreement. "You're right, Danny. While it's not a battalion of troopers, an extra hundred and fifty trained warriors in a time of war can't be a hindrance."

"An' with Red personally overseein' the new additions I'd say we're in good hands."

"I'd have to agree with you, pal," Mark replied.

Both men stood side by side silently now as the big star cruiser was towed out by the short, squat and gleaming hover lifts.

Finally the ship was slowed to a halt and settled down on the tarmac runway, its landing gear extending as the hover lifts lowered it into place.

Seeing the two men standing shoulder to shoulder a bystander would be struck at how different they were. While Mark, at six foot two inches tall, was two inches taller than Dan Sledge, he was also several inches more compact. Dan's Jovian heritage meant he was many times stronger than a normal human and much more durable. His genetics were manipulated before his birth to allow him to withstand the crushing gravity and pressure of Jupiter's moons. His family, as well as many others, had been genetically enhanced for work on a colony there that had long since been abandoned. One of the benefits of this enhancement was Dan being able to lift and carry many tons as a normal man could carry his wash basket.

But there was more to Dan Sledge than just incredible strength. He was a genius level intellect and engineer in his own right, as well as serving as the *Cagliostro's* pilot.

Mark on the other hand was all human, but incredibly intelligent. He was athletic looking with medium length brown hair. His theories had resulted in the *Cagliostro* being able to punch its way through the light speed barrier and become mankind's first successful hyperwarp ship. He had a quick thinking; ultra-sharp mind that worked on problems subconsciously, allowing him to make many last minute saves. One of those had saved the entire earth two and a half years ago.

"Who's inside the *Cag*? Who just landed it?" Mark turned with a furrowed brow and asked Dan.

"Yer girlfriend, Boss." Dan replied with a wry grin.

"Wonderful. The next thing you know she'll want to fly the *Cagliostro* into combat."

"Ah Mark, you know it's good fer her to know her way around the entire ship, includin' landing and flight procedures. An' all she did here was put the landing gear down, an' ease the bird inta place."

"It's okay, Danny. Just let me know when you want to learn the comm. I think you should know how to work that as well." Mark laughed.

He turned and walked toward the boarding ramp that had slid out of the ship's underbelly. The *Cagliostro* was magnificent. She was a thousand feet long and six hundred feet wide. She stood two hundred and fifty feet tall from the bottom of the hull to the top. The shape of the great ship was not so loosely based on a manta or devil ray, only with three tails instead of one. One tail from each 'wing' and one from the center. Those 'tails' were actually rearward aiming solar cannons.

As big and as beautiful as the *Cagliostro* was, she was also deadly. The craft was dwarfed by all manner of ships on both sides of this war. But after two and a half years of interstellar conflict none of that mattered. The *Cagliostro* and its crew proved their worth time and again, defeating terrible foes and far larger ships in countless battles.

All thoughts and musings left Mark's mind as a vision of beauty descended the ramp and smiled when she saw him. Ariel O'Conner was more than just Mark's girlfriend and communications officer; she was a gifted telepath who had long ago stolen Mark Johnson's heart. Her long wavy blonde hair cascaded over her shoulders framing a face that super models were jealous of.

"Hey, honey," she purred. "The ship is looking good. I think we're almost ready to get back into the thick of it all."

Mark leaned forward, wrapping his arms around her neck. He kissed her warmly before replying, "With you at the helm, flying us into battle?" He smirked.

"Uh no, not by a long shot," she conceded with a grin. "But you have to admit, it doesn't hurt me being able to pilot the *Cagliostro*, just in case."

Mark kissed her again before replying with a big grin of his own, "You know I like the idea of everyone being able to perform as many jobs as possible on the *Cagliostro*, especially the command crew. I'm glad you're taking an interest in piloting it, but I still need my best comm officer around."

"Don't worry, hon, I'm not going anywhere," she said with a wink.

"I'm glad to hear it. I was getting worried that you'd be going over to the side of the Agalum."

"What? You think I'd let them steal your best secret weapon, me?" She smirked mischievously.

Mark began to answer when his watch beeped loudly. He tapped its surface and said, "Johnson here."

"Mark," replied the voice of Lilly Wallflower over his comm link, "you just received a message from President Scaleia. He wants to have a meeting with you as soon as possible."

"I'll get in touch with him immediately, Lilly, thank you." Mark turned toward Ariel. "I'm going back to my office here, want to join me? When the President of the United States calls you, you have to answer ASAP."

4

"Sure." She shrugged and fell in step with him. "What do you think Scaleia wants?"

"I have no idea, Ari. It's not time for our weekly briefing. That's still two days off. Something must be up."

"God, I hope not." Ariel continued, "Everything has been so quiet since we returned from Chakix. What a terrible world that was."

They immediately entered the office complex behind the hangar and manufacturing areas. The doors slid silently apart as they neared them.

"It was *more* than just terrible, Ariel. You almost died; hell I thought you *were* dead. That was one of the worst experiences of my life. For the first time since we met I had to face a life without you in it. I was not a happy person," Mark confided.

The two of them entered a maglovator and Mark activated the controls to bring them directly to his office.

She squeezed his arm. "I know, baby. I was terrified almost the entire time I was there. But you saved me. You pulled me through it all."

"Believe me, babe, it was not easy."

They both exited the maglovator and entered Mark's plush office at the top of his world headquarters building in the Arizona desert.

Ariel sat down in front of Mark's desk in one of three plush chairs. Then she swiveled the chair to face the monitor that slipped down out of the ceiling opposite the desk. Mark sat down behind his desk and worked some virtual holographic controls he had activated with the tap of a heat sensitive pad.

The monitor blinked to life brightly. Mark spoke aloud, saying simply, "President Scaleia."

The verbal command protocols immediately recognized Mark's voice and he was instantly connected to President Scaleia, whose visage filled the screen before them both.

"Hello, Mr. President. This is a little early for our weekly meeting. Is everything all right?"

"Hello, Mark, hello, Miss O'Connor. Mark, I hate to say it, but it looks like we have a situation," the president replied.

"Care to elaborate, sir?" Mark questioned.

"It looks like there is activity from the Agalum again."

"Okay that was to be expected, though they have been staying away from us since the activity at Chakix."

"Mark, we did not believe that was something they chose to do. You knew that."

"Yes I did, President Scaleia. We all had our suspicions as to why they suddenly dropped off the radar. But for whatever reason they did I'm glad they backed off. It gave me six months to come up with some more counter measures to their new weaponry that was on display on Chakix."

"Well, since you mentioned Chakix that brings us back to the reason I'm contacting you."

Both Mark and Ariel waited expectantly for Scaleia's announcement. After a moment he sighed and said, "Mark, an operative of the Agalum has come to Chakix waiving a white flag."

"What?" Mark stood and exclaimed in surprise.

"He appeared several days ago outside of the planet's orbital proximity broadcasting an S.O.S call asking for asylum from his own people."

Mark sat back down and clasped his hands atop his desk. He looked down at the mahogany surface and then back up at the President on his monitor.

"So what did they do?"

"Our people tractor beamed his small craft into orbit and landed him in a barren area of the planet where he immediately exited his craft and obeyed all our orders. Our men half expected the ship he landed in to blow up once he exited it, like a suicide bomber."

"But?" Mark asked.

"But nothing happened. He exited the ship, gave himself up, allowed himself to be poked and prodded as was his ship after it was ascertained that it was safe to board and investigate. He's answered all questions as honestly as our most advanced devices can ascertain."

"Well, what does he want?" Ariel asked, speaking for the first time since they had contacted Scaleia.

"Miss O'Connor, he's asking for help. *They* are asking for help."

Ralph L. Angelo Jr.

Chapter 2

"What?" exclaimed Mark in surprise, "Help against who or what?"

"It actually sounds like against those aliens you battled in the other dimension."

"The Tahir Ga'Warum?" Mark answered in surprise. "How can that be? We had thought it was possible they might have followed the *Cagliostro* back, but I ran tests myself after we returned and found it to be impossible for them to follow our trail with the limited knowledge they had of our unique propulsion system."

"Your magno-disc propulsion system you mean." Scaleia offered.

"Exactly, Mr. President."

"It doesn't matter the why or the how right now, Mark, just that it's a very good possibility that they have followed you back to our dimension somehow, and that they could possibly offer a threat larger than the Agalum themselves."

"I agree, President Scaleia. You have no idea what these things looked like up close, and the smell alone was enough to make you want to vomit."

"I have seen the holo-vids you supplied, Captain Johnson, so I am quite aware of what these creatures looked like, and to say the least it was…disconcerting."

Mark nodded grimly, then said, "So what do you want of us, Mr. President, or should I hazard a guess that you want us to return to Chakix and speak to this alien? By the way, is it a purple skinned salad head?"

The President shook his head from side to side negatively, "No, Mark, it's a yellow skinned leader class Agalum."

Mark stared dumbfounded at the president a moment, and then snapped his attention back into the conversation. "And he wants our help against The Tahir Ga'Warum. Well isn't that something special."

"It's more than that, Mark. He specifically requested to speak to you. While I don't trust this fellow at all I feel this may be our best opportunity to discover what is going on over on their side of the universe. We could get some huge tactical advantages at this point."

"President Scaleia, I have no problem meeting this alien face to face. In fact I relish the opportunity to discuss this war with him."

Scaleia nodded affirmatively with a grim smile. "I'm glad to hear it, Mark. I know we can all count on you for what lies ahead."

"That you can, Mr. President."

"Good luck, Mark. I look forward to hearing your report." The president smiled at Ariel O'Connor, nodded his head, and said simply, "Ariel."

The screen went dark before the logo of Johnson Aerospace filled it once again.

"So, another day, another secret mission," Ariel commented.

"That's the way it's been since this all started two and a half years ago, Ari."

"Oh I know. I'm just thinking aloud for once."

'Yes,' Mark thought, *'you usually like to do it like this.'*

'You know I never intrude on others thoughts unless specifically asked,' Ariel replied telepathically.

'I do hon. I also know how much a...problem that must be for you to keep your thoughts in check and not eavesdrop on others' private mental wanderings. C'mon, let's go.'

They got up and exited his office together.

'*So now what?*' Ariel asked.

'*Now we recall the team, and the crew. Not that anyone has gone too far. Most are right here on the Johnson Aero base.*

'*Is the Cagliostro ready for another mission? Are all the upgrades and repairs complete? I know it's been six months, but we had a rough time on Chakix.*'

'*We did, love, but no one had it rougher than you did. The ship is fully operational with many upgrades, including a third generation camouflage unit, even better than before. Sixth generation solar canons, fourth generation star core missiles. Fifth generation shield generators. All of that and an upgrade to the magno-disc engines that should keep our edge in regards to intergalactic flight speed. We're now faster than ever.*'

They entered a maglovator across from Mark's office. The doors slid closed behind them and a moment later they emerged on the ground level, still psychically chatting on Ariel's link.

'*You know Mark, here's something I never understood,*" Ariel said telepathically, "*How is it that our tech is as advanced as the Agalum's and in most cases, better than what they have? I mean we really are the new kids on the block here.*'

'*It's actually quite simple, Ari. They got fat and lazy in their superiority. I'm sure a hundred years ago they would have stepped on us like insects because they were so far advanced of us. But we as a race have come a long way in a very chronologically short period of time. Look at the early Twentieth Century compared to a hundred years later. A man displaced in time from say 1901 that reappeared in 2001 might think he was witnessing magic and wonder on a grand scale. Think about it, paved roads, and not cobblestone, vehicles that travelled on those roads that everyone owned at least one of. If this stranger looked skyward he'd probably have a heart attack as he saw great gleaming birds soaring overhead filled with passengers. He'd have no idea what a cell phone or a computer was.'*

'The same thought,' Mark continued, *'can be applied to our weaponry and hyperwarp capabilities. Don't forget I logged thousands of hours developing and testing the prototypes. None of this was overnight. But when I was finished with all of that top secret testing that seemed to take forever I knew what I had. I knew it would work. This was no shot in the dark. I designed and created this ship, and I knew what I was doing. I had a final vision, and it's sitting on that tarmac out there. Let's take another time traveler, but this time from the beginning of this century and move him forward to today. He'd be just as much in awe of things as his counterpart would have been a hundred years ago.'*

'The Agalum tried to keep us locked in our solar system and very well might have succeeded. But in the end they did not. They never advanced their weaponry for who knows how many years; they kept their ships the same for decades. They were sure no one would ever overtake them.'

The two of them exited the corporate headquarters building and hopped in one of many waiting hover cars lined up by the doors. They activated it and hovered into the air before turning and floating toward the *Cagliostro* in the distance.

"They miscalculated," Ariel commented.

"Yes, they did. They assumed their supposed superiority was beyond anyone else's reach. As it always is with our race, our world, give us a problem and enough time and we solve it."

"What are you two talking about?" a husky and familiar voice asked as the hover car set down near the shining space cruiser.

Ariel and Mark turned toward the sound and beheld James 'Red' Robinski walking toward them bare chested and soaked in sweat. A T-shirt was flung over his shoulder. He wore a pair of nylon shorts and sneakers.

"Did you just finish your morning run?" Mark inquired.

"No, considering it's after one now it's not morning anymore. Second run of the day actually," Red replied. "First one I did five miles. This one was ten." Red shrugged his powerfully built shoulders and then continued, "I was bored from being cooped up in here. There's not much for a security chief on a star Cruiser to do when we're grounded for half a year, beside give interviews and train new security staff. Ben Smith has the security job on the campus and doesn't need me looking over his shoulder."

"Well, Security Chief Robinski, that's about to change."

"What, we're going back up there?" Red jerked his thumb skyward for emphasis.

"Indeed we are, Red. It's time to start calling up the new security crew, as well as the rest of the staff, oh and one other thing, from now on your security people are going to be called 'Rangers', or 'Red's Rangers,' if you'd prefer."

Red smiled slightly and nodded. " Naahh, I'll pass on the 'Red's Rangers' thing. Just 'Rangers' will be fine, Boss. I'm off to take a shower. Then I'll start the call ups." Red ran off, directly toward the *Cagliostro* and up its boarding ramp.

"He's in a hurry," Ariel mused.

13

"He's been feeling like a trapped animal in a cage. He never liked that I wanted all of the ship's staff not to leave the campus this past half year, unless they had security with them."

"Well he *is* the security chief. You would think he'd understand," Ariel replied.

"Oh he understood, Ari. He was more than willing to follow that order, but he'd still have liked to be out there doing something. This top secret, top secured base and corporate campus is probably the safest place on the planet against the Agalum threat. But I need Red to be here to supervise our security measures. Not once did he complain, but I knew it was chewing him up inside not to get out of here for a while."

"Mark, he knows about the shape shifters as well as those other monsters the Agalum sent against us."

"Yes, indeed he does, Ari. Which is why he never complained."

"Are we going in?" Ari asked Mark.

"Yes I just wanted to take a look around before we entered the *Cagliostro*."

Mark surveyed the corporate campus from where he stood, and everything looked perfectly normal, for the first time in two years.

"And that's what bothers me the most," Mark muttered.

"What does?" Ariel questioned.

"Everything is normal. Here and everywhere else on Earth. We've been like this for half a year now. This is what worries me the most. We have a surprisingly short memory as a race. Things that happened a year ago, no matter how horrific are easily forgotten."

"Tine heals all wounds," Ariel replied softly.

"That's the theory at least."

"So why are you threatened by this?"

Mark shrugged, "I'm not threatened Ari, I'm staying frosty as they say in the old tele-vids."

"What are you talking about?" She grasped Mark's arm and slowed him to a halt.

His gaze met hers and he answered, "We tend to forget or marginalize things as time goes by. I'm trying to stop that from happening, at least to myself. No matter what happened to the Agalum, be it the Tahir Ga'Warum or a pack of marauding girl scouts, I'm not going to forget anytime soon what the Agalum put this world through."

"You're right," she agreed, "and this is probably the best time to remind ourselves what they are capable of."

"Yes, before we meet one of them face to face," Mark replied. "And believe me if the opportunity comes to let this Agalum yellow skin know what I think of his people's actions toward Earth, I won't hesitate in conveying my contempt."

Ariel looked at Mark for a minute, almost as if seeing him for the first time. Then she smiled wryly and began to enter the ship. Mark followed her in.

Ralph L. Angelo Jr.

Chapter 3

Eddie DiGenovese was in the armory aboard the *Cagliostro* going over the new ordinance that had taken up space on his weapons shelves. Eddie was the ship's weapons officer and resident marksman. Whether he was firing the ships precision solar cannons or a rifle, his aim was true.

Like the rest of the crew he was not wearing his familiar blue and silver tech suit. He was instead clothed in a pair of faded blue jeans and a 'KISS' concert T-Shirt from the previous summer commemorating the band's one hundred and eighteenth year touring. Sure it wasn't the same people in the band anymore, they were all long dead, but they still sounded exactly the same and were still exciting to watch.

As he worked, his watch on his left wrist began to glow steadily and beeped softly. He looked down and tapped its surface. "DiGenovese here."

"Are you almost finished, Eddie?" Lilly Wallflower questioned. "Mark and Ariel just came back aboard."

"Sure, Lilly. I'll be up in a few. I'm just packin' some stuff away and inventorying some other stuff."

"I'll tell Mark you're on your way," her rather pleasant sounding voice replied.

"Okay, Lilly, see you in a couple of minutes."

"There you go with the threats again," Lilly quipped before cutting off the communications array.

Eddie chuckled. He was beginning to like Miss Wallflower.

***

Fifteen minutes later…

17

In the command conference room the primary command crew consisting of Dan, Ariel, Red and Eddie, plus the leader of the secondary crew, former Space Navy Major Matt Marek, sat around the conference table awaiting Mark to address them all. He sat quietly at the head of the table and looked them all over a moment, his face composed. Everyone was dressed in casual clothes. Red was wearing a tank top t-shirt he had just changed into after showering proceeding his run.

"We have a mission, my friends. We're going back to the planet Chakix to talk to a new captive."

"Is this another Agalum?" Red leaned forward and asked. Mark nodded and then Red continued, "What level?"

"He's a yellow skin, a leader caste," Mark replied.

"What's so special about this guy?" Dan asked.

"He surrendered voluntarily. In fact he came to Chakix looking for us specifically," Mark answered.

""Well ain't that special," Eddie remarked.

"It is," Mark said. "He claims to have inside information. According to what the President knows, this Agalum is looking for aid against the Tahir Ga'Warum."

Eddie whistled. "Well isn't that a kick in the ass. Them wanting our help against the ugly bastards from the other dimension."

"It's more'n that squirt," Dan Sledge replied. "If these things followed us back here we may all be in trouble. Don't forget they were all as strong as me. This ain't good."

"You're right, Dan. This can't be understated how serious this is," Mark interjected. "We can't decide to ignore this. If the Tahir Ga'Warum are truly here, in our dimension, it could realistically mean the end of life as everyone here knows it."

"As tough as the Agalum are, I gotta tell ya, these Tahir Ga'Warum things send a shiver down my spine," Dan commented.

Red looked at Dan and nodded slowly. "Yeah, I understand that, even with your superhuman strength and durability those things were not only scary as hell looking, but they could give you a run for your money in the power department."

"It's more'n that, Red. Something about these things broadcasts fear. At least that's what it felt like to me."

Mark nodded his head pensively. "Dan, I hadn't considered that before. But it makes perfect sense when regarding the way we all felt aboard their ship."

"Yeah but even so we rescued our people and got out of there," Dan added.

"I know, Danny. Let's face facts; there aren't many people who are as brave and as rock solid stable as this crew."

"But Mark, if these things put that inherent fear into us when we went over there, imagine what they could do to normal every day Joes? There're a lot o' people in that galaxy, a lot o' civilians who have no idea what's goin' on." Dan said.

"Yes, Danny, there are a lot of people in that galaxy and I'm sure more than just a few of them have no idea what this war between us is all about, let alone how a new alien to them threat got there and what it's doing to them. Hell, we don't even know what the Tahir Ga'Warum were doing with our people in those suspended animation pods," Mark said.

"They looked like frozen sausages to me," Red commented grimly.

19

"I hope you're wrong about that, Robinski. I'd hate to think these aliens are here to use us as a food source," Ariel commented.

"Ari, I believe that's *exactly* what they are doing." Mark replied.

"We're not gonna know anything until we get back to that crazy planet Chakix. I know we secured the place an' we're usin' it as a base, but has anything else happened there since we left that we oughta know about?" Dan inquired.

Mark shrugged. "There's nothing else I can add that's not already in the security reports we all get. The base is completely under our control and the natives have pretty much stayed away from our people. They don't trust us."

"Or Chakix herself is telling them to stay away," Ariel added.

"Ari, we found her body. She was dead," Red advised.

"Yes, but remember how she jumped from body to body, and all we have is her word, which wasn't worth two beans that she was in her real body before she got gunned down by the Agalum. She possessed me." Ariel reminded them all.

"Well we ain't gonna find any answers here standin' around talkin'. Say the word, Boss." Dan announced.

Mark stood up and addressed the table. "You're right, Danny. All this debating is just wasting our time. Let's get back into the thick of things. Launch time is in twenty four hours. It's time to see the stars again and find out what new evils are lurking out there."

Chapter 4

The *Cagliostro* glistened in the hot Arizona sun. Then with a dull roar, its gleaming white hull rose up majestically and pointed its bow toward the heavens.

"All systems are operatin' at 100 percent efficiency," Dan announced.

"All shield generators are online and fully functional," Red added.

"Weapons array is hot and ready to spread some pain," Eddie proclaimed.

Dan nodded with a wry grin and then said, "Don't forget we're goin' to Chakix to talk to this Agalum an' not to fight the inhabitants o' the planet. In fact, the last I remember about them was that we were all buddy-buddy."

"We were, but if Chakix herself is still pulling strings as I believed at that time, then just by us returning there we'll all be placed deadly danger," Mark conceded.

"So we have to be prepared for any kind of trouble and not just from the Agalum, or the Tahir Ga'Warum but from the planet and people themselves who live upon Chakix," Red said.

Mark nodded. "That about sums it up, Red. This is going to be a fact finding mission first and foremost."

"With us steppin' into a fryin' pan of hot oil," Eddie grumbled dryly.

"Stow it, DiGenovese," Mark said. "We're needed, let's do it. It's time to see what the *Cagliostro*'s new improvements can do."

Mark pulled up his virtual control panel in front of his chair with a tap on the right armrest. He touched a few of the virtual controls and then turned toward Ariel. He nodded his head.

Ari nodded toward him in reply and said, "You're on."

Mark relaxed in his seat and began to speak. "This is Mark Johnson speaking. We are leaving Earth's atmosphere on our first mission in half a year. We'll be heading back to the planet Chakix to aid in the interrogation of an Agalum leader who has surrendered himself to authorities at the base we confiscated from the Agalum and currently occupy there. We will arrive within a day at Chakix. I'm depending on all of you to keep the *Cagliostro* running like a well-oiled machine and to continue in aiding in keeping us safe. That will be all, carry on. Mark Johnson, out."

"Wow that sounded almost official," Eddie said with a grin.

"Times have changed since we were this little unofficial corporate owned space ship," Mark replied.

"You mean the first five minutes out of Earth's atmosphere two and a half years ago?" Ariel offered.

"Well, yes there is that," Mark conceded.

"Mark, anyway you put it we ain't never gonna be more'n a group of friends an' your employees runnin' this ship," Dan said.

"Sometimes I think we have to be more, Danny. There *has* to be some sort of level of order and command I think."

"Mark," Ariel interjected, "we've come too far being a family aboard this ship. Not in the blood kind of way, but in the more than friends way. Now we may have 150 new crewmembers here, but this is the same fast and loose non-military ship it's always been. That's the way I think it should remain too. It works best that way. *We* work best that way."

Mark nodded in agreement. "You're right, Ariel. Maybe I'm just pushing too much because it's been six months since we've all been out here. Maybe I just have to get back into the groove of things again."

Dan swiveled his seat around to face Mark. "An' maybe it ain't such a bad thing to make this crew realize we do run a tight ship around here. This is serious business, Boss; it don't hurt none to remind this crew that this mission is no joke."

"Agreed, Danny," Mark replied. "But there is a fine line I have to straddle I suppose."

"Don't sweat it, Mark," Eddie answered. "We trust you and we got your back too. Where you lead, we'll follow."

Mark looked around the command deck and smiled. "Thank you, everyone. The vote of confidence helps. Now let's go see what this Agalum has to say."

***

Twenty two hours later the *Cagliostro* entered Chakix's orbit.

"Hello Chakix command; this is the star cruiser *Cagliostro* seeking permission to land," Ariel spoke into her communications array.

A moment late a male voice replied, "Hello *Cagliostro*. We've been expecting you. Glad to see you and in record time too. Please follow the navigation beacon to Chakix command."

"We know the way, Command. We've been here before," Ariel replied with a slight grin.

"Roger that, *Cagliostro*; come on down. Chakix command out."

Ariel disconnected her end of the conversation and turned toward Mark. "You heard the man. They are expecting us."

"Then let's not keep them waiting," Mark replied. "Danny, take us down."

Dan Sledge nodded his head and replied grimly, "You got it, Boss. Let's go say hello."

The *Cagliostro* banked away toward the planet's surface, heat reflecting brightly off of its rearward swept manta ray shaped wings.

"Here we go," Danny commented as the ship began to slow, piercing the cloud layer and peeking through to the planet's surface.

Below them great leather winged beasts reminiscent of pterodactyls flew through the sky majestically. On the world's surface herds of great sized creatures slowly walked in packs across grassy plains.

"We never saw much o' this last time," Dan said.

"I think we were too busy fighting for our lives," Eddie replied.

Dan looked at him and smirked, "Good point, squirt."

"No sign of our red skinned pals," Red Robinski offered, while scanning his holographic security display.

"According to the intel I've kept on top of they have been rather scarce the past few months," Mark replied.

"Could they blame us for killing Chakix?" Ariel wondered aloud.

"A definite possibility, Ari," Mark answered.

"Coming up on the base now, Mark," Red announced.

"How does it all look, Red?"

"Everything seems to be legit and in normal operating procedure, Mark."

Mark nodded solemnly. "Okay, good. We can't be too careful. Put us down on one of the landing pads they installed outside the hidden base. I want us to be able to get out of here at a moment's notice."

"You don't trust our own people, Mark?" Ariel asked incredulously.

"I'm just making sure that if this base was compromised by Agalum or even Tahir Ga'Warum forces that we can blast our way out, if we have to."

"Getting paranoid, Boss?" Eddie asked with a smirk.

"No, DiGenovese, I'm just not hedging my bets." Mark turned to Ariel. "Ari, get Matt Marek and his secondary command crew up here ASAP. Tell him to be ready for anything, including blasting his way out of here at a moment's notice." Mark swiveled in his seat toward Red. "Red, a ten man security detail will accompany us inside the fortress. Ten more will surround the *Cagliostro* while it's parked here."

"You really have a bad feeling about this, don't you?" Red asked.

"I'm just being cautious, but this is the first time in two and a half years that we've heard from the Agalum in any way but threats. I do not trust them. No matter what they are claiming I want to see proof. For all we know this base has been compromised already and we're walking into a trap."

"That's a little far-fetched, don't you think?" Dan asked.

"I'm just being cautious, Danny. Something's not right about any of this."

Mark swung around toward Ariel. "Ariel, using your telepathy, are you reading anything out of sorts with these people down below us on the landing platform? Or as deep as you can probe into the base?"

Ariel closed her eyes a moment and concentrated. Finally opening them a moment later, she said, "No, Mark, nothing at all. In fact a few of them are beginning to wonder why we haven't disembarked yet. But that's about it."

Mark nodded his head. "Okay, that's fine. Let's do this. Everyone takes a blaster. Red, you make sure your hand cannon is fully charged and I want half your crew to be carrying very conspicuous solar rifles. Let's go say hello."

Eddie looked at Red who looked to Dan, then the whole command crew stood and exited the command deck on the two maglovators.

A moment later they all walked down the landing ramp and were met by several base security people as well the base commander's second in command, a young Lieutenant who looked cautiously at the armed security force coming down the ramp at him.

"Ahem, I am Lieutenant Goslov. Greetings and welcome to Chakix." First the young man saluted Mark and then he extended his hand toward him. Mark took it in a firm grip and shook it purposefully.

"Hello, Lieutenant. I'm Mark Johnson. This is my command crew. Pilot and lead engineer Dan Sledge, my communications officer, Ariel O'Connor, my security chief, Red Robinski, and my gunner, Eddie DiGenovese."

The Lieutenant greeted them all and then turned his attentions back to Mark. "I must ask, Captain Johnson, why do you have a security detail accompanying you?"

"Because, Lieutenant, I've been to this world before and know it can be somewhat unpredictable. Plus the fact that we're dealing with a supposed Agalum traitor doesn't do anything but make me even more cautious."

The Lieutenant turned and began walking toward the cavernous maw of the landing deck built under the volcano where the former Agalum base was situated. Mark looked at his friends and fell instep beside the Lieutenant, the rest of the command crew following behind.

"Has this Agalum actually explained what he wants of me?" Mark asked Goslov.

The lieutenant stopped and turned to face Mark, and then shook his head negatively. "No, he has not I'm afraid, but he refuses to talk to anyone but you. We, of course, have scanned him for any weapons and found nothing."

"All right, Goslov. Let's go talk to the Agalum. Where's your base commander anyway? Why hasn't he met me himself?"

"Commander Wilson will be meeting us at the interrogation room. *She'll* be happy to answer any questions you may have at that time, as well as to allay any lingering doubts."

Mark replied, Very well Lieutenant Goslov, lead on."

The lieutenant turned sharply on his heel and continued into the sprawling secret base.

Dan looked about himself as they walked. "Looks pretty much the same as when we were last here," he said to Red.

"Yeah, I noticed the same thing, Dan. They didn't even give this place a fresh coat of paint," Red quietly replied.

"This way, gentlemen, and of course lady." Goslov bowed graciously to Ariel. They all entered a high speed lift that descended quickly to deep within the former volcano itself.

They all exited the lift and followed the lieutenant toward what was about to be revealed as the detention area. "The engineering of this base still amazes me," Mark commented to Dan, who shook his head in the affirmative.

The group entered the detention area and found a middle aged woman with long brown hair awaiting them.

She snapped a smart salute to Mark, which he immediately returned. Then she turned to Goslov and said, "Thank you, Lieutenant, that will be all for now." Goslov saluted Mark and nodded toward the rest of the command crew, and then left the room heading back toward the lifts.

Mark turned and faced the woman. "You are obviously Commander Wilson, correct?"

"I am, and you are the infamous, at least to the Agalum, Captain Johnson, also correct?" she asked.

"I am, Commander. Perhaps you can enlighten me a bit more on what this Agalum wants?"

She sighed heavily and then sat in a wire frame chair, one of many in the observation room they were in, and then continued, "Sit, all of you, don't be bashful. All I know is he claims to have inside information on some new threat to all of us. He was sent here by his superiors, that's all I know. He claims that he will only reveal the rest to you and you alone."

"Great," Mark grumbled. "Let's get this over with."

Wilson replied, "It will only take a few minutes to get him up and out of his cell and into the interrogation area. We'll have a room with a two way glass and another room adjoining it where the Agalum will be restrained and questioned."

"That works for me, Commander," Mark answered.

"I'll have him brought up now," she replied.

Mark continued to look around the room they all stood in admiring the technology needed to carve out an entire base like this in the first place.

A moment later Lieutenant Goslov returned and said, "This way sirs and lady, follow me, please."

The command crew looked to one another quickly and all fell in line behind Goslov as he led them to the interrogation area.

The room the command crew entered was stark grey with a one way mirror embedded in one wall. A dozen simple folding chairs were the only items within the room. The room the one way mirror gazed upon only contained a steel table and one chair on each side of the table, as well as a block on one side of the table with a pair of empty wrist shackles lying there. A few minutes later the yellow skinned, leader caste Agalum was brought into the interrogation room by Commander Wilson and two of her own security staff. The shackles were placed upon the aliens wrists.

Commander Wilson entered the room the command crew was seated in and said, "He's all yours, Captain. Be careful of him though. I don't trust these Aggies at all. Anything he says could and probably is just another trap."

"I know, Commander, but it's best I get this over with sooner rather than later."

Mark entered the holding cell and the Agalum's eyes immediately widened at his approach. The enemy alien stood and stared vehemently at Mark Johnson, and then he finally spoke.

"You, the orchestrator of our doom. Of all our dooms," the yellow skinned alien spat. "Do you know what you have unleashed upon us? Upon us all? Your meddling has doomed not only the Agalum but your own people as well."

Mark looked quizzically at the alien facing him and then after a moment he replied, "What are you talking about? Are you referring to the Tahir Ga'Warum?"

"The pale fleshed creatures, yes. You did this, Mark Johnson. If not for you they would not have come."

"Again, I'm not following you. You claim to want to speak to me, and yet here I am, and all I'm getting out of

29

you are senseless accusations. Make sense or we're out of here," Mark replied.

"You led them to our universe. You led them here. They came first with one ship and then with many. They invaded the Agalum realm. They were unstoppable, a plague of flying insects, as you would say in your filthy language."

Within the observation room Eddie leaned in toward Red and with half a grin said, "I think he means locusts."

Red looked at Eddie annoyedly. "I know what he means, Di Genovese."

Mark continued, "What happened to you and your people? And how is this at all remotely my fault?"

"You led them all here. Had you not gone to their universe, obviously as some offense against the Agalum, they would not have returned with you. You must have purposely brought them to our universe to destroy us. But now they will destroy you as well."

"If you lunatics hadn't waged a surreptitious war against the Earth and her people, none of this would have happened," Mark retorted. "You were infiltrating our world for over a century, causing death and destruction wherever you went, just to deter our space program. You are a race of madmen. As far as I'm concerned you've reaped what you've sown."

"You have destroyed the Agalum Empire in six of your months! Our fleet is devastated. Our soldiers all but nonexistent now. We are in our death throes as an intergalactic race. Are you impressed by what you have done to the magnificent Agalum people?" The alien stood and with a hate filled sneer upon his face he vehemently slammed both his balled fists into the steel table top.

Mark looked disbelievingly at the being before him and after a moment his rage exploded into words. "The 'magnificent Agalum people' are mass murderers and madmen who seek to control anything or anyone that they conceive of who could possibly be a threat to them. As far as I'm concerned you did this to yourselves with your over reaching control freak issues. While I have sympathy for the innocent people on your worlds that had nothing to do with your leaders' decisions, I won't be shedding a tear for the rest of you monsters who decided amongst yourselves to interfere in the fate of my world. If your kind had never attacked the Earth in the first place, or for that matter built this base here and then sought to capture or destroy my crew and me, we would not have had to find a way to escape this planet, which resulted in us being trapped in that other dimension. You did this, all of it. Your mad leaders and their xenophobic fears of other races. This is the result of everything you maniacs have done. You've acted as if all of space was one big chessboard for you to play on. You brought about your own doom yourselves."

The Agalum stared at Mark with wide eyes filled with disbelief. Then with a roar of rage he leaped at Mark, seeking to strangle him with his outstretched, yet bound and shackled hands.

Mark took a step back and then parried with his left hand, shoving the Agalum's hands aside. He crossed his right hand under his left and then chopped it down at the Agalum's neck, dropping him to the table's surface with one blow.

Red burst through the door and was between them instantly, grabbing the Agalum by the back of his shirt and hoisting him upward. He turned and slammed the stunned alien into the table top once again.

"Hold it Red," Mark ordered. "He's had enough."

"All right Mark, you're the boss." Red set the stunned alien down in his cold steel chair.

The creature began hacking and laughing intermittently.

Now the rest of the command crew followed Red into the interrogation room, staring daggers at their enemy.

"What's so funny, you freak?" Dan asked.

The Agalum looked at Dan Sledge and smiled before answering, "I am laughing because they will be coming for you next, human. Your world, your people. In six of your terran months they did what you could not do in over two years; they all but conquered the mighty star spanning Agalum race. They will sweep over your world and leave you all for dead."

"That's where you're mistaken," Mark countered. "We were never trying to conquer you. We couldn't have cared less about you and your iron fisted star spanning empire. Your people drove us into a battle where we fought to survive. Our goal was never your total destruction. We were taking a slower path with your empire. One that would have led to your defeat eventually. You would have lost against us, there's no doubt about that as far as I'm concerned. The Tahir Ga'Warum merely finished the job we began, and where we would have shown mercy, they were merciless. Now you're going to answer some questions. First what is your name?"

The yellow skinned alien with the all black eyes seethed momentarily and then replied slowly, "Stren. I am called Stren."

"Okay, Stren. Where did you get the new weaponry from?"

The wide eyed alien opened his surprised eyes even wider before he replied, "Wh-what are you..."

"Don't play games, Stren, you know what weaponry I'm talking about. Six months ago your newest ships, the ones we call 'Predators', that attacked us over Chakix contained weapons and advancements your people never possessed. Where did they come from?"

"I, we…" Stren hesitated before finally answering. He seemed to almost deflate before them all. He placed his head in his bright yellow hands and then slowly replied, "May the goddess Azussa protect me, we found the weaponry, or at least the designs for it all buried deeply within a cavern on a long forgotten world. Those designs were ancient before your race climbed out of the swamps they were conceived in,"

"You know, Stren, you're really not winning any brownie points talkin' like that," Eddie replied with a sarcastic grin.

"I…will try to contain myself, earthman."

"Good," Mark interjected. "Now back to the weapons. Where did they come from? More importantly, what was within those cave walls you mentioned? Were there more weapons designs you didn't get a chance to develop?"

"Countless designs, human." Stren sneered, "And they were not on a wall, but in long ago forgotten computers. Buried, perhaps, as an epitaph to a great race's military prowess and engineering genius."

"Stop trying to romanticize something your race lucked into," Mark spat, "You stole those designs and found them better than anything you had designed in centuries."

"You are correct; they were better than anything we had developed in years. Our fire for discovery was dimmed by complacency. Your people, barely barbarians compared to those of the glorious Agalum Empire, were holding us at bay. After the battle on this backwater world our greatest minds realized it was only a matter of time before your world would defeat us. Even with our new weapons we would eventually fall to you."

"Where are all those weapons plans now?" Mark asked.

"A world at the far end of our empire; far away from you earthmen."

"Do you have the coordinates to that world?" Mark pressed.

"Yes, I know where it is. Why, human? Why do you want to know this?"

"I want those designs. I want them out of your hands. Furthermore, there may be something we can use against the Tahir Ga'Warum amongst those weapons designs, something your people overlooked."

"Why not just design something yourself? It is what you are known and feared for throughout the known worlds. They say you; your mind is the greatest weapon of humanity."

Mark smiled at this. "I can't take all the credit. There are plenty of other brilliant people on my world. We've all been involved in coming up with strategies and weaponry to defeat your evil empire. Now, I need those coordinates to that world where we can find the library of designs."

"I will never give you that information freely. I came to you seeking aid against a mutual foe, but I will not betray my people. I will not give you that information willingly."

"You won't have to." Mark turned toward Ariel and said, "Ariel, he's all yours."

The blonde beauty pulled up a chair and sat down opposite the yellow skinned Agalum. She stared into his solid black eyes and reached out with her mind...

Chapter 5

The *Cagliostro* flew out of Chakix's atmosphere and disappeared into space, passing the great armada EPIC (Earth Protectorate Interstellar Command) had placed there as their outermost defensive position against the Agalum threat.

"So now we're goin' into Agalum territory as a buncha spies?" Dan asked for the seventh time since they left the base.

"Yes, Dan, we are. It's not like it's any different than anything we've done before," Mark replied testily as he rolled his eyes.

"It actually is, Mark." Ariel countered. "The last time we were on an Agalum world two and a half years ago it was an out of the way little world they were using to hold poor General Abruzzi. There just wasn't that much there, at least in terms of technology."

"Well, only if you discount the replica of the Blue Ridge Mountains and a base they had terraformed there," Eddie replied.

Ariel turned toward Eddie and gazed at him through slit eyes.

The ships gunner put his hands up defensively. "Whoa, Ari, don't shoot the messenger. I was just thinkin' aloud, that's all."

"All right, all of you stop it. I know we're all nervous- and deservedly so-we've never gone this far inside Agalum territory before. But we have a twofold mission to accomplish. One-we have to ascertain exactly if it is indeed the Tahir Ga'Warum who have invaded Agalum space, and two- we have to find those ancient weapons designs. If it's

35

something I can make use of, if the whole Earth can make use of them, it'll make our war efforts that much easier."

"Course is laid in accordin' to those coordinates that Ari got outta the yellow guy's mind. Let's hope they're right an' that we ain't dancin' right inta a trap," Dan Sledge offered.

"Agreed, Danny. Whenever you're ready, light up the engines."

"You got it, chief." Dan replied. He began to push a metal handle forward on his console, and instantly the ship leaped ahead, disappearing from normal space in a trail of sparkling energy.

"Hyperwarp achieved," Dan announced.

"What's our ETA to Agalum space?" Mark asked.

"Three days until we cross their border into known Agalum territory and another two until we reach that world Ariel supplied us with the coordinates to," Red advised.

Mark nodded in approval. "Good. Have the *Cagliostro* go camouflage a day before we reach their border, just in case anyone is following us."

"You got it, Boss," Red acknowledged.

"So now what?" Ariel asked.

"Now I'm going to call up Matt Marek and the secondary bridge crew while we rest and prepare for whatever is out there. The information you were able to glean from his mind, Ariel, is better than nothing at all."

"You're right, Mark, but I really didn't get that much from his alien brain. What I did get wasn't pretty."

"It doesn't matter. Any little bit of information is a heads up for us, and that's all we need."

The maglovator doors slid open on the right side of the command deck and Matt Marek entered, along with four other junior officers.

"Permission to take command, sir?" Marek asked.

36

"Stop with all the military protocol, Matt. Just take the chair and call me if you need me. I'll be in the command crew ready room with the rest of the primary crew going over what we're going to face. We'll be holo-recording everything for your people to watch next shift."

"Understood, Mark." Matt replied.

Mark stood and Matt Marek slid easily into his chair. An air of confidence exuded from the junior officer, reminding Mark again why he chose this man to command his ship when he was unable to.

"Carry on, Mr. Marek; the rest of you, with me."

Mark turned and exited the command deck into one of the maglovators, followed by the primary command crew.

"What's with the uptight attitude?" Dan asked as soon as the maglovator doors hissed closed. "We've been in worse spots than what we're heading into now. You're more tense'n I can ever remember seein' you."

"I'm worried. This is the most dangerous mission we've ever undertaken," Mark admitted.

"How can you even say that?" Ariel replied. "Look at everything we've been through so far."

"Think about this, Ariel. I usually think two to three steps ahead of our enemies because I do my research on them. Even when we first encountered the Agalum, I knew they had clones in place of our people and I knew that world we went to was not their home world but some backwater place where they performed experiments for what turned out to be an invasion of Earth. But now we're entering a whole new arena. We're going to a world that was already hostile to us to begin with, but now it's an occupied hostile world. Occupied by a monstrous foe that we barely escaped from the first time we met."

"That ain't the way I'm rememberin' it, Boss," Dan argued. "I remember us holdin' 'em off with only a

37

skeleton crew, and then getting' all o' our people back home an' safely too. Were we in trouble? No doubt about it. But did we hold our own? Yeah I'd say, definitely."

"Maybe so, Danny, but remember they were a match for you in strength and durability; plus they could teleport as well," Mark countered.

"Mark," Red began, "we did get our people back and escape back to our dimension. If the Tahir Ga'Warum are in our dimension now, yeah, we may be in for a tough time of it, but nothing is lost. I mean you did design some stuff to take care of them the last half year, right?"

Mark slowly nodded. "Yes, I used scans from all of our tech suits to come up with a few things to use against them, to even the odds as it were."

"So why all the doom and gloom then?" Eddie asked.

"Because we're flying headlong into the unknown. Those weapons I developed to deal with the Tahir Ga'Warum? They're all experimental and I'm not one hundred percent convinced they'll work at all against them."

"Well that's sobering and confidence inducing," Eddie grumbled.

"C'mon, DiGenovese, when'd Mark make anything that didn't work exactly like it should?" Red asked.

"To be honest," offered Mark, "I'm almost one hundred percent positive that they will work against the Tahir Ga'Warum's alien physiology. But it's more than that. To be honest I feel like I'm running out of steam. I'm tired, people. The last two and a half years have been difficult on all of us, but the constant pressure is beginning to wear on me, which is why I agreed to being stationed on Earth for the past six months so I could conduct research on new weaponry as well as defensive measures to be used against both the Tahir Ga'Warum and the Agalum."

The maglovator doors hissed open once again, this time on the command crew's private quarter's deck.

"I thought we were going to the command conference room?"" Dan asked.

"No, I changed my mind. You guys get some rest. I am as well. We'll return to the command deck in ten hours. Let's all get some sleep. We can discuss more about this mission then."

Dan replied with an exasperated hiss of air. "Whatever you say, Boss." Dan Sledge shook his head and walked toward his own quarters. A moment later his door was sliding shut behind him. "Catch you all tomorrow or later or whatever," the big Jovian said before he disappeared into his quarters.

Once inside he tapped his tech suits right wrist. "Dr. Troiano." he said. Anne Troiano's face lit up in a holographic image above and projected from his right sleeve.

"Hi, Dan, what's up?" she asked with a smile.

"I'm not sure anythin' is, Anne. But I want you to talk to Mark if you don't mind. Somethin' don't seem right with him. Like he's off somehow."

"Off? How?"

"He's nervous an' shaky about this mission we're on. It don't seem right." Dan repeated, "He never gets nervous about anythin'. An' right now we need him to be the usual full o' confidence guy he normally is."

"All right, I'll have a talk with him," she replied.

"Let it wait until tomorrow though, Anne. He just went back to his quarters to get some rest. Maybe that's all it is but who knows? I just don't like the idea o' us goin' inta such a dangerous situation an' Mark not bein' on his 'A' game."

Anne Troiano's image frowned and then she answered, "You're right, Danny. Too much relies on Mark. I'll definitely talk to him tomorrow."

"You're the best, Doc." Dan said and then grinned lopsidedly.

"You keep telling me that, Dan, but you still haven't taken me out to dinner and proved it. How long is a girl supposed to wait?"

Dan was momentarily taken aback by Dr. Troiano's forwardness.

"Uh, I'll tell ya what, Doc. As soon as we get back ta Earth, I'll take ya wherever you want, how's that?"

She smiled then and said, "I'm going to hold you to it, Sledge." With that her image winked out.

"Well whattaya know. Doc Troiano's got a thing fer me." Dan let out a long low whistle in disbelief.

Chapter 6

Days later the *Cagliostro,* already in camouflage mode, emerged from hyperwarp at the edge of the Agalum galaxies.

"You see what I told you? Look at this," Red announced.

"We are…" Mark replied quietly.

The entire command crew stared at the view screen silently in disbelief.

"That's more devastation than what was floating around the Earth two years ago," Dan noted.

Slowly Mark nodded in agreement.

Before them, spread out as far as the viewer could show, were destroyed ships. A few of the blood red organic looking Tahir Ga'Warum ships lie here and there, all lights long extinguished with hulls exposed to the depths of space. But many times that number of Agalum ships also filled the void. Hulls smashed, lifeless bodies strewn about and floating in space while cascading rivers of sparking energy leaked from some ships.

"It's a graveyard," Ariel breathed.

Mark nodded. "It is. A terrible battle took place here. One the Agalum lost badly. Now we have to make sure nothing like this happens near Earth ever again."

"Take us through this mess, Dan," Mark directed. "Red, keep us camouflaged."

Both men nodded in agreement.

"Ahead one half sub light," Dan announced.

The crew sat staring at the main viewer as the *Cagliostro* passed countless Agalum and a few of the Tahir Ga'Warum's ships on its way into the solar system.

"This is bad, very bad," Ariel muttered.

"It's worse than that, Ari," Mark said. "All of this death and devastation. I have no sympathy for the Agalum, but seeing this…it's like flying into the heart of evil."

The *Cagliostro* slowly crossed the incredibly long battlefield in space. The command crew was silent and in awe as they passed vessel after derelict vessel.

"I ain't likin' this at all, Boss," Dan grumbled.

"You're not the only one, Dan," Mark quietly replied.

For hours the *Cagliostro* slowly made its way through the seemingly unending wreckage.

"Mark," Red called, "There's a ship up ahead I'm reading life signs from."

"Tahir Ga'Warum or Agalum?"

"Agalum. I'm reading half a dozen Agalum. Yellows and purples."

"So we have some commanders left alive with some worker bees," Eddie said.

"So what do we do?" Red turned toward Mark and asked.

Mark leaned forward and rested his right elbow on his knee, then his chin upon his closed fist. After a moment he said, "Go past them, leave them here. It's not our problem right now. These are our enemies too."

Dan swiveled his chair toward Mark and said, "The enemy of my enemy is what?"

Mark looked at him and then replied, "I like it better when you don't let on how smart you really are."

Dan shrugged and replied, "Just want you to think about things before we go ahead and do something we'll regret later."

"Danny, I won't have any regrets. We don't have the ability to take these people in and then to see to their injuries as well as to then incarcerate them. What do we do? Bring them back to Earth? Or Chakix? We can't do that. If we rescued them now, we'd be letting anyone in this sector of space know we were here. This is a secret mission. As usual, Earth's survival may depend upon it. We have to go on."

Dan set his jaw and nodded in agreement. "I was just layin' out our options, Mark. That's all. I ain't got no love for either o' these guys. If they wipe each other out I'd be more'n happy."

"I agree, Danny," Mark answered.

Mark sat back down in his command chair heavily, then looked grimly ahead and said, "Okay get us out of here. We have a long way to go based on those coordinates that Ari got out of that Agalum's head."

Dan nodded and moved the *Cagliostro* slowly forward and deeper into Agalum space.

"Red," Mark began, "fire a cloaked probe into that graveyard. Have it magnetically attach itself to an Agalum ship, and program it to self-destruct if anyone discovers or tries to obtain it."

Red nodded and replied, "Will do, Mark." A minute later a probe shot out of the *Cagliostro*'s bow and flew into the wreckage, disappearing amongst the debris.

"Okay, that will send constant reports back to us," Red advised.

"Good. That's what I want," Mark replied. "The last time we were in this quadrant of space it took us a week to get to that world we found the copy of Virginia terraformed on."

Eddie swiveled his seat around to face Mark, "Did you ever figure out how they did that? Terraform a world like that?"

"Eddie, I have to think that's one thing they have on us scientifically. If I'd had time to study that world in depth, things might have changed, but whatever they did there I have had no time to study with this all-consuming war going on constantly since then."

"We're clear of any remaining ships," Red announced. "It's empty space ahead of us."

Mark replied, "Okay bring us back to hyperwarp and get us out of here. We have days of travel through this quadrant before we get to our objective, and every step of the way is in enemy territory."

"Engagin' hyperwarp now," Dan declared.

The *Cagliostro* shot forward, already camouflaged and hidden from view, flying majestically through hyperwarp toward its objective.

***

"Mark, I've got something coming up on long range scans," Red announced.

"What is it, Red?"

"A cluster of ships; small most likely one or two man fighters," Red replied.

"Agalum?"

"No, Mark, they appear to be Tahir Ga'Warum."

"How many?" Mark asked.

"I count five," Red replied, then added, "No wait, Scratch that. Six total and one of those six is being attacked by the other five. It's a transport vessel of some kind. It's not Agalum or Tahir Ga'Warum. In fact whatever it is, Mark, it's taken a beating. I'm showing fifty life signs aboard, but they're not going to be alive much longer. They just lost their shields." He turned in his seat and faced Mark. "These are not soldiers, Mark, and they're going to die right in front of us."

"No, they're not. Eddie charge solar cannons and ready Star core missiles. Red, shields on full, Battle stations everyone. Danny, take us in."

Ralph L. Angelo Jr.

Chapter 7

Still camouflaged, the *Cagliostro* screamed through silent space toward the attacking Tahir Ga'Warum ships.

"Mark, should I drop the camo? I know it'll bring the shield density up if we do," Red said.

"No, Red, definitely not. I don't want them to know we're here. They may know where we are, but they don't have to know who we are."

"Comin' into weapons range now, chief," Eddie announced.

"Destroy them, Eddie. These things are ravagers. Don't show them any mercy. Ariel, as soon as they send out any kind of signal I want you to throw up a jamming blanket of static on whatever frequency they use. I don't want them to get any word to their main base about what could be happening here."

"Okay, Mark," the curvaceous blonde replied.

The *Cagliostro* fired all forward weaponry on the unsuspecting Tahir Ga'Warum fighters. Solar cannons blazed bright death and destruction at the unknowing usurpers. Instantly the nearest of the small Tahir Ga'Warum ships spun away and out of control slamming into another one in its path. The *Cagliostro* had taken two enemies out of the fight instantly.

The other three ships rotated through space and turned toward the *Cagliostro* now, their hulls and shields glowing brightly where the *Cag*'s weapons had struck.

"They're scanning for us now, Mark," Red proclaimed.

"They'll never find us under this improved camouflage field."

"Let's hope not anyway," Dan muttered.

47

"They're starting to strafe the area of space we fired from," Red advised.

"Exceptin' we're no longer there." Dan Sledge replied.

The *Cagliostro* slid silently through space, hidden and dangerous. It flew beneath the enemy craft, then up behind them, using the vastness and lack of axis in space to their advantage, the Cagliostro rotated about.

Once behind and above them, Eddie immediately fired the solar cannons once again, strafing their hulls and puncturing their shields.

"Now, Eddie, while they're turning in space, Star Core missiles, full spread," Mark almost shouted.

"You got it, Mark," Eddie answered

The Star Core missiles leaped away from the hidden *Cagliostro* and exploded brightly against the hulls of the Tahir Ga'Warum ships.

"Mark, I'm reading several impacts against the shields. They're trying to teleport their way in; like they did the first time we encountered them." Red advised.

"Keep the shields up and tight. Rotate shield frequencies if you have to. Do not let them get aboard this ship."

"They've stopped trying but I'm reading several new life forms, and there are Tahir Ga'Warum now aboard the transport vessel," Red announced.

While Red was speaking, Eddie fired the solar cannons again. The three remaining ships exploded almost simultaneously.

Mark asked, "Status reports everyone? Ariel?"

"They did try to get a signal out. I jammed it."

Red added, "They managed to clip us a few times with some energy based weapon; it was the same thing they used against us in their dimension. The new shields took a

48

pounding but held up better than the old ones did. No damage to the ship, but it was a close thing."

"I'm pullin' us in close to that transport vessel, they have boarders. Only a few, but it looks like it's gettin' bloody in there," Dan said.

"Red, get a team of Rangers over there and mop them up and do it quickly," Mark ordered.

"On my way, Mark." Red replied.

***

Two minutes later a shuttle disembarked from the *Cagliostro*'s landing bay and slid invisibly through space, sidling up to the battle damaged ship's airlock.

"It's a good thing Mark took notes on the standard style airlocks all of these ships out here seem to have," Red mentioned as the two ships softly touched.

"Red," Marks voice spoke through the tech suit's comm array, "I have you all plugged into the translator aboard the *Cagliostro*. As soon as we can get some speech to translate from these newcomers we'll get you talking to them."

"Roger, Mark," Red replied.

"Cycling the airlocks now, sir." Cane Volgers, a Ranger announced. He was a black man in his mid-thirties with fierce eyes that seemed to take everything in around him.

"Good man, Volgers," Red replied.

The Ranger team slid the airlock open carefully, standing back and to either side of the door in case any enemies were awaiting them with blazing guns.

They needn't have bothered. The corridor was empty and the transport ship was dimly lit with a dull red glow as if on emergency power only. An acrid smelling smoke drifted before their eyes.

"Volgers, you, Smithston, and I up front. Carruthers, scan for life signs. The rest of you, weapons hot. Just don't shoot each other," Red warned.

The dozen man team of Rangers entered into the smoke filled corridor following Carruthers' lead. Above the right sleeve of his silver and blue tech suit a holographic scanner appeared and showed yellow dots gathered together at one point. The bald headed Carruthers pointed toward the left in the direction of sparking and sizzling lights. Red nodded and they all silently made their way toward unknown danger.

After several feet of traipsing through the darkness, Carruthers held his hand up and they all ground to a stop.

"What've you got?" Red asked.

"Life signs. I see Tahir Ga'Warum and…something else. It must be the passengers." He turned toward Red after pausing a second and said, "They're not human, whatever they are they're not like us."

"No one out here is, Carruthers," Red replied as he pushed past the smaller man.

Red burst through the thick smoke and beheld three Tahir Ga'Warum holding down several of what Red would assume to be passengers of the now devastated vessel.

They were strange looking beings whose arms ended not in hands, but six one foot long tentacles. Their lower bodies did not end in legs either, but what appeared to be single long stems that they stood on with a multitude of very short tentacles touching the ground. Their heads were elongated slightly and their skin color was a pale golden hue that matched the hair on their longer than human heads.

50

The Tahir Ga'Warum turned as one and wordlessly leaped toward the men from the *Cagliostro*.

Red shouted, "Take 'em down!"

"You don't have to tell us twice, Boss!" Volgers replied.

The Rangers fired as one unit and the horrid Tahir Ga'Warum with their chalk white flesh, pointed ears and swirling black matter all about them were each blown through the air by the powerful ray blasts. Red instantly charged up his favorite weapon for a second shot, his shoulder mounted personal cannon. The men with him fired powerful blaster rifles.

But the Tahir Ga'Warum were not so easily finished.

Even as Red fired a second time, two of the horrific beings each disappeared in a puff of swirling matter to reappear behind the men.

"Heads up!" shouted Red, while spinning around to face the area behind where he stood.

But again the Tahir Ga'Warum disappeared in a tendril filled display.

"Red, above you!" Mark's voice reverberated about them from their tech suits.

They all looked upward as the two gruesome creatures suddenly appeared above the team and dropped down toward them, arms outstretched and hissing.

"No way!" Carruthers shouted as he squeezed the trigger on his rifle.

"Take them down, no let ups!" Red shouted above the din of battle.

Blaster fire echoed about the room within the alien transport vessel, with Red firing his big weapon repeatedly.

Again and again the Tahir Ga'Warum shouted in pain and anger before their voices were finally silenced.

"Whew," Volgers wiped his sweating brow with the back of his hand, "That was a little intense."

"It was more than I was expecting," Another Ranger named Tenant replied.

"You're not alone, mister," Red added. "I've faced these monsters before, and they still scare the crap out of me." He kicked at the one lying in a puddle of its own blood at his feet. "But we think we know why. They emit something that causes fear, and we just came to that realization on the way here. Our tech suits are sending data back to the *Cag* right now. Hopefully the smart guys will be able to figure out what it is that does this."

"What do you guys think it is?" Carruthers asked. "Psychic or pheromones?"

"How the hell do I know, Carruthers? I aim and shoot. That's my job. If you got any ideas join the other big brains back on the ship and help them figure it out," Red barked angrily.

"No disrespect meant, sir." Carruthers replied almost sheepishly.

Red sighed and shook his head side to side before replying, "I'm the one who should be apologizing, Carruthers. These things put me on edge. Don't take it personally."

"I won't, sir." Carruthers nodded.

Red turned toward the beings that inhabited the ship, which until this time had been standing nearby quietly staring on in silence.

"Mark, this is Red," He spoke into his tech suit's comm array on his sleeve. "I'm going to try to talk to these…people now. Warm up that super-translator thing."

"Already on and awaiting their speech patterns and language, Red," Mark replied.

One of the beings walked forward on their strange tentacled lower appendage and raised its right mass of tentacles to get Red's attention. "There is no need, Red Robinski. We know your tongue." The creature spoke in a strange reverberating voice, sounding as if it were speaking underwater.

"What? How?" Red answered in disbelief, "How do you know my name?"

"We have studied your race and especially the crew of the feared *Cagliostro* as much as possible since word of your many victories against the oppressive Agalum."

"So what do we call you?" Red asked.

"We, as a race are known as the 'Korai'. My name is Altlow."

"Just the same," Mark's voice interrupted from the tech suits, "We'd appreciate having some of your language on file if you don't mind."

"But of course. It is the least we can do after you saved our lives so selflessly. After all, you were in as much danger from the Tahir Ga'Warum as we were. Yet you came to our aid and saved all our lives. We are eternally in your debt."

The light golden skinned being bowed at what would be its waist, then stood upright and began to speak in a voice that could very easily be interpreted as song.

"Th-that's beautiful," Morrison, a female Ranger muttered in wide eyed shock.

"Heads up, Jenny," Red advised. "Keep your head in the game."

"I will, sir," she replied.

A few moments later the alien being stopped its song and smiled toward the security crew from the *Cagliostro*. "Is that sufficient?" It tilted its head and asked quizzically.

Red brought his sleeve up toward his face and asked, "What about it, Mark? Was that enough?"

"It was. But I have one last request. Ask our new friend to repeat his race's name in his own tongue."

Red looked at the being named Altlow before him and said, "Can you?"

"But of course, Red Robinski," The strange creature replied.

Altlow began to sing again, this time for a much shorter period of time.

"That's enough. You can tell Altlow thank you," Mark announced.

Red frowned and walked to the other side of the empty room they were standing in. Once there he tapped his sleeve's controls, allowing only himself to hear Mark's voice now. "What is it, Mark? Why'd you want him to speak his race's name?"

"It was something significant, something I had half expected. The name of these people; it means something if we have the translation correct."

"Well don't leave me hangin' in suspense, Mark. What is it?"

There was a small moment of silence from the other end and then Mark Johnson finally replied, "Their name means 'wanderer'. These people are nomads, and from what I'm able to glean from the condition and relative age of that ship, they've been out here for centuries."

Chapter 8

"So what do we do?" Eddie asked. The command crew along with Dr. Ann Troiano was in the conference room staring at holographic images of the short but deadly battle aboard the Korai vessel.

"I could send Danny over to take a look at things or go with him myself," Mark replied, "but I don't see what good it will do. From what I can discern from this end their technology is nothing like our own and our magno-disc drive is not at all compatible with whatever they are using for faster than light travel. But I think for thoroughness sake we should give a cursory look."

"I think we're gonna have to, Mark, any way you put it," Dan answered. "I'll take a tech team an' a few Rangers over there with Red. The least we can do is look at it all. But I gotta warn ya, I'm in agreement with ya."

"So why bother then?" Ariel asked.

"Ariel, what else can we do? I can't leave these people out here to die," Mark replied. "Without hyperwarp it'll take them years to get across this quadrant of space, maybe centuries."

"You said they've already been traveling for centuries, right?" Ariel asked.

"We believe so. It looks like generations have lived and died on that ship," Red answered.

"Then let them be on their way. Hell, we don't even know where they're going," Ariel said.

"What's the matter, Ari?" Mark asked. "Why such a problem with helping these people out a little?"

"Well, for one thing they've been doing just fine without us and two I'd hardly call these walking squids 'people'."

Mark looked at his girlfriend quizzically. "What's the matter with you? We've met alien races before that didn't look or weren't human."

"I don't know, Mark. Something about these…things sends shivers down my spine."

"Some empathic response?" Dr. Troiano thought aloud.

"N-no," Ari considered. "At least I don't think so. But I guess it *could* be."

"So maybe these guys are a threat?" Danny asked.

"I can't discount any possibility, Dan." Mark replied while thoughtfully stroking his chin.

"I wouldn't be surprised," Eddie offered with a smirk. 'Everything else out here is."

"The squirts got a point," Red agreed. "We've yet to meet a friendly race out in space. Everyone we've run into wants our heads. We have no idea what these guys want, if anything. And to make matters worse our cover is blown now. Our big secret mission is over if we just let them go."

Mark steepled his fingers and leaned forward staring at Red. "So what's your advice?" Mark asked.

"Look, that ship isn't that big. We can easily put it in the landing bay. It's only slightly longer than the *Stargrazer*. We can put it on board, give these people temporary quarters in one of the cargo bays we're not using, and take them with us on our way while we try to fix their ship. You already scanned them for pathogens, and you can run an anti-viral beam over them before they leave their ship so we know we're not going to catch anything from them. Am I right so far, Doc?" Red turned to Ann Troiano looking for an answer.

"Yes, Red, you are. I can make sure nothing they carry is harmful to us and vice versa. Even if we have to quarantine them in that section of the ship temporarily."

Mark began to rise out of his seat. "Well, that seems like the best course of action I suppose. I'd rather have them near us than floating around out here where they can blab of our presence in this solar system to someone else."

"So I guess we have a game plan." Red likewise stood.

Mark nodded. "We do. Ari, contact their leader, that Atlow, and tell him how we propose to aid them. Leave out any part of us wanting to keep them close by and incommunicado."

Ariel nodded and replied, "Okay, Mark, whatever you say."

Mark ordered, "Let's get a move on folks, time's a wasting."

Everyone stood and exited the conference room and headed back to the command deck, with the exception of Dr. Troiano who said her goodbyes and returned to the medical bay.

"What now?" Dan Sledge asked Mark as he walked side by side with him.

"Now we tractor beam that ship into the landing bay. After everything clears you can get a crew aboard it and try to see what makes it tick. Hopefully it's something we're at least familiar with in some way so we can replicate some parts for them, whatever they need to at least get them back on their way."

"Yeah, I kinda figured that was the plan, Boss," Dan replied.

"We've wasted enough time here as it is and we're sitting ducks, even camouflaged, out here in space with that ship crippled like it is."

"Okay, I'm goin' down to the landin' bay an' I'll work on getting' that thing aboard," Dan confirmed.

"Start the preparations you'll need, but don't do anything until I give you the word. Remember, we're only supposing these people will accept our help in the way we worked out. There's no guarantee of that."

"Got it Mark," Dan replied.

He entered the maglovator before Mark and was gone in a heartbeat. Mark waited for the next car, and entered with Red, Eddie, and Ariel, who were walking behind him and Dan.

A moment later the command crew exited the maglovator and entered onto the command deck.

Ariel immediately sat at her station and began contacting the alien craft, while Mark sat down in his command chair. Everyone else returned to their stations, allowing the secondary crew to leave the command deck. It was all done seamlessly and with a minimum of speaking. A lot of nodded heads and a few smiles and the secondary crew were gone and riding the maglovators back to their quarters.

Mark was looking over a report on the ship's battle readiness when Ariel called to him a moment later.

"Mark, Altlow of the Korai would like to speak with you."

Mark raised his head quizzically and frowned at Ariel.

'Don't ask me lover-boy.' She contacted him telepathically. *'He doesn't sound like he's too happy about them coming aboard the Cagliostro.'*

'All right, I'll take it from here.' Ariel could almost hear his telepathic sigh.

Mark stood and faced the view screen at the head of the command deck.

"Altlow of the Korai, what can I do for you?"

"Perhaps you are already doing too much, Captain Johnson. Your subordinate informs me you would like to move our vessel aboard your own to aid us in repairs."

58

"That is correct Altlow. We'd like to take you with us toward our destination and repair your ship along the way, if we can. If we cannot, we'd be more than willing to take you to your destination once our mission is complete and drop you and your people off there."

"We are doing quite well enough on our own, Captain. I thank you for your offer of aid, but I assure you it is not necessary."

"I have to disagree, Altlow. When we came upon you and your ship you were being overrun by Tahir Ga'Warum and were about to be made into someone else's next meal. We're offering the hand of friendship. We'll do all we can to aid you and your people while we're traveling to our destination. Look, the way your ship is banged up it'll take you years to get anywhere. We could cut those years off of your trip."

"And what would you ask of us in return?" the squid-like being replied.

"Just your company and a few tales about this region of space as well as where you are from." Mark paused a moment and then continued, "Look Altlow, we're extending the hand of friendship, we're not asking for anything in return. Yours are the first friendly faces we've seen out here in deep space; and seriously, would you rather we continue on and leave you to the Tahir Ga'Warum's sweet mercies?"

Altlow silenced his end of the conversation and spoke animatedly to two more of his race that were standing behind him. A moment later he turned around and activated his audio once more.

"Very well, Captain Johnson. We welcome your hospitality. You may tractor beam us aboard your ship whenever you are ready."

Mark nodded with a slight smile. "Very good, Altlow. We'll contact you shortly. Johnson out."

Ariel cut the communication link and everyone turned toward Mark.

"That was kinda strange," Eddie began.

"It looks like they have some trust issues with alien races," Ariel advised.

"I'd have to agree," Red said. "They don't seem all that trustful of us."

"Put yourselves in their shoes. Well, you know what I mean," Mark quickly revised. "They've been out here for maybe centuries and it looks like no one has treated them all too fairly."

"Do you think maybe there's a reason for that?" Red queried.

"That's a good point, Red, and one we should consider. So for now we bring them aboard but confine them to the third cargo bay. If they have any technical people with them, we'll get them to aid our engineering staff and we'll see if we can get some parts manufactured for that old bird of theirs."

Ariel spun her seat around and faced Mark. "What if this is a trap?"

"Of whose? The Agalum? Or the Tahir Ga'Warum?" Mark replied.

"Does it matter? If one of them wanted to get spies onto the *Cagliostro,* this would be the easiest way," she answered.

"Really good point actually, Ari," Mark admitted.

He sunk back into his seat and clasped his hands before his face. A moment later he said, "Red, make sure there is a guard around them at all times, at least several men. Let's not make them feel like prisoners, but let's also let them know we are not taking anything for granted."

"How many men do you want assigned to them?"

"Let's start off with three. Like I said, I don't want them to think this is us taking them prisoner. If anything escalates we'll add to their guard."

Red nodded and curled his lip. "Agreed, Mark. I'll get right on it."

"Good. Go down to the landing bay and join Dan. Make sure you have your best three men with you. They'll be taking the first shift with our new friends."

Red rose from his station. "You've got it, Mark."

Red walked away and stepped into a waiting maglovator.

'What's the matter?' Ariel's feminine psychic voice tickled Mark's mind.

'This is all happening a little too fast; everything that is except us getting the hell out of this quadrant of space.'

'You're right I think. We've wasted too much time here already,' Ariel replied.

'Call Carruthers to take Red's position at tactical. I'm going down to supervise loading that ship on to ours.'

'You're being a little too 'hands on' again,' Ariel chastised.

Mark smiled. *'My ship, my rules.'*

'Just so long as you don't take your ball and run away.' Ariel met his eyes with a mischievous gleam to her own.

"I'm going to the landing bay. I'll be right back. Ariel, contact me if I'm needed," Mark said aloud, while walking to and entering the maglovator. Its doors hissed shut behind him.

Ralph L. Angelo Jr.

Chapter 9

Mark entered the landing bay and walked up beside Dan. The big Jovian was orchestrating the docking procedures for the alien vessel.

"How's it going?" Mark asked.

Dan turned toward him, furrowed his brow quizzically then answered, "Everything's fine. Whatta you doin' here?"

"I needed to get off the command deck for a few minutes and I figured I'd use that as the excuse to meet our new friends face to face."

Dan chuckled slightly. "Yeah, I understand. We all need to get out of there every so often on these intense missions. Sometimes we just gotta clear our heads."

The battered ship settled softly down with the help of the *Cagliostro's* magnetic docking system before the two men. A hiss of steam escaped the dilapidated ship's landing gear as they began to bear the full weight of the vessel within the landing bay.

"This thing is in some bad shape," Mark remarked.

"Yeah it ain't looking too healthy," Danny replied.

"Speaking of heads," Mark began, "are we getting in over ours?"

Dan turned and looked at him straight in the eyes. "Mark, we've been over our heads since the day we left Earth and crossed the faster than light threshold. It hasn't changed at all since that day. We've been over our head then and we are now."

"So why are you still here? Why is anyone for that matter? Why do we have more people willing to sign up with us to do this? We're not the military. Hell, we're not secret agents of some kind, though we could be I guess with everything we've been through."

"I hate to tell ya, chief, but you're the reason people follow along. You." Dan poked Mark in the chest as he spoke. "You inspire people in a quiet, confident, not over the top kinda way. This crew trusts you. Hell, I think the entire planet trusts you. The Agalum hate you, an' that's more'n good enough for me." He paused a moment to let his words sink into Mark's brain and then he asked, "Why the second thoughts all of a sudden?"

Mark sighed and then replied, "Danny, it's like suddenly I have the weight of the world, maybe the universe on my shoulders. I've felt this way since we took off from Earth this time. We're going to find this ancient lost cache of weapons designs that some rogue Agalum claims is what his people have been using to counter our technology. And yet you and I along with other Earth scientists and engineers have been able to come up with something to counter everything they've created. Even those Predator ships that were plaguing us over Chakix half a year ago. I've come up with something to up our game in even those cases. Why do we really need this tech? Furthermore, with the Tahir Ga'Warum here now shouldn't I be home defending the planet? Or at least coming up with defenses against them?"

"Look, Mark, in the past six months you've studied their tech, what we have of it in scans at least, and you were able to strengthen our shields and weaponry so that we all have a better chance against those ugly buggers. I gotta tell ya, I think you're better off bein' in space leadin' this crew than you are on Earth sittin' at a desk designin' stuff. Hell, you design better under the gun than you do sittin' at a monitor and keyboard anyway."

Mark nodded. "Thanks, big guy. I think."

The comm array on both their suits began to flare to life with Ariel's face appearing holographically above their right wrists. "Mark, we have a problem. Scans are showing two Tahir Ga'Warum ships, the big ones like we encountered in that other dimension, on an intercept course with our position."

"Are we still camouflaged?" Mark inquired.

"Yes, absolutely. But Red thinks they're responding to a distress call from those small ships that attacked the Korai ship."

"Makes sense," Dan agreed with a shrug.

"Let's not waste any time," Mark ordered. "Call for battle stations. Dan, let's get that thing tied down and let's get the hell out of here."

"You and you, with us." Dan shouted at two landing bay techs that fell in running behind the two men who were sprinting toward the dilapidated ship.

Suddenly the *Cagliostro* rocked mightily.

"Uh oh," Dan muttered.

"We're taking fire!" Ariel's voice blasted out of the comm.

"But how? How can they see us if we're camouflaged?" Mark asked.

The only answer was the ship rocking with another barrage from the enemy vessels.

Ralph L. Angelo Jr.

Chapter 10

The four men, including Mark and Danny, worked quickly to secure the alien vessel to the landing bay.

"Okay, all tied down!" Dan shouted.

A door slid open on the vessel and Altlow stood at the top of the disembarkation ramp, "May we assist you? The Tahir Ga'Warum are attacking."

"No, just stay on your ship for the time being. Once we get out of danger we'll settle you in. Now go back inside please," Mark replied.

Altlow nodded his head and turned, disappearing within his own ship as its door slid shut.

"Did you scan that ship for any tracking signals?" Mark asked.

"Yeah still doin' it now. There ain't nothin' comin' outta that thing," Dan replied.

"Maybe they just saw us," one of the techs commented.

"What? What're you talkin' about?" Dan asked.

"We just towed a derelict ship into our landing bay. Maybe when they were scanning space for their ships they saw it disappearing within our stealth field," the tech replied.

Mark shook his head in the affirmative. "You're right, it's very possible. If we make it out of this one alive you're getting a raise." Mark turned and ran toward the maglovator with Dan in tow.

An instant later they both appeared on the command deck and settled into their seats.

"Shield strength?" Mark asked.

"Eighty five percent right now and holding," Red replied.

"That's better than the last time we faced these monsters," Mark said. Then he continued, "Dan, bring us around to .015 heading and Eddie, prepare to return fire, on my mark."

The *Cagliostro* shuddered again.

"How are they finding us?" Ariel nervously asked.

"They aren't," Red replied, "They're using a wide spread weapons array and just blasting dead space hoping to hit us."

"Well they're succeedin'," Dan replied, wide eyed.

"Danny, get us out of here," Mark ordered.

Dan Sledge punched the throttle controls to full speed on his virtual control console and the camouflaged *Cagliostro* leapt forward in space.

"Ariel, jam all comm signals from those ships using the new protocols I uploaded before we left Earth. Dan, take us back around. Let's show these bastards that they're not back in their home dimension anymore. Eddie, I want both fore and aft weaponry charged and ready to fire. Ready all Star Core missile launchers."

"Mark," Red interrupted, "do we really want to be taking on two of these things? Six months ago we barely survived a battle with one."

"Yes, we need to do this. We need to leave two of these things drifting here lifeless and abandoned as a warning not to screw with us."

"An' there goes our little secret mission," Dan grumbled.

"Our covers got to be blown already at this point just by our saving the Korai. No, I say we attack them and leave those that come after wondering what destroyed their two ships. No one has any way of knowing that it was the *Cagliostro* that was here."

"Except that Agalum back on Chakix," Red offered.

68

The ship rocked again from a near miss.

"They're just firing indiscriminately now," Red advised.

"Danny, take us to heading .50 and full stop when we get there."

"Are you nuts?" Sledge roared in disbelief.

"Dan, trust me. I have an idea. One that will seed doubt in our enemies' minds."

"Which enemies, a'cause we sure seem to have a lot of 'em," Dan replied.

He gunned the ship around to a new heading and stopped it, as ordered.

"Eddie, prepare both forward and aft weapons and fire on my command. Dan, be ready to hyperwarp us out of here on my mark. Red, full power to all shields."

"You got it, chief." Red replied. The other two merely nodded their agreement.

Mark silently watched his display above his command console, which was mirrored on the main viewer. Long seconds passed as the enemy ships strafed space looking for their invisible foe.

Then Mark shouted, "Eddie, Now!"

The marksman fired a full brace of forward Star Core missiles and all four forward solar cannons as well as all three rear facing solar cannons and a single rear Star Core. The two big Tahir Ga'Warum ships were fore and aft of the *Cagliostro,* and every weapon hit its mark. Both horrific looking ships shuddered from the terrible impact the *Cagliostro*'s weapons made upon each.

"Now Danny, get us out of here!" Mark roared.

Without hesitation Dan Sledge punched the controls once again and the camouflaged *Cagliostro* disappeared into space the exact second the two Tahir Ga'Warum ships opened fire on the spot the *Cagliostro* had formerly occupied.

Only the *Cagliostro* was no longer there. Each of the Tahir Ga'Warum ships weapons fire instead caught their companion ship in a horrific crossfire. One that, with the damage already done by the *Cagliostro*'s devastating attack, was too much for the weakened enemy ships' shields and damaged hulls. Both ships exploded brightly, scattering miniscule remnants of each to the four corners of the galaxy.

From a safe distance away the crew of the *Cagliostro* watched with grim satisfaction as the two Tahir Ga'Warum ships shattered and blew apart.

"Okay, Dan, get us out of here. It's time we continued our primary mission," Mark commanded.

Dan nodded his head and replied with a slight grin, "You got it…Boss."

Invisibly the *Cagliostro* shot away once more, deeper into Agalum space.

Chapter 11

Mark Johnson sat at his private work station in the engineering level. Outside this off-limits area that he shared with Dan he could hear the rest of the on shift engineering staff at work about him. Most were simply making sure everything ran correctly. Others were checking supplies and technical equipment for the hundredth time since they'd taken off from home.

Mark ran his fingers through his hair as he leaned back in his seat.

"I'm getting bleary eyed," he said to no one in particular.

'I wonder if Ari's still awake' Mark thought. He reached out with his mind looking for that tenuous link with his girlfriend. *'Ariel? Are you awake yet?'* but there was no answer forthcoming.

With a resigned sigh he stood up and exited his semi-private work area and headed for the hallway and then the maglovator at the end of the corridor. It was late based on their clock, which ran to Pacific Standard Time. *'I did it again. I get too carried away studying everything that comes along including this bizarre FTL drive on this derelict ship in my landing bay. I wonder why Ariel stays with me at all sometimes?'*

He entered the maglovator and took it to the command crew quarters deck. Exiting the maglovator he walked at first toward his own quarters and then thought the better of it. Instead he headed toward Dan's.

'I hope Danny's up. We can talk a little about the mission and just chew the fat in general.' Mark walked up to Dan's door and without thinking placed his hand over the palm reader along the door's edge.

71

Instantly the door slid opened and Mark entered the darkened room.

"Hey, Dan, are you awake?" Mark asked in slightly more than a whisper.

Suddenly his question was met by a shrill, shrieking female voice. Instantly the light came on within the room, and Mark couldn't help but grin to himself in embarrassment.

Kneeling on the bed, with the sheets pulled all around her naked form was Ann Troiano. Dan was still sprawled out covering himself up with the rest of the sheets. He waved at Mark sheepishly. "Hey, Mark, what're you doin' here?"

"What's he doing here?" Dr. Troiano repeated angrily. "Doesn't the man know anything about knocking first instead of entering someone's private room?" Her raven black hair was a disheveled mess, which she blew out of her eyes before dropping back to the bed and pulling the covers up closer. "Will you please leave now, Mark? I don't think I can ever look you in the eye again as it is, at least for the next hundred years or so."

"Okay, okay, I got it. I'm out of here. Sorry, both of you. I really am."

"It's okay, Mark, not a big deal." Dan replied with a silly grin on his face.

"Maybe it wasn't a big deal to you; you weren't the one who just exposed herself to her boss."

"And Captain, let's not forget Captain," Mark added as the door slid shut behind him. He continued to grin as he made his way to his own quarters.

"Well, that was embarrassing. Probably more for her than me," he quietly said aloud as he continued to walk toward his own rooms.

He placed his hand upon the palm reader at his own door and entered as soon as it slid aside. He began to turn the lights on when a familiar sultry voice called to him from the darkness. "You can leave those off; we don't need them, Captain."

He immediately replied with a grin, "Oh really, communications officer O'Connor. What is it exactly that you have planned in the dark?"

Ariel purred from the bed, "You'll just have to come over here and find out, won't you?"

"I suppose I will," Mark answered, slipping out of his tech suit and under the covers next to his love.

***

The next morning the crew all convened at their usual half-hour-before-shift-started meeting in the conference room.

Mark sat back and activated the holographic interface above the table. Instantly images of the star system they were in blazed to life before them.

"This is where we are now," Mark began. "We'll be crossing a deeply inhabited portion of Agalum space today; this star system alone has three inhabited planets. We have to be careful. We've been running the camouflage unit for a week straight now. We're going to have to shut it off sooner or later to let it cool down so the techs can look it over and make any adjustments it may need. But today's not the day for that. This is some bad turf we're passing through."

"Bad because of the Agalum or bad because of the Tahir Ga'Warum?" Red questioned.

"It doesn't matter. We're further than we've ever been on this side of the property line. Once again we're alone and speeding toward who knows what."

"I gotta say, Boss, I'm still not sure what we're headin' into here. I mean, do we really care if one of these guys or the other gets their dirty paws on that old tech?" Dan asked.

"We should, Dan. If that stuff is as dangerous as some of the weapons showed us so far it may be enough to overpower even our defenses.

"Aaaa, I just got more faith in our ship an' in you and me than in a buncha ancient designs."

"I wouldn't dismiss those 'ancient designs' so easily, Dan. Just remember how one of those 'Predator' ships almost destroyed the *Stargrazer* half a year back."

Dan shook his head affirmatively. "Yeah I got it, Boss. I guess I just got a lot of faith in what got us here so far. An' Mark, one other thing; the *Stargrazer* won that battle with Eddie at the controls."

Mark nodded. "Thanks for the vote of confidence, Danny, but even if we did get lucky, I don't want that luck to end. I don't want those ancient weapons to fall into Agalum or Tahir Ga'Warum hands where they have the greatest potential to do the most damage."

"You have to realize that the Agalum already have their hands on all of that information, right? I mean it's how they built those Predator class ships," Dan reminded.

"Of course I do, Dan. But if we have the information as well, it evens the playing field and doesn't make us scramble to come up with counter measures for whatever is hidden there amongst those otherworldly designs. Plus, I definitely do not want the Tahir Ga'Warum to be able to utilize those plans for their own sake."

"Like they need any more weapons," Eddie commented.

74

"Exactly, Eddie," Mark continued, "These creatures are almost an unholy monster to begin with. Let alone add their weaponry and then hand them the secret weapons plans on a silver platter."

"I gotcha," Dan said. "So our plan is either confiscate the secret plans or destroy 'em."

"That about sums it up nicely," Mark agreed.

The tech suits' comm units began to beep. But before anyone answered, they all looked to Mark, who naturally replied first. "Yes, Miss Wallflower?"

"Mark, you all better come up here, we're entering into a hot zone."

The command crew looked at each other and stood up almost simultaneously before Lilly Wallflower finished speaking.

"We're heading to the maglovators now," Mark advised.

"You better hurry, Captain. You're going to want to see this," Lilly replied.

"We're on our way," Mark confirmed after giving a cursory glance to each member of his command crew.

They all began to run toward the waiting maglovator doors, which slid apart at their approach.

Seconds later they all entered the command deck. Mark shouted, "Status, Miss Wallflower?" even before he sat down in his command chair.

The brown haired beauty turned toward him and pointed at the main view screen. "See for yourself."

Depicted on the main viewer was a scene out of a nightmare. Agalum ships battling Tahir Ga'Warum ships as far as the eye could see. Energy blasts and missiles screamed silently through space and impacted on the ships of the other fleet. It was all bloody carnage and madness rolled up into one horrific scene.

Ariel took her seat at the communication station as Lily Wallflower stood and exited the command deck. As she did Lilly she stole a furtive glance at Red and smiled.

The big security chief merely half nodded his head in reply.

"Dan," Mark said, "keep us out of the way of any stray blasts or missiles. Skirt us around the edge of this conflict. I want new video of everything that goes on here, but I do not want to be a part of this."

Dan nodded affirmatively. "You got it Boss."

Camouflaged, the *Cagliostro* turned and flew away into space.

Mark ordered, "As soon as we're away from that fight get us back into hyperwarp."

"You got it, Mark," Dan replied.

"Mark," Red barked, "we're being followed."

"By how many ships?" Mark replied.

"Two," Red answered. "They're two of those 'Predator' class ships we faced on Chakix."

"I wonder how they saw us? We should be completely camouflaged," Mark mused aloud.

"They're closing fast, and they are scanning this quadrant of space looking for us, or someone at least." Red spun in his chair and faced Mark. "I don't think they know who it is. I think they detected something and are unsure of who or what they have here."

"What do you want to do?" Dan asked. "I could hyperwarp us outta here or we could stay and fight, your call. Two of those bad ass ships are tough, but the *Cagliostro* should be able to steamroll them."

"Agreed, Dan. Stay put and power down the magno-discs. Not off, but keep the *Cagliostro* in a low powered neutral state."

"Okay, Mark, you got it." Dan replied.

76

"Red. Drop the shields. The hull is thick enough to take any punishment those two ships can dish out, at least temporarily. The rest of the systems will be stealthed by our camouflage. Let's see what this is all about. I'm curious why they didn't attack us, or where they thought we were already."

"Bad idea dropping the shields, Mark," Red cautioned.

"Trust me, Red. We'll be okay, at least for a little while against their attacks, if any are coming."

Red shrugged. "You're the boss." He lowered the shields, and the *Cagliostro* now hung invisibly in space facing their enemies who could not discern where they were.

"Status of our friends there?" Mark asked.

"They are scanning space, but our cloaking field is blocking them completely," Red answered.

"Are their weapons hot?" Mark asked.

"Yes, they are," Red advised. "But they aren't making any moves at all. Just hanging there checking out space all around us."

"Okay, keep us quiet and invisible for now," Mark commanded.

Red nodded silently as he studied his sensor display.

"Ari, anything?" Mark asked.

She shook her head negatively. He nodded in affirmation.

"I don't think they're lookin' for us," Eddie announced.

"What are your thoughts, Mr. DiGenovese?" Mark questioned.

Eddie swiveled his seat toward Mark and replied, "Doesn't it look like they're waiting for something or someone to anyone else?"

Everyone on the command deck exchanged surprised glances quickly.

"Danny, back us away from here. Keep them in our sights, Eddie. Red, continue long range scans and be ready to power up the shields at a heartbeat's notice. Ariel, scan every frequency you can find for any chatter directed at those two ships."

"What's the matter, Boss?" Eddie asked.

"I've got a real bad feeling about this," was Mark's only reply.

Moments passed silently aboard the *Cagliostro*'s command deck.

Then Red barked, "I've got something, it's coming in fast and it's big." He turned back toward Mark and continued, "Really big."

An instant later a huge ship dropped out of hyperwarp. A type of ship they had not seen in two and a half years.

"Oh no," Ariel whispered. "A command ship, like they had hidden behind Mars."

"Dan, no fooling around, get us out of here now," Mark commanded.

"You ain't gotta tell me twice," the big Jovian replied

The massive, gleaming city sized vessel with its shining spires hung in space expectantly. Then the two 'Predator' class ships spun about and began to lead it toward the battle far off in the dark velvet of deep space.

The *Cagliostro* went to hyperwarp immediately, putting distance between its hull and the monstrous command ship.

"What the hell is going on back there?" Eddie asked.

Dan shrugged and replied, "I'd have ta think some big shot Agalum was showin' up ta take charge o' the battle."

"That was not the emperor's ship," Mark added quietly, "We saw that over Chakix. No, this was some military leader, just like it was above Mars."

"So what now?" Ariel asked.

78

Mark looked at her and said, "We have to get to this planet in question, get in, find the information we need, and get out ASAP. It looks like the Agalum are beginning to get desperate. More of their ships are destroyed in every one of these scenarios we come across. That Agalum we spoke to on Chakix indicated that the Agalum were already defeated, and yet we see them still fighting. I'm not sure what is going on here, but whatever it is it can't be good for us."

"This could just be scattered remnants of the Agalum fleet coming together for one big push against the Tahir Ga'Warum," Red added.

"It could be, Red, you're right. Perhaps one big final do or die push to clear out the Tahir Ga'Warum," Mark replied.

"I dunno guys. It looked like a long ongoing pitched battle ta me," Dan remarked.

Mark rubbed his chin thoughtfully, and then said, "No matter what it is, let's go find that world and clear out that ancient information before the Tahir get it. Then we have to get back to our own sector of space."

"I'm not likin' this, Mark. I feel like a paper sailboat goin' round an' round headin' toward a drain," Dan confided thoughtfully.

"Like we're no longer under our own control and just riding a wave to our own doom," Red added

"What do you all want to do?" Mark answered angrily. "Turn around and head back to Earth to just await the Tahir Ga'Warum's arrival? Do you want to give up?"

"No, Mark, I'm not sayin' that," Dan countered. "But you gotta admit this outside lookin' in crap is startin' ta get freaky."

Mark nodded in agreement, "You're right, it is. Let's just get this mission completed and get the hell back in our own quadrant of space as soon as possible. The last thing I want to do is die out here in this hellish part of the galaxy."

"I couldn't agree with ya more, Mark." Dan concluded.

The *Cagliostro* swept through space toward its goal.

Chapter 12

Days later, far away and far deeper into Agalum space than any earth based vessel had every traveled, the *Cagliostro* had at last arrived at its goal, the mysterious world where all the weapons plans were hidden.

Down upon its surface, Red and Mark surreptitiously watched the comings and goings of their enemies.

"How do you want to play this?" Red Robinski asked with grim purpose.

Mark shrugged, his face conveying no emotion.

Both men were hiding behind a rocky outcropping watching what was going on before their eyes.

Entering and exiting a cave were enslaved Agalum of the worker class. The 'salad heads' as they had come to be known.

Standing around them were a dozen of the terrible Tahir Ga'Warum. They slinked about the worksite, walking bent half over, a murky puddle of darkness trailing behind each one of them. Their ghastly pale white flesh with their pointed ears and bare skulls gave the gaunt creatures a look akin to old vampire depictions. Every so often one would disappear in a flash of blackness to reappear somewhere else; to either crack a whip it held in its horrific hand or to simply oversee some operation or another.

For their part, the Agalum were cowed to a man or a woman as it were. Their heads were lowered and their eyes never left the dirt of the planet's surface. A seemingly never ending trail of them exited the cavern, dumped wheelbarrows full of debris and returned, dragging their feet slowly, like people pushed to the brink of exhaustion and beyond.

81

"We're not going to be able to get in there like this," Red added, "We've been watching this cave for hours now and I think this is the one we're looking for. The most activity is here."

"I know," Mark quietly agreed.

"So what are you thinking?" Red hissed.

"I think we return to the *Stargrazer* and wait until nightfall. If these Agalum are still toiling away at that point we'll have to just fight our way through the Tahir Ga'Warum present and hope that the Agalum don't join them against us all."

"We need more men down here," Red advised.

"Is that your official advice as head of security?" Mark replied with a half-smile.

"Damned straight," was Red's grim faced reply.

"I agree. Let's head back to the '*Grazer* and we'll contact the *Cag* from there."

Both men turned simultaneously and their hearts jumped. Standing before them was a Tahir Ga'Warum with a crackling whip in his hands, a silent sneer plastered across his hideous countenance and a sibilant hiss escaping his all too pleased-with-himself-lips.

Both men never hesitated, but instantly tackled the horrible creature together, knocking it to the ground in a blur of motion.

Red heaved his hand back and back-fisted the abhorrent creature with the blaster in his hand.

"Keep it quiet," Mark hissed. "We can't afford to draw more of them." He punctuated his words with a punch to the alien creature's jaw.

But the Tahir Ga'Warum merely smiled and easily backhanded both men away in one movement.

Red and Mark sprawled across the dirt, finally coming to a painful stop some ten feet away from the monstrous looking foe.

It got to its feet and wiped a trickle of its blood from its mouth with a smile.

"This thing is not going to get away," Mark growled.

He pulled his blaster pistol and fired, just as the Tahir Ga'Warum was about to teleport. The blaster bolt sliced through the swirling blackness that enveloped the deadly creature the second it began to teleport.

Instantly the creature screamed. Its roar of agony faded immediately as its black, vaporous tendrils blasted away from its body and the alien creature disappeared.

Mark leaned over and offered Red a hand. He pulled up the big security chief, who stumbled to his feet.

"What happened to that thing?" Red asked.

"The blaster interfered with its teleporting. I got lucky; I was trying to shoot it. It just didn't teleport away fast enough. But never mind that, are you all right? You shouldn't have taken the brunt of that blow. Those things are in Danny's league."

"It's my job to take that blow. I'm your head of security. I have to make sure you're safe, no matter what," Red grunted painfully.

"No. You are not my bodyguard, Red. I appreciate what you did, but don't do it again. I need you alive, and not killed by your own sense of nobility. Now we have to get out of here before that thing's cry brings more of those monsters down on our necks."

"Okay, Boss, let's get back to the *Stargrazer*."

Red looked around quickly to make sure no more of the creatures had snuck up on them, and then he led the way back to the *Stargrazer,* which was hidden a mile and half away in the midst of the sand and rock covered desert they found themselves in.

Mark touched a button on his tech suit and the side door of the camouflaged *Stargrazer* suddenly shimmered into view. With one more surreptitious look around, the two men entered the craft, the door slid closed behind them, and the door itself faded back to mirror the desert around it.

"How'd that thing find us? I thought we were as camouflaged as the ship is," Red asked.

He grimaced as he slumped into one of the flight seats at the front of the *Stargrazer*.

"We were," Mark replied. "I think it somehow smelled us. That's all I can come up with for now. Once it got close enough to us it must have heard us talking and attacked that way. They *do* have very big, pointed ears. Once we grappled with it the camouflage was broken."

"Wonderful," Red grunted, then a moment later added, "So what now? Do we take off and head back to the *Cag*?"

"I think that's a good idea for now," Mark answered.

"Yeah, let's get outta here," Red growled and ignited the *Stargrazer*'s magno-disc engines. The ship sprung to life immediately, and besides the low hum coming from beneath their feet, was almost silent as it rose up majestically-albeit invisibly-and streaked toward the stars hidden in the clouds above.

"Are we clear yet?" Red asked.

"Yes, so far no pursuit."

Ariel's voice broke in on their conversation. "Mark, we see your approach. You better get back on board fast."

Both men looked at one another before Mark replied, "What's up, Ari? Did something happen?"

"Mark," she continued, "we have an incoming fleet of Tahir Ga'Warum ships headed this way."

Mark looked at Red and immediately gunned the magno-discs to full sub-light power.

"Prepare for hyperwarp now, Ariel," Mark ordered, "We'll be aboard in thirty seconds. As soon as we touch down tell Danny to punch it and get the ship out of there. I don't care where he's going, just away from that fleet."

Flying strictly by special scanning instruments developed by Dan and Mark, the *Stargrazer* raced into the landing bay of the *Cagliostro*. The force field at the landing bay entry and exit point closed behind them as the armored door slid into place.

With a hiss the atmosphere in the landing bay stabilized and the *Cagliostro* spun about in space and was gone, mere seconds before a fleet of some twenty Tahir Ga'Warum ships dropped out of hyperwarp.

Mark and Red ran from the *Stargrazer* and headed toward a maglovator door. "A whole fleet here? What the hell is hidden on this world?" Red asked.

"Honestly, Red," Mark offered grimly, "I can only surmise it's something so powerful, so catastrophic that it will potentially mean the doom of us all, earthman and Agalum alike."

Ralph L. Angelo Jr.

Chapter 13

"So do any of you have any suggestions?" Mark Johnson asked.

The command crew as well as other high level personnel sat around the table at the center of the command conference room. Mark stood at the end of the table. Behind him floated a holographic image of the arrival of the Tahir Ga'Warum fleet.

Matt Marek stared at the image floating there with a furrowed brow. Red Robinski tapped his fingers on the tabletop in thought. Dan merely interlaced his fingers through one another and rested his chin on his hands. Eddie stared for a moment and then smiled.

"A distraction," Eddie said.

"What?" Mark asked.

"We need to distract them, like we did against that Agalum space station that had our crew captive a couple of years ago; remember?"

Mark almost laughed. "How could I forget? We had ships chasing us all over space while the rest of you jammed sixty people into the *Stargrazer*. But what are you getting at, Eddie? Tell us what you have in mind."

"Well, we could kinda do the same thing," Eddie replied with a lopsided grin.

"Use the *Cag* as a distraction and go in with the *Stargrazer* and a crew aboard her to get into that underground compound or whatever it is?" Ariel asked.

"Sure, why not. It should work fine," Mark agreed as he nodded his head.

"We'll need a big distraction to make this work," Dan added.

"You mean the *Cagliostro* will have to attack those Tahir Ga'Warum ships and then run like hell?" Mark questioned.

"Yeah that about sums it up, chief," Dan acknowledged.

"You are all getting crazier by the day," Ann Troiano interrupted. "This is insane, even for you, Mark. Last time around you had a few ships that were docked and not expecting someone to be crazy enough to make a raid on a space station. Now you want to attack twenty ships, when one of those ships almost destroyed us less than half a year ago?"

"She does have a point, Boss," Dan agreed.

"Then come up with another option, someone, please," Mark pleaded. "Because if someone doesn't come up with something else, we're going with this."

"Here we go again," Red muttered and rolled his eyes in disgust.

Long moments passed and no one said anything. Then Mark stood at his end of the table once again and said, "Everyone back to your stations for now. The command crew plus twenty five security personnel will report to the landing bay at fifteen hundred hours." Mark concluded. Everyone stood and began making their way toward the exit doors.

"Are you sure you wanna do this?" Dan asked Mark. They were standing side by side now, and Red, Eddie, and Ariel had joined them.

"Yes, I think it's our only way to make sure we have a shot at landing undetected."

"We're already undetected with our camouflage up," Dan reminded Mark.

"I know, Danny, but I don't think we can get in and out of there with such a heavy Tahir Ga'Warum presence orbiting that planet."

"I gotta tell ya, Boss, I disagree," Dan said quickly. "Look at the pattern they're flying around that world. They've got huge gaps between their ships. We could drop the *Cag* inta one o' those gaps and land near that cave. From there we could take care o' business."

"But then the entire crew would be at risk," Mark countered.

"The entire crew's at risk now," Dan replied with a shrug of his massive shoulders. "They have been since the first time we left Earth two and a half years ago. It's nothin' new, Boss."

Mark looked at his friend and slowly nodded in agreement. "I suppose you're right, Danny."

"How about a compromise?" Red asked.

Both men turned toward him.

"What have you got in mind?" Mark inquired.

Red replied, "We drop the *Cag* down low into the atmosphere through the gaps Dan found. Then we leave her amongst some cloud cover fully camo-ed. We launch a team on the *Stargrazer* to land near that cave again. I'm thinking a twenty five man security team and whoever you choose to run the mission."

"I would be choosing us, as it always should be," Mark replied.

"So the command crew, as usual," Red answered.

"Well? What do the rest o' ya think?" Dan asked.

"It sounds good to me," Eddie said. "But are we taking Doc Troiano with us too?"

"Why?" Dan asked immediately.

"Well, we've been getting into more and more scrapes where we need medical help. So *I think* either the Doc or one of her staff should be with us."

"You do have a point, Eddie," Mark admitted.

"An' it ain't even on the squirt's head this time," Dan added with a big grin.

"One thing I don't understand," Ariel interjected. "How do these monsters even know what to look for, or that there's anything worth looking for here?"

Mark looked at her and replied, "You make a fair point, Ari. But I have my suspicions."

"Meanin' what, chief?" Eddie asked.

Mark sighed and continued, "To be honest, since we heard the Tahir Ga'Warum were in this dimension, I've been wondering if it's not their first time here."

"An' you just chose not to share that thought with the rest o' us?" Dan questioned.

"No, I thought it was a long shot on my part and basically irrelevant, to be honest. They *are* here and that's enough to want to drive them out."

"But why do you think they've been here before?" Ariel pressed Mark.

"Look at them," he replied. "What do they look like? *Who* do they look like? Do you think that's just a coincidence? I don't."

"So they look like early vampire legends depicted the bloodsuckers to look like, so what? It doesn't mean they were here before, on Earth I mean," Red countered.

"C'mon, Red, look at these things. They don't look vaguely human, and are a couple of pointed teeth away from being a dead ringer for Nosferatu," Mark replied.

Dan nodded his head in agreement. "I can't say that I think yer wrong, because I really don't. It *is* too much o' a coincidence."

90

"So you think these…things were visitors to Earth sometime in the dim past and gave us our vampire legends?" Ariel asked.

"They had to begin somewhere, and these horrors would be as good a start as any I suppose," Mark answered.

"Agreed. So, what are we doin' an' how are we doin' it?" Dan asked, breaking the concentration of the last few minutes and dragging everyone back to the problem at hand.

"Tomorrow, Mark replied, "at 0700 hours we'll take the *Cagliostro* into the planet's atmosphere and stationary park it in a cloud bank. From there, we, along with twenty five of Red's finest Rangers, will take the *Stargrazer* out and land upon that planet's surface again. Only this time we're not coming back until we find what we want."

Ralph L. Angelo Jr.

Chapter 14

"Are you afraid?" Ariel propped herself up on one elbow and stared down at Mark below her on the bed.

"What? Where'd that come from?" Mark asked. He sat up and looked at her, propping his back against the headboard. He continued to look at her with a bemused smirk spread across his face.

"Are you afraid?" she repeated. "I've never seen you like this before. This mission, this time, you're, well, different. You seem more cautious. I think you're scared."

Mark looked at her silently for a moment, then reached over and pulled her naked body close to his own. He hugged her tightly momentarily, then gently extricated himself from her. He held her by the shoulders and stared into her eyes, making sure he had her attention.

"Ariel, do you know the last time I was afraid, I mean ever, in my entire life?"

She looked at him, not sure how she should reply. Then he continued, "I was last afraid, and I mean really afraid, when my father left our house when I was twelve. I knew he wasn't coming home that day, or ever again. It was just a feeling. Something wasn't right. He looked at me differently. I saw it in his eyes. He knew he was never going to see me again. In that moment when he walked out the door and looked back at me one last time I felt genuine fear. I felt terror. I knew, I just knew I'd never see him again. When that door closed and he was gone, the terror grew until that night. I kept hoping, no, praying I was wrong, that he would return. But he didn't. He never did. My parents had a lousy relationship; I knew that even as a kid. They didn't get along. I always thought they did, that they must have earlier on, before I had memories of our family life together. But I don't know. All I do know is that that was the last time I felt fear, real, true terror, ever.

"Years later, my dad came back to me. I think he realized I owned a company that was making a lot of money and that I had turned into the genius he always thought *he* was. He was down on his luck and looked like hell, but his eyes were still the same as I remembered them sixteen years earlier."

"So you were twenty eight at the time?" Ariel asked in a whisper.

"Yes, it was seven years ago."

"What'd he want?" she asked.

"What do you think? He wanted money."

"What'd you do?" she continued to whisper.

"I gave him money." He shrugged. "I wanted to be better than him. I wanted to make sure I wouldn't leave a family member out in the cold when they needed me. I wanted him to be the one I gave help to. It was a dream come true. It was the revenge I waited half my life for."

"Did it give you some kind of closure?" she asked quietly.

"No. It didn't. What it did was something I never expected. It made me happy to see the man who walked out of my life so many years earlier. The man I hated so thoroughly for so many years. I hugged him and he returned the hug. We both cried. I told him I hated him, he told me he was sorry, that he had made a mistake. Then he left."

"Did you ever see him again?"

"Yes, he works for me now as a janitor in the main labs. I see him several times a week actually."

"I don't understand, why tell me this now?" Ariel asked.

94

"Because nothing could instill in me fear like knowing I'd never see my dad again. I'm not afraid of anything, Ariel. You asked if I feared the Tahir Ga'Warum, or the situation we're currently in. The answer is no. I do not. I don't have any fear left inside of me. All I have is determination to conquer every obstacle that gets put in my path, no matter what it is. The Tahir Ga'Warum and the Agalum are not things I fear, no matter how ugly or terrible they appear. They are problems that have to be solved, and when it comes to problems like these, I am the cold, calculating problem solver."

Ralph L. Angelo Jr.

Chapter 15

Dan Sledge spun his seat around and faced Mark Johnson. "We've just dropped outta hyperwarp. We're on approach to Agalum 32, as you called it."

"Okay, Danny, good work and thanks. Start the approach we came up with," Mark replied.

"We're on our way in," Dan answered.

The command deck was decidedly tense as the great ship arced invisibly through space and began to slide between the alien Tahir Ga'Warum vessels. They were miles apart in orbit above Agalum 32, the world hiding the mysterious caverns with their hidden treasure of ancient technology.

"I almost feel like this is a trap," Red muttered.

"I've got the same issues, Red," Mark said. "But we have to go in there; we have to find whatever it is that's buried in that world's depths before either of those two races find it."

"Well are we goin' in or not?" Dan asked, his hand poised over the throttle control on his virtual control panel.

"Go in, Danny. We have to. Red, make sure the camouflage is at full power and working properly once again."

"Everything's working the way it should, Mark. I just checked it three minutes ago."

Mark nodded in silent agreement, then added, "Danny, take us in."

The *Cagliostro* invisibly scooted between the horrible looking Tahir Ga'Warum vessels and invisibly began its descent.

"Slow our descent, Danny; I don't want our friends up there seeing our heat signature piercing the atmosphere."

Dan grimaced and looked at his friend. "Relax chief. This ain't my first rodeo."

Mark nodded and sat back in his command chair, steepling his fingers in front of his face while he silently contemplated the ships entry into the mysterious world's atmosphere.

'You're not looking too relaxed,' Ariel's psychic voice purred within his mind.

'Is it that obvious?' he replied.

'It is. Relax, cowboy. We'll be fine, and everyone here is very good at their jobs.' Ariel countered.

'You're right. I just keep thinking this is the most dangerous thing we've done so far,' Mark answered.

'I know. I keep thinking the same thing,' Ariel nervously admitted.

"We're buried in the atmosphere now, Mark," Dan announced.

"Find a nice heavy cloud bank somewhere and keep us within it," Mark ordered.

"You got it, Boss." Dan answered.

The *Cagliostro* skated through the atmosphere and came upon some heavy storm clouds. Dan slipped the camouflaged ship within them and slowed it almost to a stop, matching the clouds' speed with the ships.

"We're in and we're invisible," Dan confirmed.

"Good," Mark replied. Then he touched his virtual control panel. "Secondary command crew to the command deck," he ordered.

A minute later Major Matt Marek, Lori Westin and the rest of the secondary crew entered the command deck.

The primary crew stood, relinquishing their seats.

Mark shook Marek's hand and said, "Take care of my ship, Matt. Any trouble, get her out of here."

Matt grinned. "You mean any trouble we can't handle, right?"

"You know what I mean, Matt." Mark said as he headed toward the maglovator with the rest of the command crew.

The doors hissed shut behind them.

"Is everyone's tech suit fully charged?" Mark asked. Everyone nodded.

"Okay good. Red, gather your twenty five best Rangers. Make sure everyone is armed properly. I want four in heavy armor suits. Everyone make sure your weapons are fully charged and that you have spare power cells with you when we board the *Stargrazer*. Dan, notify Dr. Troiano that it's time to meet us on the landing deck."

"Okay Mark, you got it," Dan replied quietly.

Mark ordered, "Rendezvous at the *Stargrazer* in fifteen minutes, people. Take whatever you may need, because once we leave the *Cagliostro* there's no going back until the mission is over"

The maglovator doors hissed open on the command crew living quarter's deck and everyone exited and dispersed to their own quarters.

Ariel entered Mark's quarters five minutes later. While they were a couple and were very serious about one another, she kept her own quarters aboard the *Cagliostro* simply for times their schedules did not coincide. Most of her belongings were within her own rooms.

"Do you have everything you need?" he asked her as she entered.

"Yes," Ariel replied. "I'm ready, how about you?"

"Just about there." Mark was zipping up a roll bag as he spoke, not looking at her.

"Hey mister, are you sure you're okay?" she asked tenderly, wrapping her left arm through his right, and giving him a squeeze.

He relaxed a moment and leaned over to kiss her. Their lips pressed together for a long few seconds as his arms wrapped around her until they slowly broke the embrace.

"I'm fine, Ari. Let's get out of here."

He slung the small bag over his shoulder and picked up Ariel's for her.

"I can get that," she protested.

"No, not this time. I've got it." He hefted her bag over his shoulder and headed toward the corridor outside his door.

Mark and Ariel left his quarters and the door hissed shut behind them both.

Two minutes later they exited the maglovator in the landing deck where most of the mission team was waiting for them.

"Where are Eddie and Dan?" Mark asked Red, who was standing nearby checking off personnel on a pad he was holding as they entered the *Stargrazer*.

"Hhhmm? Oh, Dan's inside doing a preflight check, I think. Eddie hasn't shown up yet."

"Okay, thanks, Red," Mark replied. He tapped his suit's right sleeve and called, "Where are you, DiGenovese?"

Immediately a voice replied, "On my way. I just picked up a few extra goodies from the armory."

"Okay, snap to it. It's time to go," Mark ordered.

The last of the Rangers Red was checking in had boarded and were aiding the engineering team in clicking modular seats into position in the forward section of the *Stargrazer*, then buckling themselves in. The ship was reconfigured now to sleep the twenty five man crew plus the command crew. It was sixty feet long with an eight foot forward section for the five man flight team, though it could just as easily be run by one person in a pinch and two normally. Five rows of five seats were in the fifteen foot space behind the flight area.

The next thirty feet were behind a bulkhead door that was also a modular section and installed in the last few hours. This was a sleeping area with mostly bunks two high behind five more comfortable rooms for the command crew.

The last ten feet were jammed with weapons and equipment. In a section under the floor and accessible from outside the *Stargrazer* were stored five of the sky cycles the crew had used on previous occasions.

Dr. Troiano entered the *Stargrazer* with trepidation. She looked about and called to Mark, "You're sure you need me, right?"

"C'mon, Ann, it won't be *that* bad," Dan said.

"You know how much I enjoy away missions," she replied testily.

"Find a seat near the front, Ann. It's time to go," Mark advised with a grin.

Dr. Ann Troiano sat her diminutive frame in the front row behind the command chairs and buckled herself in. The Ranger, Cane Volgers, sat down next to her, looked at her, and smiled, then said, "Relax, ma'am. This will be a piece of cake."

She turned toward him. Her long black hair spun over her shoulders and she looked at Cane over the top of her ever present metal framed eyeglasses, and then said, "I'll be the judge of that."

"Okay, you last stragglers buckle in," Red ordered. That was when Eddie finally bounded in the door with an armload of extra weaponry.

"What have you got there, squirt? Dan asked.

"Two bandoliers of white light explosive grenades, two extra charging clips for my sniper rifle, and two extra fine calibrated blast pistols."

One of the Rangers leaned forward and asked, "What does 'fine calibrated' mean?"

"Eddie likes to calibrate his own weapons for accuracy. It's almost an art form for him," Mark replied.

Eddie stowed the gear in locking units behind the flight seat he was about to buckle into.

A moment later the *Stargrazer* hummed to life as its magno-discs began to spin.

"Engines are hot, we're good to go, Boss," Dan announced.

"Take us away, Mr. Sledge."

The *Stargrazer* majestically hovered upward a few feet, its landing gear retracted into its skin, and the ship moved forward toward the force screen at the end of the landing bay. An instant later it burst free of the *Cagliostro* and headed toward the planet's surface.

"Camouflage is up and running at one hundred percent efficiency," Red announced.

"Engines and controls are also at peak form, Mark," Dan confirmed.

"Weapons are ready to fire," Eddie affirmed.

"*Cagliostro* says we are invisible," Ariel added.

"Okay, as of now we are silent running. Shut down all communications and head toward that mining area the Agalum and Tahir Ga'Warum are digging in," Mark commanded.

The *Stargrazer* peeled invisibly off, heading toward its starboard side and the caverns in the distance.

"How far do we have to go until we get there?" Dr. Troiano asked.

"Another few hundred miles. We'll be there in a few seconds," Dan replied.

"Why couldn't you just park the *Cagliostro* over this spot and let us just fly straight down to it?" she asked.

"Because it's dangerous to put all our eggs in one basket," Mark replied. "By leaving the *Cagliostro* some miles away there is far less of a chance that it will be discovered, and if we need help escaping, it could be here to aid us in seconds."

"Or it could be too late by the time it gets here," Dr. Troiano said nervously.

"Glass half-empty, Ann," Mark replied with a smirk.

"Blah," was her only answer.

The *Stargrazer* slowed to an almost crawl, then set straight down behind a rocky outcropping near the caves. The surface of this world was all sandstone colored with barely any vegetation. The craggy surroundings similar to the one the *Stargrazer* hid behind seemed common across its broken surface.

"Camouflage is running and the *Stargrazer* is hidden," Red advised them all.

"Okay, let's reconnoiter," Mark said.

"You heard the man," Red said. "Let's move out."

The twenty man security force fanned out around the command crew, Red at its forefront.

A few moments later a Ranger named Jennings returned, "All the workers are away in their camp and only a few Tahir Ga'Warum remain on site as guards," Jennings reported to Red.

"Let's make our way to the nearest cave entrance," Red suggested.

"Good job Jennings." Mark praised, "Everyone make sure your tech suits are switched to the camouflage mode, and keep your eyes open."

Red and several of his team slowly and carefully entered the clearing before the cavern entrance. The rest of the team was hidden both by their tech suits' stealth ability and the natural rocky outcroppings. Everyone's eyes were darting back and forth, up and down. Red and several of his security team entered the cavern first, then he motioned the others to follow from their concealment.

When the entire twenty five man unit plus the command crew were within the cavern, Red turned to Mark and said, "No guards. This doesn't seem right."

"You're right, it doesn't," Mark replied.

"Do you think it's a trap?" Eddie asked.

"I would not be surprised, Eddie," Mark answered.

"Ramirez and Markowitz, you both have guard duty. Keep an eye on that cave entrance while the rest of us go deep. If you have any sign of trouble you notify us immediately, got it?" Red ordered.

The two men, both husky Rangers, nodded and took positions on either side of the cave entrance.

"Let's go," Mark commanded, and everyone fell in behind him, Red, and Dan. Directly behind them were Eddie, Ariel, and Dr. Troiano.

'Are you okay, Ann?' Ariel asked telepathically.

'Not really, Ariel. I'm not used to this...planet-side stuff. I prefer being in my med bay one hundred percent of the time,' Troiano replied.

'Relax Ann, we'll be fine,' Ariel replied reassuringly.

'That's easy for you to say, you're used to this stuff. I'm not and I'm scared spit less.'

Ariel smiled and put her arm around her friend's shoulder.

'Let's talk about something else then while we walk.' Ariel began. *'So what's this I hear about you and Dan?'*

'Mark told you?' Ann's telepathic voice raised an octave.

'He didn't have to. The rumor was going all around the ship. Even with a hundred and fifty new crewmembers we're still only a ship of two hundred and fifty people. News travels fast.'

'Like a rocket fuel fed fire you mean,' Ann replied testily.

Ariel shrugged and smiled. *'It is what it is, Dr. Troiano.'*

Ann sighed, *'I suppose so, Miss O'Connor.'*

"Hold up." Red's voice drifted back to them. Both women turned toward the front of the group, where Red, Mark, and Dan were. Eddie was with the security team scanning for enemies hiding amongst the stalactites and stalagmites of the cavern.

"I don't get it," Eddie said breathlessly. "Why no guards, why no one here at all?"

"They must be really secure in their thoughts about this place being safe from intruders," Mark whispered.

"Or it's a trap," Eddie replied.

"Or it's a trap," Mark agreed.

"How are we going to find whatever it is we're looking for, which we're not even sure of what it is, while these guys have been digging through this place for weeks, maybe months?" Red asked.

"I've been wonderin' about that myself," Dan admitted.

Mark did not reply. He simply headed deeper and deeper down into the cavern. They all walked a path that slanted downward into a much larger room. Water fell from somewhere ahead and splashed loudly, echoing back to them all.

It was hot and humid in the cavern, and everyone felt it, even through the tech suits they all wore.

"How deep are we?" Dr. Troiano asked.

"Ask your Tech suit, Ann," Mark replied.

"Just tell me already, will you please?" she replied angrily.

"We're two hundred feet under the surface," Dan replied after checking his suit's display.

"Thank you, Daniel," She answered quietly.

"Look at this," Mark proclaimed.

Everyone followed to where he was standing, which was a wall that had been excavated. This was no stone wall with hieroglyphs spread upon its surface. No, it was a crystalline wall filled with what appeared to be very modern equipment. But all of it was covered in dust and silt, making it appear to be very ancient.

"Lookit this stuff," Dan Sledge spoke aloud.

"Yes, it *is* impressive," Mark agreed.

"But none if it is running. It's all turned off, whatever it is," Ann Troiano announced.

"Right now it is, yeah. Who knows what it was doin' yesterday?" Dan replied.

"Is this what we're looking for?" Ariel asked.

"No, it can't be. They found this sometime ago and from the looks of it had this piece of equipment up and running at one point. My guess is this is some sort of ancient computer that held weapons designs." Mark said.

"Like the stuff we encountered on Chakix," Eddie said.

"Should we fire this baby up and see if we can get what's on its hard drive, or at least what passes for one with this thing?" Dan asked.

"No, on the way out maybe. For now, let's keep going deeper," Mark answered.

Everyone nodded at Mark and began to trudge after him. For his part Mark was single mindedly walking deeper below the world's surface. The group followed him and

106

every so often one of the party would 'Ooo' and 'ahh' over something that would lie half-buried, as if it was dug out of its resting place.

"This path looks like it goes on forever," Red grumbled.

It doesn't matter. Once we find what we're looking for we don't have to go any further at all," Mark answered.

They continued downward, their tech suits' illumination displays lighting a path for them all.

"Look," Ariel said while she pointed ahead of them, "there's another excavation area."

The path ahead of them evened out to a landing.

"I see," Mark replied quietly.

Cautiously the group began to explore the newest dig, with Mark and Dan using their tech suits' equipment to take video recordings of everything they saw.

"It's real quiet down here," Dan commented.

"Yes, I noticed as well," Mark replied. He turned toward Red. "Are you getting any movement down here? Anything at all?"

"Nothing, Boss. No signs of critters of any size, and no signs of our enemies at all."

"I don't know if I should be happy about that or concerned," Mark mused aloud.

"Probably a little of both," Eddie commented.

"Ari, are you picking anything up telepathically? Be careful though, I don't want you doing anything that goes beyond just 'listening' to what's out there."

Ariel furrowed her beautiful forehead a moment, and then shook her long blonde hair negatively. "Nothing at all. It's totally quiet here."

"Did you guys get all of the pictures you needed?" Red asked.

Both Mark and Danny nodded in the affirmative.
"Yes," said Mark. "We've taken images of everything they uncovered down here. Let's move on."

They began to spiral down an ancient stone pathway that had been cut into a circular pit deeper and deeper into the darkness below them.

"I ain't likin' this," Dan admitted.

"Getting claustrophobic?" Ann Troiano asked.

"No, Doc," Dan replied. "I'm not likin' how far we're underground an' how long it's gonna take us ta get back to the surface. We're walkin' for a long tome already, in case you didn't realize it."

"That's a valid point," Mark admitted. "I should have left half the force up top with the two men at the cave's entrance."

"It doesn't matter, Mark," Red interjected. "If those two guys get over run by hostiles, how long do you think a dozen would have lasted? This is a spy mission, not a battle."

"This whole endeavor is a spy mission," Mark countered.

"No kiddin'," Dan said.

They continued trudging downward for a second hour, descending further and further until they came to the end of the ancient stairs.

"End o' the line, kiddies," Dan remarked.

"You men tighten up and form a perimeter." Red commanded. The remaining twenty three men did as they were ordered, guarding the stairway against anything that might come from above.

"You do know we're trapped down here if anything goes wrong?" Dr. Troiano asked.

Mark looked at her with a lopsided grin and replied, "What could go wrong?"

No one said a word, expecting the other foot to drop, but it never came.

"See?" Mark said after a few moments. "Nothing to worry about."

"Now what?" Eddie asked.

"Now we see where they left off," Mark answered.

"That's what I'm worried about," Dan added quietly.

"Let's have a look and see what we've got here," Mark said.

Mark and Dan began to image the strange wall in front of them, recording both videos and static images.

"What do you make of all of this?" Mark asked Dan.

"It's some kinda computer and monitor system. It could be eons old for all we know, but whatever it is it's still up and runnin', or at least it was recently."

"Why do you think it was running?" Mark asked curiously.

"Well look at it," Dan began. "It's wiped free o'dust an' sediment, an' look at all the footprints in the dirt in front o' it."

"Good points, Danny. Let's see if we can get it turned back on."

The two engineers began working around the front of the panel.

"Why d'ya think this stuff is buried in a cave? I mean this ain't no pre-historic society what made this stuff?" Dan asked.

Mark grinned and replied, "I love when you get nervous."

"How'd ya know I was nervous?" Dan asked in surprise.

"You have less and less control of the language when you do; it's almost funny."

"Aaaa yer ass," Dan muttered testily.

"Anyway, I have to assume this was a bunker that was being used during some long standing war. I believe this planet was once a lush, green world, much like our own, but some weapon or another was used here. One that deforested it at an amazing rate."

"D'ya think that's what was on these boards?" Dan cocked a thumb at the eerie floor to ceiling monitors behind them.

"I doubt it. A weapon like that wouldn't be used on one's own world; at least I hope not," Mark replied thoughtfully.

"Why do you think this world was once lush?" Dr. Troiano asked.

"Well, to begin with," Mark answered, "it's very earth-like in a lot of respects. It's got the same atmosphere, relatively the same distance from its sun, about ninety five million miles compared to our ninety three. If anything it should be slightly cooler here, and yet it's almost arid. Something burned away this planet's surface very quickly, either as a terraforming device or a final option against the people who lived here."

"Either way that's awful," Ann admitted.

"This may have been the place where the last stand of a race took place," Mark commented; he looked around the empty cave and in his mind's eye saw an unknown humanoid race running around frantically as the cavern rocked around them. Debris fell from above and each scientist, for that is what they surely were, frantically added something to the very new looking equipment that now looked ancient in today's world. Mark shook his head a moment, trying to focus his eyes, but still the mad display seemed to fly before them. Then he noticed that Dan was staring also.

"A-are you seeing this?" he asked quietly.

Dan nodded slowly. "Yeah I am."

"No one else seems to be," Mark noted.

"Any ideas why?" Dan whispered.

"I hate to say it, but I think it's because we two are the smartest ones here," Mark offered candidly.

"I know; same thought I had. Maybe somethin' to do with scientific knowledge or somethin'?"

"Yes," Mark observed, "same thing I thought."

The two men watched silently as the scientists in their vision hurried about adding calculations and conferred with one another again and again.

Finally one of them turned and began speaking, as if he was speaking directly to Mark and Dan.

"If you are seeing this, this is the last record of an entire race. We were one of the first races, a race of scientific genius and intellect. We were explorers who lived to discover. Our entire existence since the beginning of time immemorial was simply to perceive and understand the unknown. We waged no wars, not even amongst ourselves. As a race we were united in scientific discovery. Our world was peaceful. It was a world of love and honor. We worked hard and in our off time played just as hard. But overall we as a people were obsessed with discovering what was out there as well as in here." He pointed at his own chest, indicating his heart.

"Our ships scoured the galaxies, waging discovery wherever we went. Did we have great weapons? Yes, of course. In our time we met many a violent and evil race who sought to steal our secrets and who were not worthy of them. Yet none ever posed a threat to us until we met...them."

"I almost hate to see who he's talkin' about," Dan admitted.

"Shhh," Mark admonished.

111

The alien figure continued. Its features were blurred somehow so the men could not see exactly who they were listening to. "When they arrived they at first seemed friendly enough. They claimed to want nothing from us save our hand in friendship; and at first we allied with them in a sense of destiny, in a sense of coalition building. We would create a great union of universal harmony and understanding. We would welcome new races in a great galactic alliance."

The alien sighed dramatically, looked down, and then continued, "We were fools."

Both Dan and Mark looked at each other, and then back at the electronic ghost before them. "They were methodical. They came and we believed their offer of friendship, of interstellar camaraderie. For many years they played their hand, and for many years we became more and more...comfortable with them.

"Then the day came when they betrayed us all. Their ships converged over Plaxia, the world you stand upon now. They said they came for a great celebration of peace on the one hundredth anniversary of our meeting. But they lied. While our world stood with open arms, prepared for festivities and celebration, their ships opened fire upon us. For one hundred years we had stood shoulder to shoulder as cosmic brothers and in an instant all of that was dashed away. We fought back, recalling our fleet from the depths of space, but all the ships we had here were unprepared and were among the first things they destroyed."

'What are you two doing?' Ariel's psychic voice interrupted.

'Shhhh, link up with me and Dan, and include Red, Eddie and Dr. Troiano,' Mark replied.

Ariel did as Mark bade her. Instantly the rest of those linked stopped in their tracks, turned and faced the same direction as Mark and Dan.

"What the hell?" exclaimed Red.

"Just watch, big guy," Dan said.

A moment later the alien continued, as if awaiting them all to stop speaking.

"Our greatest vessels were far superior to anything the invaders had. Our weapons would have decimated them on any equal field. But our most powerful ships were far away, and those upon our world could not get off the ground. Those that did were quickly destroyed with all hands lost as they streaked heavenward.

"But still we battled on for weeks; our once pastoral skies were filled with smoke and fires burned constantly. Our once beautiful world was in ruins in days. Our loss of life is catastrophic." The change in tense did not slip past any of those watching.

"We know our time is at an end. We know not when you are watching this. It could be countless millennia from when I am recording this, but it matters not. Our time is at an end now. But our vast scientific knowledge is here for posterity. We have made sure none but those of like minds will be able to access it. Explorers and scientists. Those men who are above petty squabbles and terrible wars; and most especially those that do not share blood with our foes."

"But who were their foes?" blurted out Dan.

The image they all saw stopped moving momentarily and all the images behind the alien of frantic moving associates stopped and disappeared, leaving the sole alien standing with his head down. Then his blurred image looked up and began to speak again. "Accessing," he said. Then a moment later he continued, "What we have named them, for the name they have called themselves will be forgotten in the years to come, we have seen to that. The name we call them, it is a curse to be called such. A name that literally means 'accursed' in our tongue. It is a small vengeance by us, but one that will dog them for the rest of their days. They are called the Agalum."

Chapter 16

"Is that it?" Dr. Troiano asked. "There are no magical secret weapons or plans we can use against the Tahir Ga'Warum and hell, the Agalum too?

Again, the ancient alien image spoke, "Accessing."

An instant later the screen behind them all began to flash images and data.

"Quickly," Mark ordered, "record all of this. We need it all, every last drop of it."

Dan touched the sleeve on his right arm and instantly a beam of light shot out of his sleeve, and played across the ancient screen behind them.

"How have the Agalum been able to get weapons out of this thing if it's keyed not to allow them any access?" Eddie asked.

"Good question," Mark agreed. He turned back to the image of the alien before him and asked, "How have the Agalum been able to access weapons designs out of your data banks?"

"Accessing," the alien scientist spoke again, and lowered his head. Then a moment later he raised his head and answered, "They have not. They use a man from another world to access our secrets. A man with seemingly good intentions. He does not realize what he has done. But now he comes no longer. Now they send only those who shovel dirt to seek our answers. The Agalum are no longer in charge of their own fate. They have become fat and lazy in their dotage."

"It stopped transmitting. I think I recorded it all." Dan announced.

"How are we even able to record or decipher it?" Ariel asked.

"We've been studying everything we could find from the Agalum ships we defeated for the last two years, including their language data feeds. This races, the Plaxians' language was in there, so all of that studyin' we did helped," Dan said.

"But if the Agalum had this great world crushing weapon that destroyed this planet, how come they didn't use it on us?" Red asked.

The image that burned in their minds of the Plaxian scientist looked up and answered, "The weapon was not theirs, it was ours. You must try to understand. Billions of our people were dead already. Those that had escaped to space, and of those there were very few, were already beyond our galactic rim and we knew no more would escape. Yet our world was a lush beautiful place filled with the secrets of a society so ancient that we were new when the universe was. That weapon you speak of was a final solution. One that was destined to turn our world into an arid wasteland. Its documentation is not within the data you have just received. It is forever eliminated. A weapon that terrible should never be used against another foe, only as a final solution against an enemy who would seek to usurp a race's home world."

Mark's face turned angry and then he replied, "No. I do not agree with your 'final solution'. There is always another way. Always a better way than to annihilate what remains of an entire race as well as its world. I refuse to see what you did here as acceptable."

The Plaxian scientist merely added, "It does not matter whether you agree with our choice or not. It is done, and it has been done many centuries ago, across the vast breadth of time. The Plaxian people wish you well. May our scientific knowledge aid you as it did not aid us.

The image began to waver and shake as a violent cataclysm seemed to explode across their very minds' eyes. The Plaxian scientist seemed to crumble and melt as did those who were seen once more working behind him. They all began to shout and scream in fear of what was to come, but they all knew to a man what they had released.

Then the image disappeared from all of their minds.

"What just happened there?" Eddie asked.

Mark slowly and almost reverently replied, "We saw the end, the extinction of a race, perhaps the greatest and oldest race that ever flew the stars."

"This is terribly sad," Ann said, "just terrible. The emotions I'm feeling…"

"We're all feelin' them, Doc," Dan agreed.

"The despair they must have felt…" Ariel commented. She shook her head in almost disbelief.

"We should get out of here," Dan announced. "We have everything we could get out of this place."

"You're right, Danny. Let's start heading to the surface," Mark ordered.

"Wait! Do you hear that?" Donaldson, one of the Rangers said suddenly,

"Hear what?" Red asked.

"I hear it too now," Eddie replied.

And then they all did; it began as a distant, dull, low roar and continued from there, escalating in volume as if the creature making the sound was drawing ever closer.

Because it was.

"It's comin' from behind the monitor!" Dan shouted "Get away from it!"

They all backed up quickly and the ancient monitor exploded before them. Standing in its place was a creature from nightmare. A gargantuan hairy beast with snow white fur and four arms stood before them all, bellowing madly.

117

Its shining black face had four eyes as well, along with tusks pointed upward from its lower jaw.

"What in hell is that thing?" Red asked.

"I have no idea," Mark answered, "but judging by its fur you would think it's a cold weather creature, but there's not cold weather anywhere on this planet."

"I have a feelin' there might be deep within its core." Dan commented.

The beast roared again, bellowing as if to frighten the men and women facing it.

"I would say let's back up the staircase and get out of here, but I have a feeling it's not going to matter. That four armed monstrosity is going to follow us no matter where we go," Mark commented.

"Let's just get out of here. If it chases after us we can kill it and just move on," Red advised.

"Yeah I gotta agree with Red," Dan said. "That thing is all animal and musta been hunting down that tunnel behind the monitor screen when it heard us."

"Actually it probably smelled us," Dr. Troiano said.

"Set your blasters to heavy stun," Mark ordered. "I'd rather not kill a beasty that thinks it's defending its home if I don't have to."

The beast roared again and charged them.

Eddie immediately shot it before it got two steps into its charge. Red was a heartbeat behind him, followed by the rest of the security team who had come running at the creature's first roar. An instant later the great white beast fell over and lay still and silent.

"Well, that was easier than I thought," Eddie admitted.

Almost immediately Eddie turned his head toward the blackened ceiling so far above, squinted his eyes, and shouted, 'Everyone get back!"

The group as a whole hugged the walls and an instant later two bodies slammed into the floor before them.

Instantly Dr. Troiano leapt to two burned and crushed bodies. She looked up a heartbeat later and said, "It's Ramirez and Markowitz."

"Okay Ann, move back closer to the wall," Mark ordered. "There's nothing you can do for them now."

"Who is down there?" a voice hissed from far above in the shadow darkened tunnel. "Perhaps earthmen? Like those who visited our world, our universe once before? Hhhmmm?" the voice of the unknown Tahir Ga'Warum continued to taunt.

"Come up and we will not harm you," the voice added, "But if you make us come after you, you will meet the same fate as your two companions."

"Mark," Red began, "They could be teleporting down here any second. We should back up through that tunnel that monster just came out of."

"No, Red, that's too dangerous. There may be more of those things hiding down there. Let's play it by ear a few minutes and see where it leads us."

While the two men were talking Dan began to work on something he pulled out of his pack. They all had small packs with them. Some had slung them over their shoulders; some wore them as full backpacks, such as Dan did.

Mark turned to him. "Are you almost ready, Danny? They could be here any second."

"Yeah, I'm activatin' it now." Dan pushed a button on the device's side. It was a cylinder about six inches across and ten inches tall. At its top he screwed a portable parabolic antenna that he then fanned out. Dan quickly jammed its legs into the hard sandy surface in the center of the floor.

119

Dan turned back toward Mark, "Okay, boss, it's on."

Mark nodded and looked toward the ceiling so far above them. "Any second now..." he muttered.

As if in response to his words a dull thud sounded above them all followed by another. Each thud was punctuated by a bloody splash in the air above their heads, as if an invisible dome had been erected above them, and in truth it had.

"Force field's holdin' with no problem," Dan advised.

"Yes, I knew it would. The Tahir Ga'Warum are trying to teleport through it and are being splattering like bugs against a windshield," Mark confirmed to them all.

"How long can that thing last?" Red asked.

"I ain't sure. I'm thinkin' at least a few hours, as long as the power cells hold out; though that depends on what they throw against the force field itself," Dan admitted.

"Uh oh, look," Eddie warned.

Everyone turned toward where he was staring and saw the white furred four armed monster groggily getting to its feet.

"Great. That thing is blockin' the only way out of here," Eddie said.

"I don't think we want to go down that tunnel," Mark reiterated.

"I don't think we have a choice," Ariel replied. She pointed to the top of the invisible dome where more and more body sized blood red splotches appeared against its imperceptible surface. Tahir Ga'Warum were teleporting into the shield without regard to their own safety, and splattering against it again and again.

A sudden roar turned everyone's attention back to the four armed, white furred beast. They all turned in time to see it charge toward them, its arms gesticulating and it bellowing madly.

120

Eddie dropped to his knee and fired his hand held blaster repeatedly at the fur covered horror. Red fired his rifle and was joined by the rest of his security team. This time no one's blaster was set to stun. They were on full power, full kill.

But surprisingly, even though the monster showed blotches of blood now staining its fur it continued to move forward against the energy volley.

"What the hell? We stunned this thing into submission not five minutes ago, now we're not even slowing it down?" Red boomed.

"Maybe it was playin' possum," Dan shouted.

"Or maybe it somehow adapted to our blasters," Mark offered.

"It's getting closer," Ann Troiano yelled above the deafening din of close quarter's blaster fire.

"Hold yer fire, I got this," Dan roared angrily. "I been getting' itchy fer a fight anyway."

The big Jovian hurled himself at the beast in one leap. Cocking his right arm back, he let it fly in an incredible right cross into the thing's upward tusked jaw.

Both man and monster hurtled back toward the tunnel the beast had appeared from, impacting with the wall behind the white covered monstrosity.

But then all four arms grasped Dan, seeking to pull his arms and legs off of his body.

"Arrgggh!" he groaned painfully.

"Danny!" Dr. Troiano shouted.

Mark, Red, and Eddie opened fire once again, peppering the beast across its left side. It immediately

dropped Dan's right arm and sought to cover its face from
the blistering attack.

That was all the opening Dan needed. He swung his
right arm again and connected with the thing's shiny black
face, staggering it immediately.

"It ain't gonna be that easy, Hairbag," Dan growled.

"Hold your fire," Red cautioned. "We may hit Dan."

"I got this," Dan shouted over his shoulder.

But even as he was charging the beast, it swiped its two
right arms at him, knocking him to the ground.

Again the monster charged him, but Dan did not
hesitate. The instant the great beast came within range he
kicked out savagely with both of his very powerful legs. He
caught the creature squarely in the chest and sent it flying
through the air and into the wall behind it. The monster
staggered forward, its body's impression left in the solid
stone wall as it struggled to pull itself free.

But Dan Sledge was not waiting for that to happen.
With a roar like a mad beast himself he attacked again. His
fists swung through the air like pile drivers, hammering the
larger monster back, ever back. The beast roared its
displeasure and pain as it continued to swing-and miss-its
powerful arms at the Jovian powerhouse.

Dan ducked and weaved away from the beast's frantic
swings, but he himself was now connecting on every blow.

The small confines were rocking with each impact.
Finally Dan reared back and punched the monster in its
stomach, doubling it over painfully. Then he reached both
his hands up over his head and with a roar he brought them
down on the thing's head, knocking it out cold before its
body hit the ground.

"Yeah, try adaptin' to that," Dan growled as he wiped
his hands together.

"Good job except for one thing," Eddie shouted.

"What?" Dan questioned.

"That!" shouted Eddie, while he pointed behind the powerful engineer.

Dan looked where Eddie was pointing and his eyes grew wide in shock. Behind him, the force field generator lie crushed. During the battle it had been destroyed.

"We have only seconds until they're down upon us, get into that tunnel," ordered Mark.

"I got our backs," Dan replied.

"No, you go in front," Red argued, "in case this thing has any big brothers waiting for us. I got the rear. Don't argue with me, just go; this is *my* job."

"Okay, okay you got it," Dan agreed.

"Eddie," Mark instructed, "you and half the Rangers go up front with Dan. The rest stay back with Red and follow us in immediately after the last of us enters the tunnel. Then blast that opening closed on your way in."

"Mark!" Ariel asked in surprise. "Are you sure?"

"We have no choice, Ari. Hell, they could probably teleport beyond the stone walls anyway, so I have no idea if this is going to help or not. We may be in trouble either way."

"Hurry it up, this is clear," Dan admonished from somewhere ahead of them in the tunnel.

As the last men cleared the tunnel's maw, the stench of brimstone reached their noses. Red turned back to see the horrific Tahir Ga'Warum teleporting in behind them in the clearing. Without hesitation he and his eight man team opened fire. At first they fired at the incoming invaders and then secondly, the walls and ceiling of the tunnel area. They dropped untold tons of debris into the tunnel entrance. The impromptu avalanche blocked them from the creatures who were angrily trying to force their way through the rain of rock and sand.

"They're closed off, Mark," Red said. "This may not do us any good though if those things can teleport past this."

"I'm playing a hunch that for some reason they can't, Red. Otherwise why would they need the workers to dig down here? I'm hoping that something in the planet's makeup doesn't allow them to teleport through these stone walls."

"That may be all well and good, but now we're trapped in here with nowhere to go," Ann Troiano said.

"You're wrong Ann. we do have somewhere to go. Down," Mark replied.

She shook her head angrily. "Why did I know you were going to say that?"

"Because you're brilliant?" Mark answered with a lopsided grin.

"Don't try to make me laugh. I'm really mad at you right now. I don't need this. I should be back on Earth with a nice practice out in the country somewhere where I could do the most good."

The group began to walk deeper into the tunnels. Their tech suits' right sleeves shot a beam of light outward, illuminating their path easily.

"At least we can see what we're walkin' into," Dan grunted.

Mark turned his attention back to Dr. Troiano as they walked deeper into the tunnel. "Ann, if you weren't an important part of this team, this crew, would you really be happy? Look at all you've done in the past two plus years. Also the fate of the Earth is something we're fighting for. All of us, including you, are integral to the world's survival. Heck, probably the entire human race's survival. You have to know how important your contributions have been."

She sighed, obviously exasperated. "I know all about that, Mark. I'm just tired of feeling like I'm in above my head all of the time."

He leaned toward her conspirationally. "I'll let you in on a little secret. That's how I've been feeling since all of this began two years back. I've been making a lot of this up as we go."

She shot him a withering glance and then continued, "Yes, but it's different for you. You're this super genius and tactical wizard. When you come up with something that gets us all out of a last second jam, no one is really surprised. Me? Every time we do something that I can help out with, I'm stunned it worked."

He put his arm around her shoulders and gave her a quiet kiss on the head. "Don't underestimate your contributions, Dr. Troiano. Without you we would not have made it anywhere near as far as we have."

"So you keep saying. I'm still not sure I believe you or not," she answered with a slight smile.

"Mark, we're coming into some kind of large cavern," Red called back. He and his men had moved to the forefront of the group after closing the tunnel entrance off.

"I'm on my way," Mark replied.

He pushed his way past the security men, and joined Red, Eddie, and Dan at the front of the pack.

"Lookit this," Dan spoke in a barely audible voice.

"I am," Eddie replied.

The tunnel ended in a great cavern, so large the other side was not visible. The walls glistened with light as stones embedded everywhere the eye could see gave off bright, glowing white luminescence.

"Shut your tech suits' flash beams off. We don't need them and we can conserve some energy now, just in case," Mark commanded

125

"What are those stones?" Dan asked.

"I have no idea," Mark replied. "I've never seen anything like this that glowed that brightly."

'Mark,' Ariel's psychic voice intruded on his thoughts, *'we're not alone. I'm 'hearing' another mental voice. I can't make out what he's thinking, but I hear some sort of language.'* She pointed toward the other side of the cavern where a furtive, black cloaked and hooded figure crept surreptitiously away from them and into the shadows.

'He's running from us,' Mark said.

"Should we go after him?" Dan asked aloud.

"No. He's too far away. Let him go. Whoever it is did not want to be seen, and reacted fearfully to our presence. Let him go, there are too few of us and he's already too far away, I'm sure we'll end up catching up to him later on. To chase him now would just separate us all and put some of us in danger from an unknown source," Mark reiterated.

Dan nodded, "You got it, boss."

Mark looked around carefully, and then said, "Let's move out. It may take us hours to get across to that other side."

"What do you want to do? Follow that mysterious figure?" Dr. Troiano asked.

"Yes Ann, that's exactly what I intend to do. That mysterious figure is going to tell us how to get the hell out of here and back to the surface and the *Stargrazer*. Now let's move out."

"How do we get down there?" a Ranger named Ryerson asked.

"There's a stone trail going down to the cavern's floor, Ryerson," Red answered, "Just watch your step. It's not very wide, and one misstep-well, let's just say it's not a good idea to have a misstep."

Ryerson nodded his sandy colored head of hair and half grinned nervously, then followed the man in front of him down the craggy, ancient pathway.

The group moved as one, following their leader down the ancient stone path and out into the huge cavern's floor.

"Well I'm glad that's over with," Dan admitted.

"Scared of heights, Chunky?" Dr. Troiano asked, smiling.

"Let's just say they ain't my favorite thing ta deal with, Doc," Dan replied.

Mark walked up to Red who was using his tech suit's scanner system hooked up to a set of small electronic binoculars.

"See our mysterious friend at all?" Mark asked.

Red shook his head negatively, "No, he's gone."

"How far behind him are we?" Mark asked.

"Honestly, with this terrain? Probably two to three hours would be my best guess. Of course if we had a sky cycle or two, we could be there in a few minutes easily," Red answered.

"Let's get moving then." Mark said, "Those strange rocks seem to be giving off a lot of light down here and there probably isn't a natural night time rest period in this underverse. We'll try to get to the other side and then camp for the night if we have to."

"What are we doin' here anyway, boss?" Eddie asked.

"We're going to try to find a way out of this place," Mark replied, "either another tunnel that heads up, or we'll track down that mystery man and hopefully he'll know a way out of here."

Ariel looked at her boyfriend and smiled slightly, then said, "We're in uncharted territory, again."

"No kidding," Mark replied with a hint of angry acceptance. "The last thing I wanted to be doing was traipsing around the inside of a world somewhere."

"Think about it this way," Eddie interjected. "Right now we got something those Nosferatu things don't have and that they want, so all we gotta do is stay one step ahead of them."

"Is that supposed to be a good thing, DiGenovese?" Mark screwed his face up and asked. "You do realize they *are* going to be hunting for us all the more right? Exactly because they will figure out that we have that information they've been hunting for and getting nowhere finding."

"An' then we traipse in an' get it all without a hiccup," Dan added.

"Exactly Danny," Mark finished.

"I know Mark. I figured it all out already," Eddie said. "But you gotta admit it feels good to get one up on these ghoulish bums just by we bein' who we are."

"You're nuts sometimes, Eddie," Red uttered as he shook his head side to side.

"Maybe so big guy, but we did pull a fast one on those things, so score one for the good guys," Eddie replied.

"Okay all of you, enough, let's get out of here before they blast their way into that tunnel and catch up to us. We have to move out now," Mark ordered.

Nervous glances passed between everyone. Then they all turned and headed out across the rocky and barren terrain, through a path sometimes only wide enough for one person to walk in with thirty foot tall stone walls on either side of them. Other times it was a flat plain of sandstone as far as the eyes could see.

The minutes turned into hours, and mostly quiet ones as the group walked steadily through the underground maze.

Finally after several hours they stopped for a short break at a wave of Red's hand.

"Do you notice anything strange?" Mark asked Red, Dan, and Eddie.

"Like what could be stranger than any of this?" Eddie waved his hand around and replied.

Red and Dan both shot him annoyed glances. Then Red answered, "What, like we haven't seen hide nor hair of another one of those creatures that attacked us?"

Mark replied, "Yes exactly, Red."

"What're ya thinkin', Mark? That that thing was the hooded guy's pet?" Red asked.

Mark nodded his head to the side slightly and half smiled. "Yes I am. It's definitely a possibility at the minimum."

"So that guy sicced that thing on us like a mad dog? If that's what passes fer a dog on this cockamamie world I'd hate ta see a wolf," Dan grunted.

"What are you complaining about? You took that thing apart like nothing," Red said.

"I dunno about 'like nothin', Red. I had a tough time with it. That was one bad ass monster."

"Yeah maybe so, Sledge," Eddie chimed in, "but our blasters weren't having any affect at that point. It was like it suddenly became impervious to the blasts, like it adapted."

"That's exactly what happened, Eddie," Mark agreed.

"Somehow that thing changed on a molecular level and the energy blasts no longer affected it."

"What a curious creature," Dr. Troiano admitted.

"That thing would have torn us apart if not for Danny. I'd hardly call it curious, Ann," Mark replied.

"I hope there aren't any more of those things hidden here waiting for us," Eddie added.

"You're not the only one squirt," Red replied.

"You're worried? Now I know we're in trouble," Eddie countered.

"I didn't say I was worried, short stuff," Red answered. "I just think it'll be better if we don't have to fight our way through miles of this place."

Eddie shrugged. "Makes sense, but yeah, I'm worried." He held up his rifle and looked at it. "If this is useless, what use am I here?"

"They're not useless. Neither are you," Mark quipped as he began walking forward into the stalagmite heavy cavern.

"Wait up, Mark, let me lead the way." Red pushed forward impatiently.

"If you want to lead, Red, then lead. We can't sit still any more like this. We have no idea how far behind us the Tahir Ga'Warum are."

Dr. Troiano asked, "Do you think they're following us, Mark?"

Mark nodded and replied, "I know they are, or will be once they dig out of that cave-in we caused. They want what we have, what they couldn't get. The Agalum had to know how to access that information, it explains their recent advances in ships and weaponry, but they're not sharing with the Tahir Ga'Warum."

"From what we seen, they're still fightin' 'em," Dan rumbled in reply.

"Yeah but it doesn't look like it's going their way, does it?" Red answered.

"Nope, not at all," Dan admitted.

"Hey! Look up there." Eddie pointed to something gleaming in the distance.

"What the hell is that?" Red wondered aloud.

130

"Time to find out," Mark answered. He turned and began to walk toward the gleaming object in the distance.

Whatever it was, it reflected light like a polished mirror, instantly drawing their attention to it.

The group moved forward toward the object, then Mark turned around and said, "Turn your tech suit to camouflage mode."

Many complied immediately, some a little slower than others, but the group as a whole faded from sight.

"Make sure you don your spectroscopic goggles, it's the only way we'll be able to see each other," Mark said.

"Done and done, boss," Dan replied.

"Ditto," came Eddies answer as well.

Soon everyone had acknowledged that they had the goggles on and powered up.

"Let's take a roundabout route through these stalagmites," Red advised.

"You've got the lead, Red," Mark acquiesced.

The big man nodded and said, "Follow me."

'I'm linking us all telepathically,' Ariel advised the group.

'Are you going to be able to handle this many minds?' Mark asked.

'It's not a problem,' she replied.

'Okay let's do it this way then,' Mark answered along her link.

'Jackson, Brevard, and Coops with me,' Red ordered. *'The rest of you hang back a little. Let us get there first. I want the rest of my Rangers surrounding and protecting the command crew, is that clear?'*

'As crystal,' Brevard, a buxom brunette in a very tight fitting tech suit, replied. She looked more like a swimsuit model than a trained security officer.

But she was deadly and dangerous, as were all of Red's handpicked crew of professionals.

'Move out,' Red ordered tersely and the three man security detail followed his lead toward the glittering, sparkling object.

'What do you think?' Dan asked Mark.

'Of?' Mark questioned.

Dan pointed at the glittering object in the distance, *'What do you think it is?'*

'Either a trap to draw our attention to it, or God only knows what else.'

'So you're bettin' it's a trap?' Dan asked.

Mark nodded. *'I am. Let's hope we can turn the tables.'*

Dan shook his head side to side and grimaced. *'Great, just what we needed.'*

***

Red and his team moved silently and invisibly through the great stalagmite filled cavern. Their view of the others had now been obscured by the upward growing rocky outcroppings. The floor had leveled out, so the team was no longer looking down across the valley like floor of the cavern.

Still, they could see the flickering light ahead of them.

'What do you suppose that is?' asked Brevard.

'We're about to find out, soldier,' Red replied.

The team split up at Red's finger pointed instructions and surrounded the zone the gleaming light was coming from. Then they slowly entered the area ahead of them. In the center of the small clearing was a gigantic pointed gem mounted on a circular device that was turning constantly in circles, rotating the gem so it reflected the cavern's light.

"What the hell?" muttered Cooms, the shaven headed security officer.

Instantly all hell broke loose around the still camouflaged team.

Dark figures, shorter than an average man's height and wearing what appeared to be ragged cloaks pulled up over their heads, leaped from behind stalagmites and swung pointed staves of some unknown metal through the air at the invisible security men.

Two of the cloaked figures struck at Cooms, their staves giving off a glowing shrieking burst of what appeared to be electricity. Cooms arched backward in pain, his mouth wide open and immediately his tech suit's camouflage unit shorted out. He dropped to the ground, his body smoking.

Red wasted no time, and had his blaster out and firing at the ragged attackers, dropping several in their tracks with each well placed blast. Jackson and Brevard were likewise firing their hand blasters almost feverishly.

But still the unknown assailants came, in almost a wave of hooded, stave wielding fury.

'Back up!' Red shouted along the psychic link.

'Red!' Mark's telepathic voice intruded on the desperate melee. *'What's going on? Are you okay?'*

'Stay back!' Was Red's only reply.

'What's happening there?' Mark pressed.

'Can't talk! Under attack,' Red answered tersely.

Mark turned toward his team and psychically shouted, *'Let's go!'*

The group began running invisibly toward the sounds of battle.

Dashing into the clearing they found no signs of their friends, or their attackers, save for the body of Cooms.

Ralph L. Angelo Jr.

Chapter 18

Red awoke with a start. Surreptitiously he looked around and realized he was in a steel cage being transported by several of the cloaked beings.

"Don't move, Chief. Stay down," a feminine voice suggested.

"Brevard? Is that you?" he hissed.

"It is," she replied.

Red, without moving from the position he lay in, looked to his left and saw Brevard sprawled out next to him in the same cage. She opened her left eye and winked at him, then closed them both back to slits again.

He did likewise. "Where are we?" he whispered.

"You got me, boss." I woke up a few minutes before you and found the predicament we were in."

"Where's Cooms and Jackson?" he continued to whisper.

"Dead, at least I assume as much. Neither one is here." she replied almost inaudibly.

"Great. Where the hell's Mark and the rest of the team?"

"I have no idea, Chief," Brevard replied despondently.

"Don't sweat it, Joanie. They'll show up and get us out of here. These tech suits have trackers built in with redundancies," Red said. "We'll be okay."

"What should we do in the meantime?"

"We play possum, and wait for our rescue. If things look bad, we may have to fight our way out."

"But they took our weapons," Joanie Brevard said.

"I assumed as much. I'm not worried about that right now. We'll either get 'em back or take some of theirs, when the time comes. My biggest concern is where's Mark and the rest of the team?"

***

"Where is Red and the rest of his team?" Mark asked no one in particular.

"We'll find them, Mark, don't sweat it," Eddie assured him.

"Ari, are you reaching out with your telepathy?"

The blonde beauty looked at her boss and boyfriend and shook her head negatively. "No sign of them yet, Mark. Either the natural rock formations are blocking my telepathy at any distance or there's something else working against me here."

"Wonderful, and from what I can see here in this mess they left behind, those staves that a few of their attackers dropped pack a real electrical wallop. Definitely enough to stun or kill." Mark looked sadly at the two covered bodies nearby.

'Are you okay?' Ariel asked.

'Yes. I don't like losing men on missions. It's not something I'll ever get used to,' he replied.

'And that's what makes you a good man and a great leader. At least one of the things,' Ariel said.

'Thanks for the confidence boost, Ari, but at this point we need more than a pat on the back.'

"Rangers," Mark said aloud, "I want you to break into groups of three and spread out. These…people we're tracking move fast, and don't leave any obvious trace. Furthermore I think those energy staves shorted out the tech suits somehow. I can't track Red or Brevard. Be careful. They know this land. We're the invaders here, don't take anything for granted. We caught up to where they were in two minutes once we realized what was going on and they were already gone. Keep that in mind. Now move out. Maintain your camouflage and use the telepathic link Ariel provides us with. After this no shouting, no talking, unless you are somehow attacked. Then do whatever you have to, to get someone else's attention and get help for yourself. Am I clear?"

"As crystal, sir," The Ranger named Rayborn confirmed. He had taken over as commander of the Ranger team in Red's absence. He was a burly man with his brown hair in a short military cut. He wore a full beard and a serious demeanor. He was not as tall or as a powerfully built as Red, but he was still a bruiser.

"Good, Rayborn. Move out your men and lets go find our friends," Mark ordered.

Rayborn saluted Mark, then turned and led his three man crew into the stalagmite wasteland all around them. The other teams followed his lead, leaving Dan, Eddie, Ariel, Dr. Troiano, Mark, and three of the security team as a separate unit.

'Spread out wide and stay within sight of one another. Make sure your goggles are down and turned on so you can see one another,' Mark commanded.

A chorus of *'Yes sir's'* echoed within his mind. He turned and smiled at Ariel who warmly returned his smile. He took her hand and led her through the maze of brightly glowing stone.

***

The cage containing Red and Joanie Brevard was dropped unceremoniously to the ground, jarring both badly. It was a purposeful move to force them awake.

Both feigned grogginess, but the pain they were exhibiting was real enough.

"Where are we?" Brevard asked breathlessly.

"We're about to find out," Red replied.

The top of the steel cage was opened and for the first time in over an hour Red and Brevard could stand. The way the cage was set up they were lying flat within its confines. Red was not able to stretch out all the way because of his height. Brevard had no such problems, but still it was tight.

Rough hands grabbed at them and pulled them upward.

"Watch it," Red growled menacingly, only to have an electrical stave shoved in his face as a threat.

Remembering its bite Red put his hands up to show he was not going to fight them. They dragged both he and Brevard out of the cage and shoved them roughly ahead through the stalagmites that thinned with each step.

"Any thoughts on how to get out of this?" she whispered.

Immediately she received a smack in the back of her head with one of the shining metal staves. She dropped to the ground in pain.

Red spun. "Grrraaahhh!" he howled and swept the legs of the hooded figure behind him out from under him, throwing the man to the ground. Reacting with lightning quick reflexes, Red snapped the stave out of midair and began battling the tight group centered on him.

"Dammit! I can't figure out how to turn this damned thing on," he grunted aloud.

An instant later he had a second stave in his left hand he had wrested from a now insensate foe.

Brevard began to fight her way to her feet at his side. He looked at her and that proved to be his undoing.

One of the aliens smacked him across the back with a charged stave, sending him tumbling. He hit the ground, fought to stay conscious, and kicked out for all he was worth, sending the nearest ragged attacker tumbling into a stalagmite. With a solid 'thunk' the being hit the stony outcropping head first and slid down its length to the floor, insensate.

But Red was already being overwhelmed the instant he had fallen to the floor. Charged staves darted in and out and he couldn't block them all, even though he tried mightily.

Another minute and it was all over. His unconscious form was dragged out of the crush of bodies and into what appeared to be a village hewn into the side of the cavern walls which reached up hundreds of feet, disappearing into the darkness above. What appeared to be windows were carved into the face of the underground cliffs the rocky cavern walls dotted with them.

Joanie Brevard looked at Red's body being dragged and a shiver ran down her spine. She saw him breathing so knew he was still alive, but not much else.

The next instant she was grabbed roughly and prodded along behind the unconscious security chief.

"Get your damned hands off of me!" she shouted, pulling loose of her captor and throwing a left cross to where its jaw would be under the hood. The hooded, ragged creature fell to the ground like a sack of potatoes. Instantly half a dozen sparking staves were pointed at her face. She raised her hands in compliance and followed along. This time none of the silent creatures grabbed her.

***

'Did you see that? We have to get in there and help them,' Dan Sledge told the rest of the group.

139

'Dan, it's too dangerous right now. We'll end up just like Red and Brevard,' Mark answered along the telepathic link.

'We can't just stand here and watch this. We have to do something,' Eddie said.

'We will, Eddie,' Mark replied. *'These things have to have a sleep cycle. When they do, we'll make our move.'*

'What if that's too late? What if they sacrifice them or something?' Dan asked.

'I won't let that happen, I promise,' Mark responded.

His eyes narrowed as he watched the strange creatures drag Red and force Joanie Brevard into their stone, multi-floor village.

***

'What've we got?' Dan Sledge asked. Several hours had passed while the group stood about invisibly with their camouflage units keeping them from sight.

Dan and Eddie were pacing with anxiety while Mark, Dr. Troiano, and Ariel were sitting behind a particularly tall stalagmite watching the hooded creatures that guarded the entrance to their village. Two of the creatures stood stock still with their staves at the ready, resting on their shoulders guarding the entrance to the village in the cliffs.

'Nothing's changed, Danny,' Mark replied. *'If we don't see anything happen soon we'll have to sneak by these guards and into the cliffs.'*

'We'll haveta do what we'll haveta. We've been waitin' fer hours now. If somethin' don't break fer us soon, we're gonna haveta charge in there. There's no tellin' what's goin' on inside those walls,' Dan said.

'Actually there is. Red's tech suit self-repaired and I've been able to get a feed on his vitals. He's okay, but apparently still unconscious.' Mark said.

'Well, that's a mixed bag,' Dan telepathically grunted, then as an afterthought he turned toward Ariel and asked, *'How are you feelin', Ari? Are you okay?'*

Ariel smiled at her friend and replied, *'I'm good, Danny. This is no strain to me.'*

Dan Sledge nodded grimly, and then replied, *'Okay, Ari, I'm glad ta hear it. I just wanted ta make sure you were okay.'*

Mark and Rayborn were both staring at the guards in front of the strange town built into the cavern wall. Finally Mark turned toward the Ranger and telepathically asked, *'What's your opinion of all of this? Do you have any suggestions? I usually rely on Red's input in situations like these.'*

Rayborn squinted his eyes in deep thought, then said, *'I gotta tell you, Boss, I just don't see a way into this place without eventually having some kinda conflict with these guys.'*

'I agree, Rayborn. But I think a small group of us could sneak in past these guys and free the others,' Mark replied.

Rayborn thought about it for a minute and then added, *'Maybe while the others create a diversion out here when needed. Ariel could signal the rest of the team out here and tell 'em when to attack, when it'd cause the biggest distraction. What do you think?'*

'I think it's a good idea and plan, Rayborn. Ariel, did you read all of that?'

'I did, Mark,' she replied.

'Okay. We're coming back to you to finalize everything. We'll have our people back, and then these mole-men will

realize what the rest of our enemies already know. Don't mess with the crew of the Cagliostro.'

Mark, Dan, Rayborn, and two other men from the security team all stood behind a rocky outcropping staring into the entrance to the strange town. The guards had just changed to a new set of two as the previous guardsmen called it a night.

'So now what?' Eddie DiGenovese asked.

'Now you and the rest of the Ranger team get ready to raise some hell out here on our signal, Mark replied, *'Ariel,'* he called out to her, *'Are you sure you'll be able to keep in contact with us after we enter this place?'*

'Yes, it's not a problem, Mark, really. I still hear Red's and Brevard's thoughts; at least Brevard's. I think Red is starting to come to,' Ariel noted.

'Just bear in mind that there could be hundreds if not thousands of these guys attacking you in a matter of seconds. They seem to pop out of the woodwork.' Mark reminded them all.

'In this case it's rock,' Eddie corrected.

'Shuddup, squirt,' Dan telepathically grumbled.

Mark fought back a grin and then said, *'Okay, it's show time.'*

As one, Mark, Dan, Rayborn as well as the two additional Rangers, Hopkins and Neely, stealthily walked toward the entrance to the wall city. They skirted the immobile guards and quickly hustled past them, as silent as a leaf touching down on a fall morning.

Rayborn led the way into the ominous wall city that disappeared far above them.

'This is incredible,' Mark thought.

'Mebbe so, boss, but we're in enemy territory an' I think less sight seein' an' more concentratin' on gettin' our people outta here is the ticket,' Dan replied crisply.

Mark nodded, the lenses of his goggles reflecting light from the glowing stones about the walls of the corridor they were in. *'You're right, Danny. I know better than to not keep my head on the job at hand.'*

'That's what I'm here for, Mark, to make sure things go smoothly,' the big powerhouse replied.

'Any idea where they are?' Rayborn's thoughts intruded on their conversation.

Mark looked at the sleeve of his tech suit while a holographic display danced over it.

'Ahead and up.' He pointed as he 'spoke' toward a staircase cut into the stone at the end of the corridor.

'How far up? They carried Red up that thing?' Neely asked. He was a thin man, lean but muscular. His own hair was a mop of red and his light complexion and freckles spoke of his Irish descent.

'It looks like only one level,' Mark replied.

Mark began to walk, but Rayborn held up a hand and halted him. He carried a big rifle and had it aimed at the ceiling. *'I've got this, boss. Stay behind me and just tell me where to go.'*

Mark nodded and grinned. *'Okay, up that staircase there for one level, then head to your right when we come up to that next level.'*

'You've got it, boss,' Rayborn acknowledged.

As silent as cats walking on feathers the team went up the staircase. Silently they scanned all about them.

'All clear to the right,' Hopkins advised. He was a shaven headed black man with a Van Dyke beard.

'Not so much to the left,' Dan rumbled.

Everyone stole a glance to the left side of the landing they were on and saw several of the ragged creatures sitting on the floor cross-legged. They had a fire roaring in the midst of themselves, warming their hands near it and yammering on in some language no one understood.

'How come the tech suits aren't translating that for us?' Hopkins asked.

'We're too far from the Stargrazer or the Cagliostro to connect to the mainframe on either ship ta do the translatin', ' Dan replied.

'Straight ahead,' Mark said, *'they're both directly ahead of us.'*

The five man crew continued into the now poorly lit rock wall city. It seemed the deeper they went the less of the strange glowing rocks were present about them.

'Switchin' goggles ta infra-red,' Dan announced.

The rest followed suit. Now instead of seeing everything as they normally would, or at least close to it, now they saw bright colored masses which were hot spots. The hooded and ragged creatures were small hot blobs to their enhanced vision.

But ahead of them two larger figures, one very large and glowing a very bright red immediately grasped their attention.

'Wow, I guess he really earned his nickname this time,' Dan said.

'Let's get them and get out of here,' Mark ordered, *'Eddie, it's go time.'*

'You got it, boss,' came the marksman's terse reply.

The crew stood to the side of the aliens surrounding a bound Red and Brevard as an instant later explosions rumbled the stone city from without.

Immediately the hooded creatures ran toward the outside of their city in the walls to deal with the unknown attackers.

Two were left to stand guard over Red and Brevard.

'I got this,' Rayborn said.

'Stun them. I don't want them dead,' Mark ordered.

'You're the boss.' Rayborn replied.

He lined up the scope on his solar rifle to his eye and fired twice. Twin blips of energy streaked through the air and impacted with both of the guards before they could react. They hit the ground with dull thuds.

Quickly and professionally the five man rescue team swarmed forward, cutting Red and Brevard free.

'Are you all right?' Mark asked.

Red shrugged then answered, *'I've been better. Those sticks of theirs pack a wallop.'*

Mark nodded. *'What about you, Joanie? Are you okay?'*

'I'm fine, boss. They kept their distance after I slugged one of them, except to tie me up, which they did with more of those sticks in my face.'

'Mark, you better see this,' Dan interrupted.

'What is it?' Mark replied.

'Look,' Dan said.

He had peeled away one of the hoods the creatures in rags wore and revealed a pale almost sickly yellow colored face with big black eyes devoid of all hair.

'Look familiar?' Dan asked.

'The beings in the vision we all saw. These are their descendants; changed from thousands of years underground, but the resemblance is undeniable,' Mark replied.

'So now we know what happened to these guys after the Agalum came from wherever they did,' Dan offered.

146

Another explosion followed by repeated blaster fire woke everyone from the trance they were in staring at the strange creatures before them.

'*Let's get outta here,*' Dan said.

'*Yeah, let's move out.*' Red agreed; then he and Joanie Brevard picked up their weapons and gear that was neatly stacked nearby. They had never lost their goggles, which were still in place when the team found them.

A savage roar permeated the air suddenly followed by more. With a look of surprise in his eyes Dan led the team and bounded down the steps toward the exit to the sandy and stone cut courtyard they had come in from.

'*They brought in reinforcements.*' Mark noted.

Six of the four armed, four eyed white spider/ape-things were trying to attack the invisible invaders.

'*Either those eyes can see in the infra-red spectrum, or they can smell our people,*' Mark allowed.

'*It don't much matter, Mark, 'cause here they come!*' Dan shouted. Mark spun and saw another of the fearsome beasts hurtling toward him, teeth gnashing, all four of its arms outstretched and a terrible roar bursting from its horrific mouth!

Ralph L. Angelo Jr.

Chapter 20

Mark didn't hesitate. He pulled his blaster and fired directly at the creature's chest. The beast stumbled a few feet but shook off the effects of the weapon and aimed itself toward the spot Mark was standing invisibly to once again renew its terrible attack.

Mark began to back away and continued firing his blaster. Each time the monster slowed momentarily and then howled in agony before charging once again.

Mark reached into the bandolier he carried and pulled a shock grenade. He ran backward and hurled it at the creature. On impact it exploded brightly, tearing the beast apart with its concussive force and knocking Mark from his feet.

"Whoa, that was loud enough, dontcha think?" Dan asked aloud, helping his friend to his feet.

"Yes it was. My ears are still ringing," Mark said.

"Let's move out. The others are up to their eyeballs in these little creeps."

Nearby Red ducked under a swinging stave, stepped through, and back fisted the hooded attacker across its jaw, instantly knocking it unconscious.

"One punch, not bad," Dan said to Mark.

"He's angry I think," Mark replied, "and embarrassed about being taken down by a bunch of five foot two inch tall stick wielding fanatics."

"Look over there." Dan pointed at Eddie and the rest of the security team. They were all hurling shock grenades at the monsters now, in lieu of their blasters. Explosions began to rock the ground beneath their feet almost continuously.

But each explosion meant one less monster. It also meant more of the small attackers were beginning to swarm out of the wall city toward the invisible attackers.

'When the monsters go down, switch back to your blasters for their masters!' Red telepathically shouted.

The roughhewn courtyard before the wall city was awash in charging hooded attackers and invisible opponents.

Blaster fire reverberated noisily off of the confines of the underground city, but slowly and surely the diminutive denizens were losing their battle against their unseen opponents.

"Stop all of you!" A voice boomed out.

Everyone, *Cagliostro* crewman and underground dweller alike stopped and stared toward the sound of that voice.

'How are we understanding him?' Ariel asked.

'He's speaking a dialect we've heard before. I think it's one from that world where we first encountered the Agalum,' Mark answered.

'The planet with the two bruiser mechanics that were running a fight game in that bar?' Ariel asked.

Mark nodded and said, *'The same'*

"Stop your fighting, please. We mean you no harm." The figure seemed to almost plead. He was taller than the creatures about him. He stood about six feet tall, and wore gold and red trimmed robes that seemed almost foil-like. His head was covered by the hood of the robe he wore.

'What d'ya think?' Dan asked, *'Should we trust him?'*

'I don't trust anyone from this galaxy,' Red grumbled.

'No, I agree with Red. Let him make the first gesture toward peace, and not mere words.' Mark said.

Mark suddenly stepped away from the others.

'Wait, whattaya doin'?' Dan asked.

150

'Stay back,' Mark ordered. *'If this is all a ruse and they attack I'll be the only one standing in this spot, and I'll still be able to get away from these stick wielding maniacs before they can strike at me.'*

'If you say so, boss,' Dan replied unconvincingly.

Mark looked at him and grimaced, then turned his attention toward the hooded figure standing silently in the courtyard of the wall city.

"Remove your hood," Mark shouted. "I want to see who I'm dealing with."

He stood awaiting a renewed attack by the ragged and hooded minions.

It never came. The hooded being slowly reached up and pulled his hood down, revealing a face they had all seen only recently before.

"It's the guy from that video!" Eddie exclaimed aloud.

Now it was the strange being's turn to speak. "Reveal yourselves, please. We will do you no harm."

Red immediately countered, "Yeah? Tell that to the two people your devil dwarves murdered."

"I-I did not know of this, m-my apologies." the being stammered. "Please, none of that was ordered by me."

"So you speak for these murderous beings?" Mark inquired.

"I am their...leader. But I was away from here. I was on the up surveying our enemies' renewed interest in this world."

Mark looked back at his crew, and then touched his sleeve. Instantly the camouflage shut down and he stood revealed to his counterpart.

"What is this 'up' you speak of?" He asked the being before him.

The wide black eyed creature shrugged before continuing, "It is the above world. It is the 'up'." He pointed his thumb toward the surface so far above them all.

"Are you telling me it is accessible from here?" Mark pressed further.

The being nodded his pale yellow head. "It is, through our city." He waved his hand back toward the wall that seemed to go up forever into the darkness above.

"Who are you?" asked Mark.

"I am called Delrin, and I am the last of the Plaxian race."

Chapter 21

"How is that possible?" Mark asked, "I saw that vision of you. You have to be thousands, or perhaps millions of years old. It was you in that video, there's no doubt of that."

"Please, come inside our city. I will explain everything," Delrin pleaded.

"Inside your city? Naaah, I don't think so, bub," Dan replied, eyeing the alien cautiously.

"Please I mean you no harm," Delrin reiterated.

"Yeah well after your people already killed two of our crew you'll have to forgive us for being a bit cautious," Dr. Troiano said.

Delrin hung his head, as if giving in to an eventuality. Then slowly he raised it again and met Marks gaze. "Please, I cannot bring your friends back to life, but you must believe me I am not your enemy. My people have devolved somewhat over the many centuries. They are not as intelligent as they once were."

"Judgin' by your video I'd have to say that's an understatement," Eddie replied.

Delrin nodded his head affirmatively before replying, "Yes, you are correct. We are not what we used to be. As a race, the Agalum have cost us much. We, at one time were rulers of all we surveyed. Yet we were benevolent." He looked at Mark once again. "Please come inside, it will remain warmer there. Also there are wild creatures that prowl these wastelands during the sleep period. I have no doubt they will smell us all and come looking."

"Wilder than those monsters you sicced on us?" Eddie asked.

Delrin's large black eyes locked on Eddie's before he replied, "Much wilder I am afraid. That is why we had sentries posted here. I promise you we mean you no harm, and besides, even if we did, it appears as if you would have no problem subduing us all."

"Thanks for the ego stroke, Delrin," Mark answered, "but we're still going to play it cautiously. You lead the way, and we'll bring up the rear."

"As you wish. When we have settled down for a meager meal, I will explain all to you."

"That sounds fair," Mark agreed. "Lead on."

Delrin spun on his heel and led the way back into the city built into the cliff wall.

Mark looked at Ariel first, then Dan, Red, and Dr. Troiano before shrugging his shoulders and following the pale skinned alien into the naturally made structure.

***

A half hour later the crew was seated on the dusty stone floor. A fire burned in their midst. Most of the security team was standing around them all facing outward, holding their solar rifles tentatively, looking for any sign of trouble from their supposed hosts. The small, hooded rag wearing people huddled about. Some sat cross legged on the floor, others milled about behind the crew talking quietly to themselves.

"All right, Delrin, how is it possible that you are here and still alive after all these years?" Mark questioned his host.

"The answer is a simple one. I am not the man you saw in that video. I am his clone."

Dan shook his head in disgust. "More clonin'. This galaxy gets crazier an' crazier with each step we take."

154

Mark looked at Dan. "It's not the first time we've run into cloning. You know as well as I do, Dan, that was how the Agalum infiltrated all forms of our government a few years back."

"The Agalum like to play God with the lives of others," Delrin said. "That is not what we of the Plaxian race have done. We are-or rather were-a peaceful race."

"We know, we all saw the vision you, or rather your predecessor left behind." Red acknowledged.

The strange being nodded slowly. "Yes. We were a people used to peace and peaceful intentions, though we could defend ourselves when called upon to."

"As the Agalum found out, at least to some extent," Ariel commented.

The alien turned toward her and nodded in agreement. "Our weapons were great, and the Agalum wanted them for that reason. They killed so many of my people, so many…" he trailed off.

"But what happened then? This cloning stuff how'd that happen?" Eddie asked.

"It was a failsafe put in place in case our race was ever on the verge of annihilation. The idea was that if we as a people were beyond saving that a thousand years hence our deeply hidden automated facilities would use long stored DNA and recreate our race from the best and brightest of our people. From there they would repopulate this planet, and the Plaxian race would once again stride amongst the stars."

"How many years has it been since the Agalum overcame your people?" Mark asked.

"It has been many years. Many thousands of years."

"How many?" Mark pressed.

The Plaxian named Delrin exhaled slowly and replied, "Nine thousand of your years."

155

"That's insane!" Eddie exclaimed.

"No, it is the truth," Delrin confirmed.

"I-I'm sorry Delrin, I wasn't doubting you. I'm just kinda stunned by how long your people have been gone," Eddie explained.

"No offence was taken, I assure you," Delrin replied.

"Do you notice anything similar about Delrin's story compared to our own?" Mark asked. His eyes darted across the group seated with him.

Ariel replied before the others. "The Agalum attacked them because they perceived them to be a threat."

Mark smiled and then said, "Yes, that's right, Ari. They were attacked without any provocation and they were attacked surreptitiously, almost from within, which is exactly what the Agalum did to us."

"You are fighting the Agalum?" Delrin asked in surprise.

"We are, Delrin," Mark answered, "they are our enemy as well."

"We have much in common," Delrin allowed.

"But what about you? How come yer the only one alive down here, an' how come those guys look like devolved versions o' you?" Dan asked.

"In truth that is what they are. Many of our people who were left escaped to the planet's inner catacombs. Catacombs so well hidden that only a genetic marker installed at birth on all Plaxians could unwittingly guide them down here."

"Wow. So some kinda system that gave directions without the person knowin' it. Pretty slick," Dan congratulated.

"Yes, Dan Sledge, our genetic code enhancement was useful in keeping our people-or what was left of them-together," Delrin acknowledged.

156

"But what happened then?" Mark asked.

"There were only a handful of us left. We had hidden much scientific equipment down here over the years. Our equipment was of incredibly stout design. It would prove to be many, many centuries before it became unusable. It was determined that my predecessor would serve as the template for one final Plaxian, who would survive through our scientific genius, by being reborn as a fully formed adult every century. I am one such reiteration of the final Plaxian."

"But why only one of you?" Ariel asked, "If you had the technology, why not many of your people?"

"Alas, it was not to be, Ariel O'Connor. There was only one cloning tube fitted for use here. No time allowed to install more. When those of us who had escaped finally were able to rendezvous here we simply did what we could to make sure our vast knowledge did not fall into the hands of the accursed Agalum. Those who escaped lived out their lives in these depths. Many had progeny down here the natural way, a way that had not been used in many, many centuries by my people. After many generations down here our people became smaller and more barbaric. The thirst for knowledge dimmed and the thirst for revenge and battle brightened."

"My God, this sounds awful," Dr. Ann Troiano commented.

Delrin turned toward her. "It was not as bad as it may have seemed. Dr. Troiano. With times passing, the memories of living above ground faded to mere legend and those left thought more of revenge for their ancestors than for any wish to escape these catacombs."

"Did the Agalum ever leave this place?" Eddie asked.

"Oh yes, almost immediately upon our arrival down here," Delrin replied.

157

"I don't understand why they would just get up and leave," Mark inquired.

"They did not. We had our final revenge upon them."

Mark tightened his jaw as he awaited Delrin's next words.

"You of course noticed the planet's blasted surface, correct? Nothing has grown there for many years."

"Since your people destroyed all life upon the surface, including the planet's ability to sustain life. Your people did that, didn't they? It wasn't the Agalum. As a final act of defiance you razed the planet."

Delrin nodded his hairless head. "We did, Mark. If the Plaxian race was no longer allowed to live upon the world they had been born to, no one else would have that honor, especially not the evil that was the Agalum."

"Wonderful," Mark spat. "So you effectively killed your planet and transformed your people after countless millennia into little more than beasts." Mark waved his hand toward the rag wearing beings awkwardly limping around the room near them. "This was your great decision to end your problems with the Agalum."

"What else were we to do?" Delrin asked, perplexed at Mark's reprimand.

"Fight back," Dan interjected. "You an' yer people hid here for how many centuries? An' yet you couldn't hide some tech down here that you could have created with to defeat the Aggies? Lemme tell ya, we, the people of Earth would never surrender like this an' torch our own world. This is ridiculous. Yer 'scorched earth' policy did nothin'. The Agalum are still here, after all these centuries, only now they finally discovered yer secrets an' have been makin' off with 'em to use against us. An' guess what? We still beat 'em, at every turn."

158

Ariel stood up and walked between Dan and the stunned Delrin. "Dan's right. What you people did here, it's insane, and unthinkable. You destroyed your entire civilization, all your knowledge. How do you reconcile that? It did nothing for you, at all. You're the last surviving Plaxian and you're a clone. God only knows how much you've degraded over the years."

Delrin hung his head sadly. "I-I am sorry. I did not mean to make this mistake, to doom our race. We believed that we would rise again one day, centuries later. We erred. Our planet was destroyed so irrevocably that it has never recovered. This was not our intention."

"What happened to that weapon, the plans for it I mean?" Mark asked.

"T-they were on the machine you used to learn our secrets."

"You mean the machine that the Agalum finally figured out how to access, by using someone who was more than a glorified crook or thug to gain information from it? A machine they finally decided to use a scientist or engineer to access?"

"No, you do not understand. It had to be someone greater than just an Agalum scientist. The machine was created and geared to deny any with Agalum genetics from ever operating it."

"What are you saying, Delrin? That someone from another race operated that machine earlier?" Mark growled menacingly.

Delrin shrugged. "Perhaps it was someone who was a copy of a being from another race. A clone or worse."

"A shape shifter?" Dr. Troiano asked.

"Yes, both are possibilities to our long lost science," Delrin confirmed.

"The Agalum have used both against us in the past," Mark affirmed.

"And they probably are right now too," Eddie added.

"This ain't good," Dan grumbled.

"No it's not, Danny," Mark replied.

"What're you thinking?" Red asked.

"I'm not sure yet, Red, but it would explain a lot, including that ship that attacked us two and a half years ago that resembled the *Cagliostro* in function if not shape."

"An' the new weapons the Agalum had suddenly," Dan added.

"It would explain a lot," Mark agreed, almost fearfully.

"Oh no," Ann Troiano blurted out. "I think I know what you two are talking about in your secret code."

"Whaddaya think Ann, is it possible?" Dan asked.

"Yes, I have to admit it is," Ann agreed.

"What is?" asked Red.

"They cloned us, or at least me," Mark answered. "We've been fighting against my designs for the past few years. Distorted, warped designs that I would have come up with."

"They learned cloning from our records as well as many other dangerous weapons designs," Delrin said.

"So between your people's weapons and what they were able to glean from my possible clone, the Agalum have been fighting against us with my own creations and theoretical designs, as well as whatever they could discover from your long lost records."

"But how come they ain't beatin' the Tahir Ga'Warum? I mean you would've come up with somethin' by now to at least slow 'em down."

"Would I have, Dan? I haven't yet, not really at least. We didn't know the Tahir Ga'Warum followed us home until recently, so I didn't spend a lot of time on them as a threat because we were dealing with the Agalum. But if all of this conjecture is true, well either way, we're in trouble."

Ralph L. Angelo Jr.

Chapter 22

A rumble passed through the cavern, then another.

"What the hell was that?" Joanie Brevard leapt to her feet and asked.

"That felt like an explosion. Or rather a sequence of them," Red offered.

"I got a bad feelin' about this," Dan commented.

"You're not the only one, champ," Eddie replied.

Now everyone was on their feet, including the rag wearing subterraneans. Their faces were forever cloaked within the hooded shadows that obscured their heads, but the group immediately felt the small creatures' unease.

"Delrin," Mark asked, "is this normal? Have you felt anything like this before?"

"No, Mark Johnson, I have not."

"They're bombin' this place," Red growled. "Maybe trying to kill us, or drive us to the surface."

"I hate this stuff," Dr. Troiano mumbled. "I belong on a space ship, not running around a mile underground."

"We're not a mile underground, Ann, a few hundred feet at best," Mark corrected her.

"Whatever, but I think we better get out of here, and soon," Ann replied.

"I'm not going to argue with you on that," Mark agreed. "Delrin, is there another way out of here, one that the enemy definitely does not know about?"

Delrin nodded his head quickly. "There are many ways to the surface, Mark Johnson. All, at least as far as I know, are unknown to our foes."

"Get us to one that they cannot possibly know about, Delrin, and get your people to safety too," Mark said.

"I will. Quickly now my friends. We have a long journey ahead of us." Delrin turned and quickly walked over to one of the small, hooded people who were once of his race. After a terse order the diminutive being quickly left.

"Where's he goin'?" Dan asked.

"I'm not sure…" Mark replied.

Almost simultaneously a gong began to sound from the direction the rag wearing alien had hurried off to.

"Well I guess that answers that," Eddie announced. Delrin began walking toward a stone staircase leading up. He paused and turned back to face the *Cagliostro's* crew and said, "Quickly my friends, follow me."

"What about your people?" Ariel asked.

"They will follow us, I have given them orders on what to do exactly," Delrin replied

"Brevard, Rayborn, take two others with you and go join our host up front, but keep an eye on him, just in case," Red breathed almost silently to his subordinates. Rayborn nodded grimly with his eyes slit and Brevard merely activated her solar rifle.

The group as one began to ascend the ancient stone staircase. Soon the depths beneath them disappeared into smothering darkness.

"This path ain't too wide," Dan grumbled. He was now walking sideways up the stone steps with his back to the wall. His width made this type of travel difficult.

"I hate heights," Eddie said quietly.

"Yeah I ain't too fond of 'em myself, squirt," Dan replied.

Mark aimed his right sleeve up the trail they were taking and activated his tech suit's scanning system. Instantly a holographic image popped up above his sleeve.

164

"The steps widen about a half mile up and it looks clear as far as I can scan," he said.

"Alright. Good," Dan replied.

Within minutes the group reached a plateau of sorts.

"Take a rest break here," Red ordered. "It's flat and defensible, at least for a few minutes."

"Where are your people, Delrin?" Ariel asked.

"They have dispersed and hidden in the caverns below. They know how to avoid our enemies. But they have never raided this far into our lands; they must want you all badly to come this far," the alien replied.

Screams suddenly tore at their ears from the darkness below.

"No! My people!" Delrin shrieked.

"We have to go back and help them," Red announced, "We can't leave them to suffer for us being here."

Ariel touched his arm, stopping him from running back down the stone stairway. She shook her head, "No Red. It's too late," she said quietly, "I don't hear their thoughts any longer, I hate to say it, but they're all dead, I-I'm so sorry Delrin." She touched the side of her head to indicate her telepathy.

Delrin fell to the ground and moaned.

"Help him up," Mark ordered.

"We gotta make a decision; either we fight these bastards or we get the hell outta here," Dan growled.

"You know I hate to run," Mark said. "It's not in my nature; but what we have here, the information we've been able to discover it's more important than just us. It could mean the survival of our race. We have to get back to the *Cagliostro* and back to Earth with it."

"Then let's get out of here before those ugly bastards find us," Eddie replied.

"What about Delrin?" Ann Troiano asked.

"You're with us now, Delrin. We'll keep you safe," Mark said.

"My people..." the alien muttered.

"I think he's in shock; we better get him out of here," Dr. Troiano advised.

"All of my people, gone..." Delrin muttered.

"Yeah I'd say that's about right, Doc," Dan replied.

Suddenly the air sizzled about them and a dozen Tahir Ga'Warum appeared, teleporting in.

Instantly like a well-oiled machine the crew sprang into action. Red and his team fired their blasters. Mark pulled a shock grenade off of the bandolier he still wore and hurled it into the crowd of fast moving Tahir Ga'Warum. The explosion threw the enemy from their feet, blinding them at the same time. The crew of the *Cagliostro* still wore their goggles that allowed them to see one another when camouflaged, and these instantly turned black, protecting their eyes.

"Move it!" shouted Mark, "Head up, Red, lay some covering fire."

"Not gonna do us any good, boss," Dan shouted, "these guys teleport."

"I know, Danny. Everyone stay near one another. Don't get so far apart someone else can't help you if you get grabbed by them," Mark answered.

The crew ran up the stone steps half dragging the dazed Delrin with them.

"These punks just disappear every time I shoot them, and I know I'm hitting them," Eddie yelled over his shoulder.

"Just do your best," Mark replied. "They must be teleporting out before the beams hit them; or maybe using something unknown to deflect the beam as they teleport?"

166

"Who cares? Just run. We need to get outta this tomb an' to the surface. We gotta activate our camouflage too." Dan said.

"But once we do, Delrin won't be able to see us. We'll lose him. Hell, we'll be condemning him to death," Mark shouted.

"Make up yer mind, Mark. The fate o' the Earth or one guy?" Dan answered. He was punching his way through Tahir Ga'Warum who appeared in his path. His powerful blows scattered the enemy, knocking them into the dark abyss alongside the stone staircase that ascended toward freedom.

"These guys may be almost as strong as me, but they ain't got any fightin' skills," Dan observed.

Suddenly three of the enemy appeared simultaneously around Dan, grasping him and with a whoosh they all disappeared!

"Danny!" Dr. Troiano screamed.

Rayborn grabbed Troiano roughly and scooped the diminutive doctor up over his shoulder and ran for the surface.

"Let me go!" she shouted, "I have to help Dan!"

"We will," Mark replied. "I'll find him, I promise. But we're no good to him dead. Let's get to the surface."

A group of the horrific Tahir Ga'Warum teleported in ahead of them, hissing and growling like mad beasts. Immediately the team peppered them with heavy blaster fire, and another of Mark's solar shock grenades sent them flying in all directions.

Moments later the entire group exited the catacombs to the darkness of the night sky above Plaxia.

Instantly they were surrounded by Tahir Ga'Warum hissing and spitting all about them.

"Where's our friend?" Mark roared.

167

"Dead;" one stepped forward from behind the others and replied, "he was teleported into orbit and left there."

Shock was written on everyone's face, but none so much as Dr. Troiano, who slumped to the ground in despair.

Chapter 23

Mark Johnson slowly raised his eyes to meet those of the Tahir Ga'Warum who stood opposite him. The horrific alien leered at them all triumphantly.

Before Mark could say anything however, the left sleeve on his tech suit began to blink red. Almost immediately a corresponding green began to flash out of the same sleeve, as if in reply.

Without hesitation Mark tapped his right sleeve and instantly faded from sight, his camouflage reactivated.

But what was surprising was that the rest of the assault force's tech suits also activated at the same time. All that were left standing in sight were the stunned Tahir Ga'Warum and the despondent Delrin.

"I've got him," shouted Red. He invisibly tackled Delrin and carried him off, the sallow skinned alien seemingly flying through the air with his arms flailing while borne away by Red.

The Tahir Ga'Warum commander shouted, "Get them! Do not let them get away!"

Eddie slid up next to Mark while firing his blaster repeatedly and said, "You turned all our suits into camo mode? What'd you do? Override our tech suits' controls?"

Mark nodded. "I had to. Time is of the essence. We have to get out of here," he replied while firing his own weapon.

The ghoulish Tahir Ga'Warum charged their invisible foes, slicing the air with taloned fingers to no avail.

Energy beams from the solar blasters exploded across the open area, searing the Tahir Ga'Warum, driving them back.

"What now?" Eddie asked Mark.

"We fight until we kill every last one of these bastards," came Mark's terse reply.

Both men knelt side by side firing their weapons over and over. The security force was spreading out, driving a wedge into the Tahir Ga'Warum, and splitting their forces apart.

Behind a rocky outcropping near the entrance to the underground catacombs, Red and Dr. Troiano knelt near Delrin, who was mumbling incoherently to himself.

"I've gotta get back to the fight, Doc. Take care of this guy." He began to stand then turned toward her and added, "And don't worry, I'm sure Danny's fine. I don't believe a word these slimy ghouls say."

"Go help the others," she nodded, smiling weakly.

He placed a hand on her shoulder and then was gone, running back into the battle.

'How's it going, boss?' Red asked over their still running telepathic link provided by Ariel.

Mark answered, *'There are more of these things coming, Red. We're holding our own right now, but it's going to get worse fast. We have to get out of here ASAP.'*

The ground rocked around them as their own people hurled solar shock grenades at the Tahir Ga'Warum, scattering them. Solar blasters fired again and again, nailing the horrific creatures and dropping them in their black swirling mist-filled tracks.

But more and more began teleporting in. While they could not see the assault team from the *Cagliostro,* they were able to attack a few simply by charging the spot the energy blasts erupted from.

"We will crush your bones and rend your flesh," one of the Tahir Ga'Warum bellowed angrily.

He leaped toward the spot a blast had just issued forth from and slashed at a quickly back peddling Ranger. The claws tore through the durable tech suit, barely missing the man beneath.

The Ranger fell on his back and kicked out, slamming his feet into the charging Tahir Ga'Warum. It was like kicking a stone wall. The horrible alien was upon him instantly tearing into the startled man, killing him in an eye blink.

"Roberts!" shouted Red, bringing his weapon to bear on the enemy who just murdered his trooper. Firing madly, he charged the Tahir Ga'Warum, slamming the muzzle of his blaster rifle up into the creature's leering face, finally succeeding in blowing its head clean off of its shoulders. The pale skinned horror dropped to the ground, lifeless.

'Move it, Red!' Mark shouted telepathically.

'We have to get out of here,' Ariel said.

'I'm working on it now. I need another few seconds,' Mark replied.

All around them the ghoulish Tahir Ga'Warum drew closer. They fought without weapons, merely relying on their great strength and teleporting ability. Wisps of black smoke rose and fell with each teleport as blaster beams pierced empty veils of shadow and smoke a split second after each creature teleported away.

"This is no good!" Red shouted. "We can't get a bead on them. They're coming and going too fast."

"Speak for yourself," Eddie replied. His blaster made quick work of two of the alien marauders before his sentence was finished.

"How the hell are you doing that, squirt?" Red asked.

"I figured out their rhythm and I'm firing between the beats of their teleporting," Eddie answered.

"You are one scary little man," Red finished.

"I ain't that little, you're just freakishly tall," Eddie replied with a grin.

Red grunted. Meanwhile the Tahir Ga'Warum continued to get closer and closer to their small circle of protection.

'They can't see us yet, keep moving,' Mark ordered.

'They don't have to see us. All they have to do is drive us tight together and take us out all at once,' Red replied.

'Don't sweat it Red. We're getting out of here now,' Mark announced.

The Tahir Ga'Warum were now tightly around the remaining crew members of the *Cagliostro* when a beam of light stabbed down from above, illuminating the sand and stone slab they all stood on.

Instantly everyone-including the crew of the *Cagliostro*-looked upward in surprise. Hovering there in full sight now was the *Stargrazer*.

Dan looked at Mark and through their telepathic link said, *'Remote control?'*

'Yes, now hang on,' Mark replied.

A beam suddenly touched the ground from the ship's belly, enveloping the crew and tractor beaming them inside almost instantly.

The stunned Tahir Ga'Warum sneered and hissed at the small ship, then began to teleport toward it, trying to gain egress, only to bounce off the force field Mark had raised.

"Let's get out of here," Red grumbled.

"Not yet," Eddie replied. "One more sec."

He was holding the fire control and began shooting the gathered enemies with the *Stargrazer's* solar cannons. Many disappeared in puffs of swirling black smoke, but many more were immediately hit and destroyed.

"Okay enough," Mark commanded. "You scattered them and sent more of them to hell. Let's get out of here, *now!*"

172

Ariel sat in the pilot's seat and powered the ship away from the planet's surface, streaking skyward toward the heavens.

An instant later it broke into space. In the near distance could be seen several of the blood red Tahir Ga'Warum semi-organic heavy cruisers floating in space as if watching for something or someone.

"Poor Dan," muttered Ann Troiano despondently.

"Dan's fine, Ann," Mark replied. "The *Cagliostro* picked him up a minute after he was forced into space. I saw his red emergency signal flare to life on my suit's left sleeve. The *Cagliostro* answered with a green signal. His own natural durability and his ability to hold his breath for a prolonged period of time saved him."

"What? You couldn't have let me know sooner?" she yelled angrily.

"Doc, we were in the middle of something at the moment. I'm sorry," Mark apologized.

A light flashed on the *Stargrazer's* control panel. "The *Cag* just signaled us. The *Cagliostro* pulled out of orbit and is a half a light year away awaiting us in a desolate area of space. I have the coordinates," Ariel said.

"Get us out of here but don't go to hyperwarp until we clear those ships. Thread us through here carefully, Ariel."

"I'm on it, Mark," she replied quietly.

The *Stargrazer*, camouflaged and invisible, spun about and flew through space, dipped its wings in a turn, and then accelerated away into hyperwarp once clear.

Minutes later the small ship dropped out of hyperwarp at the coordinates they were given by the *Cagliostro*.

The moment they arrived the *Cagliostro* shimmered into view.

"Welcome home," Major Matt Marek's voice greeted them all over the *Stargrazer's* comm system.

173

"Thanks Matt," Mark replied. "Get us back into hyperwarp the instant the *'Grazer* is secured on deck."

"You got it, boss," Marek answered.

The *Stargrazer* flew into the *Cagliostro's* landing deck and settled down in its marked parking spot beside the smaller shuttle craft.

"How's Danny?" Dr. Troiano asked.

"I'm fine, Ann," came Dan's immediate reply over the comm unit.

"Dan? What are you doing on the command deck? Get to the medical deck. I have to make sure you're not suffering from exposure."

"Ann, relax, hon. I may look the part, but I ain't exactly human, remember? At least not earth-man human. I was genetically enhanced ta make me an' my fellow Jovian's survive Jupiter's crushin' gravity. When they say I'm 'Jovial' it ain't meanin' I'm happy, doll face."

"I know all about it, but you're not getting off that easily. Get to the medical deck. I'm giving you a thorough going over. I don't care how hard your head is," Ann angrily retorted. She stepped off the *Stargrazer* onto the landing deck at the same instant the ship rumbled slightly, signaling the leap into hyperwarp.

"I'm heading up to the command deck," Mark announced. "Eddie, Ariel, Red, you're with me. Doctor, take our new guest, Delrin, to the medical deck. Brevard and Rayborn will accompany you and once you make sure our new friend is okay, I want you to check them out as well, along with the rest of the landing crew."

"What about myself?" Ann Troiano replied. "Aren't you going to order someone to make sure I'm okay, now that I've been scared half to death."

"I'll let that decision defer to your own knowledge and ability," Mark answered as he stepped into a maglovator.

174

Ann stepped in behind him and the rest. The maglovator rode up to the medical deck where she stepped off first, followed by Danny, who looked back at Mark and shrugged his shoulders. Then Delrin, surrounded by Brevard and Rayborn exited behind Dan. Rayborn looked back at Mark and Red and nodded slightly as he left. They disappeared as the doors hissed shut behind them, leaving the command crew-minus Dan-within the maglovator and heading to the command deck.

"The Doc ain't happy," Eddie quipped.

"No, she's not, at all," Red added.

"She's just letting me know she doesn't like going on landing crew missions, that's all," Mark said. "C'mon, let's get to the command deck. After we make sure everything is in order, I'm going to take a quick shower and then get back up there."

"I think we all need that and a few dozen hours sleep," Red replied.

"Yeah that about sounds right," Eddie said.

"I couldn't agree more. I'm dead tired, but it was fun flying the *Stargrazer*," Ariel said with a twinkle to her eyes.

The four people exited the maglovator onto the command deck. Marek and his crew began to rise but Mark waved them back. "Relax, Mr. Marek. I wanted to make sure everything was good to go here before we took a rest cycle."

"Actually, Captain," Matt Marek began, "we all need a cycle ourselves. We're over twenty four hours up here now. If it's all right with you, I'll call in the tertiary crew."

Mark looked at his second crew leader and realized the bags under the man's eyes. Then he scanned everyone else's face on the command deck and saw the same thing mirrored there.

175

"All of you go take a break. Lily, call in the tertiary crew before you leave. But tell them to rotate in in a half hour. We'll take it from here. The rest of you have twenty four hours off. Go get some rest," Mark ordered.

Communications officer Lily Wallflower smiled and put the call out for the tertiary crew.

Eddie, Ariel, and Red slid into their consoles and sat down. Mark stood for a moment and joined them. The secondary crew all stood and after a quick report headed toward the maglovators and off the command deck.

"What now?" asked Eddie a moment later.

"Fly us home," Mark answered. Aiming his reply toward Barton Samuels, the young pilot who was part of the secondary crew, the only remaining secondary crew member left on the command deck.

"Don't worry, Mr. Samuels. As soon as Danny returns after his checkup you can take off and get some rest, or when the tertiary crew finally arrives."

"Not to worry, sir. I'll stay on as long as you need me here," Samuels replied.

Mark smiled and replied, "Good man, and thank you."

"Mark," Ariel interrupted, "I'm getting a distress call from the forward base on Chakix. Mark, they're under attack."

Chapter 24

The *Cagliostro* raced through deep space, invisibly avoiding both Agalum and Tahir Ga'Warum ships in battle in various quadrants.

"Full hyperwarp, Samuels," Mark ordered.

"Sir, even at that speed we're days away from the planet Chakix," the young pilot replied.

It doesn't matter. Get us there as fast as this ship can carry us, Mister," Mark replied tersely.

"Will do, sir," Samuels answered.

The maglovator doors slid open and Dan Sledge entered the command deck, followed by Dr. Troiano. He excused Samuels and quietly took his seat. Samuels nodded toward Mark and entered the maglovator.

Mark looked at Dan and asked, "Are you all right? You had us all worried, you know."

"Hey, pal, no one was more worried than me, believe me," Dan replied with a slight grin tugging at the corners of his mouth.

"He's none the worse for wear, Captain. Those hearty Jovian genes of his saved his tough hide once again," Dr. Troiano said.

"Still mad at me, Ann?" Mark queried.

"I was a little nervous, that's all. I-I'm sorry I snapped at you before and all that. I'm not much of a warrior, that's all," she replied.

Mark's face softened. "It's okay, Ann. I know you were under stress. I thought after the last landing crew mission we took you on back on Chakix that you had gotten better used to this sort of thing. I'm not going to say it won't happen again, if we need you, but I'll try to remember you'd rather remain on the ship."

"I-I'm not trying to shirk my duty, Mark. I'll do whatever you need me too," Ann offered.

"Ann, it's okay. Go back to the medical deck. Look over the crewmen who were down on the surface with us. Make sure they're all right."

"I'm on my way, Captain," she replied and left the command deck via the maglovator.

"What about those that didn't make it back?" Red asked.

"Red, I'll need a list of names of those who perished below. Please get that to me when you have a chance. When this is all over I have to write some eulogies and deliver them to the President's office so he can add his own and make sure they are all delivered to the families."

He turned toward Ariel. "Ariel, contact Captain Nagata onboard the Coronado and see what his position is in regards to Chakix. Maybe he has a better idea of what's going on there."

"Okay, Mark," Ariel replied.

A moment later Ariel announced, "Mark, I have Captain Nagata on the comm."

"Patch him through to the main viewer, Ariel."

The view screen at the forward end of the command deck lit up with Nagata's dour countenance and he began to speak. "Hello, Captain Johnson. I see we both received the same distress call."

"Hello, Captain Nagata, yes. I was trying to ascertain if you had any more of an idea of what was going on there than we did."

Nagata leaned back in his command chair, his light green military uniform in stark contrast to the *Cagliostro* crew's electric blue and silver tech suits. "No, Mark, I'm afraid not. We were guarding a border, along with several

178

other ships-which was quiet, mind you-when we received the distress call."

"I'll fill you in on where we're coming from, as well as what we've just been through when I see you in person. As of now I think both our ships should get to Chakix ASAP. What's your ETA?" Mark asked.

Nagata looked at his console before him and replied, "Three days at current speed. It seems no matter how fast you geniuses make these things, it's never fast enough."

Mark nodded in agreement. "I know. Right now we're almost five days away at our top speed."

"All right, Mark. I'll keep you informed if I find anything before you arrive there. Nagata out."

"See you in a few days, Captain," Mark replied as the monitor went blank.

"So what now?" Ariel asked.

"We head to Chakix, and hopefully we won't be too late to stop whatever is going on there," Mark replied.

"How's our new guest?" Eddie questioned.

"Good question, Eddie. Ariel, contact the med deck and see what Troiano has to say about Delrin," Mark asked.

"I'm on it, Mark," Ariel replied.

A moment passed and Ariel turned to face Mark. "She says he's seems to be okay. His physiology is different from ours, but not that much different. He's still in what she terms as shock. He's not taking the death of his people very well," Ariel concluded.

"I don't blame him, really. He was the custodian of his entire race and he just watched them all die. I'd give him some slack myself because of that," Mark concluded thoughtfully.

Against the back wall of the command deck the tertiary crew waited patiently and professionally for their turn at the controls.

Mark looked back at them, and then said, "Let's get out of here and get some rest. Jacobs," Mark addressed the tall thin black man who led the tertiary crew, "If you have any problems or encounter anything strange you don't hesitate to call me, and I mean immediately, got it?"

Jacobs nodded and then replied, "Yes sir, got it."

"Let's go get some sleep. I know I need it," Mark ordered.

Mark, along with the rest of the command crew, stood and exited the command deck. Once within the maglovator everyone leaned back against the walls of the maglovators interior as if decompressing.

"I'm exhausted," Eddie admitted.

"You're not alone," Ariel replied.

"Let's all try to get some rest, and keep our fingers crossed that nothing else happens along the way. God knows we could use a break," Mark added.

The maglovator doors slid open on the command crew living quarters deck and they all exited.

"Let's all try for eight hours of sleep if we can. I know I could use it," Mark said.

"Yeah after my little spacewalk I could some rest too," Dan offered.

"Are you sure you're okay?" Ariel asked.

"Yeah, thanks fer bein' concerned, Ari, but I'm fine. Ann checked me out thoroughly."

Ariel smiled. "How thoroughly?"

"Aww, not you too, Ari? C'mon, I can't put up with more 'o this jabbin' from you now."

"Relax, Jupiter Jones, no one's going to ride you about this, for too long anyway," Red replied with a snicker.

"Get outta here, ya red headed rooster. There's only so much garbage I'm willin' ta take," Dan grumbled, playfully angry.

They went their separate ways into their respective living quarters, Ariel of course following Mark into their essentially joint quarters.

"Finally alone at last," Ariel said.

"Not that it'll do us any good. I know I'm dead on my feet," Mark replied.

He flopped into his bed and kicked off his boots. Ariel turned her back to him and began stripping out of her tech suit.

"Keep acting like that and you're likely to give a girl a complex," she said.

When Mark didn't answer, she turned back to face him. "Are you kidding me?" Ariel asked no one in particular. Mark was out cold on his back with his mouth wide open, sucking air.

She looked at him for a moment, then her smile softened. She finished removing her tech suit and slid into bed next to him, covering him with the light sheet.

She reached over and tapped the nightstand. Instantly a blue light glowed beneath its surface. "Sixty two degrees," she said. The light blinked once and then went out, as did the lighting in the suite. An instant later they were both sleeping quietly.

Ralph L. Angelo Jr.

Chapter 25

In what seemed like only minutes later a voice intruded upon Mark and Ariel's sleep. "Captain Johnson, we need you on the command deck."

"Acknowledged, Lori. I'll be there immediately," Mark answered groggily.

"What is it?" Ariel asked sleepily.

"I don't know. They requested me to the command deck, but there are no alert klaxons going off, so whatever it is can't be that serious," Mark replied.

"I'm sensing anxiety from the command deck. They see something out there but we're far enough away that I'm not getting a clear image of what they see telepathically," Ariel added.

"Okay, stay here. If I need you I'll call," Mark said.

"How long have we been asleep?" Ariel asked.

A disembodied computerized voice replied, "Six hours nine minutes."

"Longer than I thought," Mark admitted.

He slipped his boots back on after donning a new tech suit from his closet and bounded out the door.

'No shower?' Ariel asked.

'I can do that when I get back from the command deck. Right now the ship needs its Captain,' Mark answered across Ariel's telepathic link.

He ran down the hall to the maglovator and tapped the panel to the right of the door. Instantly the doors whooshed apart and he stepped inside. Tapping the panel within he was whisked up toward the command deck, which he entered a few seconds later.

"Status?" He asked an instant before the image on the main view screen caught his attention. "Never mind, I see it."

Displayed on the main monitor was an ancient and derelict looking ship. Its engines had long ago gone out. It merely hung in space.

"Is there any reason you called me out of a sound sleep to look at a long dead ship of unknown origin?" Mark inquired.

"That's just it, sir," Jacobs replied. "It's not that dead. We're reading power, minimal, but it's there nonetheless. Also we've been detecting a life sign."

"A life sign? As in one and only one?" Mark asked.

"Yes sir, only one. But it's barely registering, like it was on life support or something."

"Or in suspended animation," a scientist named Cirillo chimed in. He was standing along the wall of the command deck reading a scanner that was focused on the unknown vessel.

Mark turned toward the sandy haired young man and said, "Good point, Cirillo. Jacobs, hold our position. I'll be back in fifteen minutes, Lori, recall the primary command crew. But first and foremost if there's anything that can be construed as hostile coming from that ship get us out of here immediately. Is that clear?"

"As crystal, sir," Jacobs replied.

"Good. I'll be back in fifteen minutes," Mark concluded before he spun and exited the command deck.

***

Fifteen minutes later the primary command crew was back at their stations when Mark reentered the command deck. He took his seat relieving Jacobs.

"Thanks for your help, Mr. Jacobs. You're off duty until further notice," Mark said.

"Thank you, sir." Jacobs replied and left the command deck.

"Ariel," Mark began, "contact Nagata; relay to him what we've found out here. Tell him I'd like to investigate before returning to Chakix. If he'd rather we continue on to rendezvous with the *Coronado*, we'll leave a marker buoy here. But if he can stand for us to be a few hours later, I wouldn't mind checking this out first."

Ariel called up her virtual control panel above her console and contacted Nagata aboard the *Coronado*.

A moment later she turned back toward Mark and said, "He said the *Triumphant* has been recalled to the area and should beat both of our ships to Chakix, so we have a few extra hours, if not a day to discover what's going on here."

"Good," Mark answered with a smile. "While I hate to ignore a call for aid, a mystery like this dumped in our laps really can't be passed up. Hopefully this will be nothing and we can get on our way."

Mark turned toward Red and asked, "Red, what's the atmosphere look like over there?"

The big security chief shrugged noncommittally and then replied, "It's breathable, but stale. We might want to carry our own oxygen units with a helmet on the tech suits or the heavy armor, depending on what we use."

"Recommendations?" Mark asked.

"A six man team of Rangers with a doctor along for the ride, just in case. Everyone wearing heavy suits for protection," Red answered.

"Red, you're going to lead that team. Take your best people. I'll talk to Troiano and get her best doctor to accompany you."

Mark looked at Dan and ordered, "Mr. Sledge, bring us alongside that thing. Red, if there's any sign of hostility warn us immediately so Dan can get us out of here."

185

Red nodded and replied, "You got it, boss."

The *Cagliostro* slowly maneuvered into place alongside the strange craft. It was shaped with rounded fore and aft sections. Three huge engines hung off its tail section. It was roughly the size of the *Cagliostro,* but looked ancient compared to it.

"How long do ya think this was here?" Dan asked.

"I have no idea," Mark replied quietly, "but I suppose we're all about to find out."

"I found a hatch about two thirds of the way up its side," Red announced.

"Good," Mark answered. "Dan, bring us up alongside it where our umbilical can connect."

Dan nodded and said, "You got it, boss."

Slowly the *Cagliostro* crept forward until it was alongside the other ship's entry portal.

"I'm lining up and releasing the umbilical now, Mark," Red announced.

"Good. As soon as that's done, Red, I want you and your team to go across and secure that ship. If there's a survivor and he needs aid, we'll give it to him," Mark ordered.

A few seconds more and Red stood up from his console and said, "We're all lined up. My crew is in the armory and we'll be heading over there now."

"Okay, keep us informed of everything you see and find there. I want constant contact, is that clear?"

"Like my momma's crystal, boss-man," Red answered.

"Good, then get over there and let us know what you find." Mark turned toward Ariel and continued, "Ari, who is Troiano sending with Red and his crew?"

Red entered the maglovator before Ariel replied.

"She's sending Dr. Rothstein. He's down in the armory now with Red's men donning a heavy battle suit," Ariel replied.

"Good, Rothstein's a good man. He's not Troiano, but he's still top notch," Mark said.

Two minutes later and the command crew watched as the umbilical began to move to the side of the other ship.

"We're extending the umbilical now," Red's electronically modified voice announced over the comm system.

"Very good, Red. Be careful," Mark cautioned.

"Will do, boss," the security chief replied.

"Ariel," Mark began, "switch to their suits' vid feed. Use one of the Ranger team's suits and not Red's or Rothstein's. I want to keep an eye on both of them just in case."

She nodded her agreement and said, "Okay, Mark. Switching to Rayborn's suit."

"Thank you, Ariel," Mark replied. He leaned forward and rested his jaw on his fist as he watched the main monitor at the front of the command deck.

The view was astonishing. The Ranger team walked into a dimly lit ship of dull metallic walls. They were unpainted as if made of bare metal. Lights ran along the floor on each side of the corridor the team found themselves walking in. As they walked the lights nearest them grew brighter, illuminating their path with each successive step.

Dr. Rothstein was watching a scanner displaying a hologram on his heavy suit's right sleeve, as he led the way with Red a half step behind him.

"This way," the doctor advised, pointing down the corridor they walked in.

Red pushed his way past the smaller man. Rothstein was five feet seven and decidedly thin; some would say gaunt almost, with a very bald head that was now hidden beneath the heavy suit's helmet and its sealed environment.

"How much further?" Red asked.

"Another hundred and fifty feet, Mr. Robinski," Rothstein replied.

Red looked back at the doctor who followed him closely and said, "Drop the 'Mr. Robinski' garbage, Doc. My name's Red."

"Very well, Red, whatever you prefer," Rothstein answered.

"What I'd prefer is to be in the crew lounge with a cup of java right about now. Either that or a tall glass of good Kentucky bourbon," Red admitted.

"I can't say that I blame you, Mr. Robi-uh Red," the smaller man stammered. "I'll gladly join you for a drink or two when we get back. My nerves could certainly use it."

Red smiled slightly beneath his helmet and said, "Don't sweat it, Doc. We'll be back aboard the *Cagliostro* before you know it."

"I sincerely hope so, Red," Rothstein earnestly replied.

The seven man team slowly made their way through the darkened ship, the floor mounted lights flaring up and illuminating their way with each step. Each security team member held their weapon at the ready as they progressed.

"Sensor's within the floor or walls," Rothstein murmured.

"Yep," was Red's only reply.

"Turn left here," Rothstein advised.

Red nodded and made a left, leading the way carefully.

"The life sign is stronger down this way. We're getting closer," Rothstein commented.

"Good. Let me know approximately how many feet until contact, and anything else you can tell me about this mysterious life sign."

***

Aboard the *Cagliostro*, the command crew were entranced by the scene unfolding before them on the main monitor. Mark Johnson leaned forward in his command chair, his right arm resting on the arm of his chair as he held his chin. His brow was wrinkled in thought.

Ariel looked at him from her position at the communications console. Finally she touched his mind with her own, *'Why?'* was all she said telepathically.

'Hhmm? Why what, Ariel?' Mark replied.

'Don't 'why what' me, mister. You know damned well what I'm asking. Why aren't we down there with Red doing the investigating? This entire mission you've been playing it safe. That isn't like you. Everyone here, all your friends, are wondering the exact same thing. Hell, even Red was surprised you didn't just order us all off the command deck and into action. You gave me that story about your Dad earlier on but I'm thinking that's just an excuse. There's something more going on here that you're not being honest about. I could dig a little deeper and find it out for myself, you know.'

'I also know you promised never to use your unique psychic ability to invade my, or anyone else's mind without their permission,' Mark answered testily.

'Then tell me why we're not down there doing what we do best? Why aren't we exploring and diving head first into the unknown?' Ariel pressed.

'Because I'm trying to be mature about this, Ariel. I'm trying not to be the cowboy so many accuse me of being. A lot is riding on us this mission. The fact is we should be heading back to Earth as quickly as possible, and not

stopping here or even at whatever emergency is happening on Chakix. Dammit, Ariel, we all just traipsed around an underground city and nearly got killed because of it. That scientific information we were sent to find, our entire mission and reason for being so far back behind enemy lines might have been lost if that had happened. How would that have aided our cause at all?' Mark countered.

'But it wasn't. We won and got what we were looking for, and maybe came up with the reason the Agalum were able to suddenly come up with scientific advances that looked familiar to you. You have to be out there, on the front line. It's where you work best. Mark, why are you shying away from getting your hands dirty on this mission?' Ariel asked passionately.

'Because I can't drag you into danger all the time, Ariel. I almost lost you the last time we were on Chakix and I'm not going through that again. You died. At least I thought you had. I can't risk you like that anymore.'

'What is wrong with you? Have you lost your mind?' Ariel telepathically shouted. *'You don't even sound like the same person anymore.'*

'Ariel, it's me. I'm just…I don't know, maybe sensing my own mortality and becoming concerned with yours. I can do just as good a job sitting here and overseeing my people in the field than being out there with them.'

'You've completely lost your mind,' Ariel practically screamed. *'Maybe the Agalum replaced you with a clone and that's who I'm talking to. Because this sure isn't the Mark Johnson I know and fell in love with.'*

"Mark, we have a problem," Joanie Brevard interrupted the silent argument. She had taken Red's place behind the security console.

"What is it, Joanie?" Mark asked.

"I'm losing contact with their heavy suits' transponders. Ariel, can you get in contact with them?" Brevard asked.

"Hang on, Joanie, let me see," Ariel replied.

"*Cagliostro* to security team, *Cagliostro* to security team, do you copy?" Ariel called.

A scratchy reply came back over the connection. "Robinski here. I can barely hear you, Ariel. Something's interfering-" and then his connection went dead.

"What the hell?" Mark shouted. He jumped out of his command chair and ran to the communications console. Then he looked toward Dan at the engineering console and said, "Danny, are you seeing anything on your end that could explain this?"

"Nahhh, boss," the big Jovian replied. "I ain't got nothin' leapin' out at me here. Whatever's blockin' us is comin' from over there."

"Ari, try to reach Red telepathically," Mark ordered. He was still leaning over her console, their shoulders barely touching.

Ariel narrowed her eyes in concentration as she reached out across space, '*Red, can you hear my thoughts? Are you there?*'

Almost instantly Ariel and through her Mark, Dan, Eddie, and Brevard heard Red's telepathic 'voice' reply, '*Ari, something's wrong here. We're hearing something powering up. It's like this place is coming to life.*'

'*Get out of there now, Red,*' Mark ordered.

'*Already ahead of you, boss,*' Red answered.

***

Onboard the alien craft the team in their heavy suits were running down the corridors, back from whence they had entered the alien vessel.

191

"Move it!" Red shouted, half dragging Rothstein behind him.

The remaining crew was fast on their heels. Desperately they ran through the now pitch black corridors, their heavy suits' own illumination the only lights within the rumbling ship.

"Something's happening here. We set something off with our presence here. It's powering up the ship," Rothstein yelled. We have to get out of here!"

"Workin' on it, Doc," Red replied.

"Red, look!" Rayborn yelled.

The entire group ground to a halt as the walls of the ship suddenly seemed to step forward and block their path.

"I don't believe it!" Red barked.

'What is it?' Mark asked through the psychic link.

'Mark, you're still there?' Red queried.

'Yes, Red, we're coming to get you. Hold tight.' Mark replied.

'Don't bother, boss. We're in trouble and things are getting worse.' Red's words were punctuated with the scream of blaster fire.

"What the hell is going on there?" Mark shouted.

'The walls, boss, the walls are alive!' Red telepathically shouted over Ariel's telepathic link, until the roar of blaster fire drowned out his psychic voice.

"Danny, Eddie, you're with me. Ariel you stay here and keep that psychic link open. I need twenty security men at that umbilical with every weapon they can carry and I need them there now."

'Now that's the Mark Johnson I know,' Ariel replied.

'Damned straight, lady, I'm not second guessing anything this time,' Mark growled.

The three men ran to the maglovator when a rumble ran through the *Cagliostro* itself.

"What the hell was that now?" Eddie asked.

Dan pulled up a holographic interface on his right sleeve as they entered the maglovator. "That damned ship is powerin' up its engines," Dan roared. "It's pullin' away from us!"

Another shudder ran through the *Cagliostro* and Ariel's voice spilled out frantically from their comm units. "Mark, the umbilical just broke free; that ship is taking off!"

Mark's fingers danced over the control panel in the maglovator and it reversed direction returning them to the command deck.

The three men burst forth from the maglovator when the doors split open and returned to their seats, each pushing the secondary crewman who had taken his place out.

But before they could even react, the ship they had been next to glowed with power and shot away from them, disappearing in a burst of light.

Ralph L. Angelo Jr.

Chapter 26

"Dan, pursue that ship *now!*" Mark roared.

Before the words had even finished being spoken the *Cagliostro's* magno-disk engines were ramping up to speed and the great ship leaped into hyperwarp.

"Joanie, status on that ship?" Mark asked

"I-it's pulling away from us, Mark," she looked at him in disbelief.

"Danny…" Mark implored.

"Hang on, Mark, I'm bypassin' the safeties now."

"I don't care what you have to do, just catch that ship," Mark ordered angrily.

"We're no longer losing ground," Brevard noted.

Mark looked at her, intensity writ all over his face. "Are we gaining on it?"

"N-no," she stammered, "but it's not pulling away from us either, at least for now."

"What's our heading?" Mark asked.

"An uncharted sector, Mark. One we never had any reason to believe had any life in it," Dan replied.

"What's there?" asked Eddie.

"A nebula. The Palmaris Nebula, actually. AKA the Vanishing Nebula. Named after Professor Arthur Palmaris. It was discovered in 2054," Mark answered.

They all looked at him. He wasn't reading this off of a screen; he was reciting it from memory.

"How'd you know all o' that?" Dan asked.

"I studied Palmaris when I was studying stellar cartography. I remembered his research. This damned nebula was hidden somehow behind star matter, almost as if it was being shielded. Palmaris varied frequencies on his atomic telescope. He realized that the nebula was somehow

195

fading in and out of view by changing the frequencies of the radiation it emits. When this war is over I intend to research it. It was always part of plan for the future."

"This radiation changin' thing, is it some natural cloak o' this place? Or is it an intelligent manifestation?" Dan asked.

"I have a feeling we're going to find out on this trip," Mark replied quietly. He turned toward Ariel. "You better contact Nagata and apprise him of our situation. Tell him we'll get to Chakix as soon as possible, but right now our main concern is retrieving our people."

"I'm on it," Ariel replied, and turned to her holographic interface console.

"Any response from that ship since it took off?" Mark asked Ariel after she was finished speaking with the comm officer on the *Coronado*.

"No, and I'm sure you realize I've been sending a cease and desist request since it flew away," Ariel answered.

"I know. I saw you sending it on the looped send protocol," Mark acknowledged.

"So what do we do?" Eddie asked.

"We keep after them until we can gain ground," Mark answered.

"What if the magno-disks overheat?" Eddie asked.

"They won't squirt," Dan replied. "These babies should be able to take this speed for days, at the minimum."

"We'll be all right," Mark assured.

"What about them?" Ariel asked. She nodded toward the monitor at the front of the command deck and the alien ship depicted upon it.

"That's what I'm worried about," Mark replied.

Everyone stared nervously at the main monitor and the ship far in the distance ahead of them.

Mark punched the right arm of his command chair and the holographic display sprang to life before him once again. "This ship is leading us somewhere. That's its purpose," he muttered almost under his breath.

"Whattaya sayin', Mark?" Dan asked.

"It's leading us into a trap, without a doubt," Mark replied. He steepled his fingers under his nose as he studied the holographic star chart before him.

"Want me to shoot its engines? That may be enough to stop it," Eddie said.

"It may also blow that ship up. No, Eddie, we can't risk it," Mark said.

"So what do we do?" Eddie asked.

"We stay in pursuit and at the highest of alert levels. If that ship and its mysterious occupants think they're leading us into a trap we have to show them we're ready for anything they might try to throw at us. If they fire at us we do our best to avoid their fire. Double shields up in the fore section of the *Cagliostro*. Ari, call up Matt Marek and the secondary crew. The rest of you, convene in the command conference room in five minutes. We have to discuss strategy."

***

"So what now?" Eddie asked. "Red's stuck on that ship with the rest of the security guys he took with him. Hell, we don't even know if they're still alive or not."

It was five minutes later, and Mark sat, as always, at the head of the conference table. To his right sat Dan, to his left sat Ariel. Next to her sat Brevard in Red's usual spot and Eddie sat next to Dan. Matt Marek sat in also, as did Dr. Troiano. Ben Jacobs was watching on the holo display built into the command chair where he sat with the secondary command crew in control of the ship's functions.

"Honestly, I have no idea where this ship is leading us, or why," Mark said. "All I know is it's doing it purposefully and with intelligence. Someone or something, be it living or artificial intelligence, wants us to follow that ship. It's not pulling away from us. I don't know if that's by design or if we really are just keeping up with it. What I do know is that this is a very dangerous situation, especially in regards to whatever is happening on Chakix."

"We'll have to do something to that ship to stop it, whatever it amounts to. We can't let them get into that 'Invisible Nebula' or whatever it's called," Joanie Brevard advised.

"Vanishing Nebula, and I'm really hesitant to start taking potshots at that ship, Joanie," Mark replied, "for the reasons we already discussed. I don't want to kill our own crewmen. I want to rescue them."

"That bein' said, boss," Dan interjected, "what do we do if we actually have ta enter that nebula? You know that's gonna play havoc with our instruments. We could be flyin' right inta the biggest ambush this side o' Custer an' the Little Big Horn."

"I know, Danny. Believe me I did think about that. But what choice do we have?" Mark questioned.

"You could try to cripple that ship and then board it. We could rescue our people then and escape with them," Dr. Troiano suggested.

"Ann, I have no idea what we'd be stepping into. There could be a thousand armed aliens of who knows what race waiting for us within that ship. No, I think it's better if we just let this play out and keep our options open for now," Mark replied.

"Yes, this can't go on forever. They'll have to reach some destination sooner or later," Ariel said.

"It's just a matter o' when," Dan replied.

"I suppose we'll all find out sooner than later. Dan, what's our approximate time to the edge of the Vanishing Nebula?" Mark asked.

"Figure about sixteen hours at our present speed," Dan Sledge replied.

"I know you said the *Cagliostro*'s engines could take it, but that's almost another day full out. Are you certain we'll be okay without burning something out?" Ariel asked.

Mark smiled slightly. "We'll be fine, Ari. I built those engines to take a lot more than sixteen hours plus at full hyperwarp. We'd be able to go weeks at that speed if need be."

"But our friends there don't know that," Matt interjected.

"I was wondering if you were going to give us your opinion, Matt. Any suggestions?" Mark inquired.

Marek shrugged and then said, "We could fake an engine malfunction and see if they slow down or stop."

Mark shook his head and replied, "No that's too risky. What if they just continue on and we lose track of them? We're traveling at incredible speeds. It would be very easy to lose track of them at this parsec consuming rate."

"I realize that, Mark," Matt replied, "but I really can't think of any other way to slow them down, short of a full out assault."

"I know, Matt, which is why we're just going to hang back and hope they don't pull away from us. We really are at a hundred and ten percent of our theoretical peak right now. We're overstressing everything, but this entire ship is built to take it. When Danny and I designed it, we took a lot of things into consideration."

"Mark, do you think they're trying to make us break down or at least cause us some sort of damage?" Ariel asked.

"That is a possibility, Ari, but if it is what they, whoever 'they' are, are trying to do they don't know the *Cagliostro's* build quality or the level of stress it can take. That will work in our favor, if it comes down to it," Mark said.

He leaned back in his seat and stared across the table at everyone before him, also knowing Ben Jacobs was watching and listening as well on the command deck. Then he said, "We may have to just let this play out to its end, but that doesn't mean we can't play this game to our strengths and use that to gain the upper hand when the time comes."

Chapter 27

The *Cagliostro emerged* from hyperwarp sixteen hours later right behind the alien craft that had absconded with Red and his people.

"Battle stations," Mark rumbled. "Let's not give them a chance to fire upon us. I've had enough of this game at this point."

"Mark, that ship is pulling forward again, it's entering the nebula," Joanie Brevard announced.

"Danny, follow them, but keep our distance," Mark ordered.

"I'm on it chief," Dan replied. The big Jovian throttled the engines up and the *Cagliostro* began to follow the mysterious ship into the nebula.

The maglovator doors slid open then, and the alien guest named Delrin slowly entered the command deck. He looked around carefully, cautiously, seemingly noting the location of everything he saw. He was taking in the command deck and familiarizing himself with it all.

"Can I help you, Delrin?" Mark asked carefully.

"No, Captain Johnson. I have come to aid you." Delrin walked onto the command deck and continued to take in the sights before him.

"How can you aid us, Delrin?" Mark asked, intrigued.

"My people, at least my true, unspoiled people, have a developed sense of danger. I am sensing a great deal of it coming from that nebula before us."

"Is there any more that you can tell us about what lies in that direction? Perhaps what the source of the danger is?" Mark questioned.

Delrin shook his head negatively. "No, Captain Johnson, I'm afraid not. All I can tell you is that I sense

201

grave danger, a terrible threat to this ship and all of those upon it through that nebula."

"I thank you for your input, Delrin, but we really have no choice in the matter at this point. We have to get our people back," Mark affirmed.

"Are you certain they yet survive?" the pale, full black eyed alien asked.

"Our tech suits and the heavy suits they are wearing all send a signal back to this ship that allows us to monitor their vital signs. We'll be able to go directly to them when we finally get aboard that ship."

"That would be fortuitous, Captain, for I sense great evil and danger that way," Delrin replied slowly.

"Thank you for your input, Delrin. If you discover anything else that can be of help to our mission please don't hesitate to inform me of what you discovered," Mark concluded and turned back toward the main monitor just in time to watch the smooth hulled alien ship disappear into the strange void before them.

"Okay, I'm not likin' that," Dan muttered.

"It doesn't matter what you like, Danny. Just stay with that ship," Mark ordered.

"I'm on it, boss," Dan confirmed.

The *Cagliostro* slid into the seemingly all enveloping void of the nebula, and suddenly everything went berserk!

Emergency klaxons rang repeatedly as the *Cagliostro* was rocked again and again by violent gravitic waves within the nebula while it slid into the strange multi-hued void.

Almost immediately all the lights on the command deck went black and emergency lighting took over.

"What the hell is that?" Eddie asked in surprise.

"We're losin' power, squirt, across the board. The ship just had its energy stores drained." Dan said.

"Magno disk status?" Mark asked.

"Both engines *seem* all right, but I can't be certain, at least not yet. They're not firing though. That's fer sure," Dan assessed.

"I assumed as much, Dan," Mark replied. "What about restarting them?"

"Give it a couple o' minutes and that shouldn't be a problem," Dan replied.

"Good. Now where is that other ship?" Mark asked aloud.

Brevard replied, "I have a sensor lock on it, Mark. Well, actually on the heavy suits of our people. That ship is heading toward what looks like a world out there."

"There's a world out here? In this void?" Eddie asked in surprise.

"Yes there is, Eddie, and that ship we've been following for the past day is moving into a landing attitude toward its surface," Joanie answered.

"I don't get it," Eddie stated. "It's like this whole sector of space is devoid of anything but this one world. How is that possible?"

"I don't know, Eddie, but I do know that this is not a nebula in the truest sense of the word, but rather a screen to hide that world," Mark replied.

"So whole races give this place a wide berth an' meanwhile there's this planet hidin' out inside o' it." Dan commented.

"I think that sums it up succinctly enough, Danny," Mark noted. "How are our engines?"

Dan shrugged. "Ready to fire up again. Power's back to almost halfway across the ship. We should be able to fire up the magno disks any time we want."

"Okay good, do we still have forward momentum?" Mark asked.

"Yeah, yeah we do. In fact that planet's gravity is pullin' us right toward it."

"Just like I thought," Mark confirmed. "Keep everything shut down, Danny. Let that planet pull us toward it for now, but be prepared to fire up the magno disks on command, got it?"

"Yup, I hear ya, boss," Dan replied.

"What are you doing?" Ariel asked.

"Playing the Trojan horse," Mark answered.

"That's a really big risk to take, even for you," Ariel noted.

"I know, Ari, but I think it's our best chance at the moment. Whoever these beings are, they are hostile and they have seven of our people. I'd rather have them underestimate us if at all possible." Mark turned back toward Dan and asked, "How much longer until we begin our descent to that world's surface?"

"Two minutes at our current speed, Mark."

"Okay just be prepared to power everything up on my mark. This may be tight."

An emergency klaxon began to go off and everyone looked to their respective consoles, including Mark.

"Tractor beam," Dan said.

Mark nodded after looking at his display and then replied, "I see it. They're pulling us down, but it looks like gently for some reason. They could easily cause any ship that wanders too close to this world to crash with this tractor beam, but that doesn't seem to be what they want."

"I wonder what their game is?" Ariel asked.

"We're about to find out. Have you tried to telepathically contact the security team?" Mark asked.

"Yes, I've been trying for hours, but we're either out of range or they're just not answering, or unable to answer."

"You know, I can blow this tractor beam emitter apart with one blast of the forward solar cannons," Eddie offered.

"I know, Eddie. I'm counting on just that. For now continue to play it as if we're powerless, but keep your hand near the triggers."

"Okay, Mark, you got it," Eddie replied.

"Uh, Mark," Dan interrupted, "we got a problem. I really can't get the magno disks up an' runnin'. Somethin' in this tractor beam is negating the power output, like it's syphonin' the energy off somehow. We're really in trouble." He spun his seat around and looked at Mark.

Mark silently looked at his own holographic console for a few seconds and then finally replied, "Okay, get your engineering crews on this right away. We have to negate that beam somehow. Where are they taking us?"

"Looks like an empty field. That emitter seems ta be hidden in the middle o' it," Dan rumbled.

"I don't have enough power for the cannons to fire, Mark, unless we can cut that thing off at the source," Eddie advised.

"Forget it for now, Eddie; do we have enough power for the force fields?" Mark asked.

Dan shook his head negatively and said, "No, boss, we gotta take that thing out first or at least hope it shuts down when we land."

"We're in trouble then. Joanie, get all security staff to the armory and have them armor up. We're going to have to fight our way out of this and I don't care if we have to use pointed sticks to do it. Whoever this is, is going to learn the tremendous mistake they made today by capturing us and our crew," Mark said.

A slight rumble made its way through the *Cagliostro's* hull.

"What was that?" Brevard asked.

"We landed. We're on the ground," Dan advised.

Mark stood up and said, "I want armed security all over that entry ramp. Let's give these aliens a greeting they won't soon forget."

"Mark, we have incoming," Brevard announced.

"How many, Joanie?" Mark questioned.

"A lot. But look at them, they look like hippies or something," she replied.

"What the hell?" Eddie barely spoke. He was staring at the main monitor in slack-jawed disbelief.

Over a hill came white robed alien natives. They all looked like teenagers. They had green skin and golden hair with twin antenna poking through it, and wore white robes with a simple rope belt. They danced down the hill with flowers in their hands and in their hair. Their bare feet seemed to barely touch the ground as they skipped and ran toward the *Cagliostro*.

Dan looked and shook his head in stunned disbelief, then said, "This is freakin' surrealistic. We're bein' surrounded by children."

"Is that tractor beam still on us?" Mark asked.

"No, it shut down when we landed," Joanie replied.

"Put up the shields," Mark ordered, "if they're working."

"They are," Brevard confirmed.

She tapped her virtual control panel and the ships shields sprang to life about the *Cagliostro*. The natives were seemingly oblivious to the shimmering barrier before them; that is until they walked into it and bounced off, enmass.

"What the hell?" Dan rumbled.

The gathered horde of seeming teenaged aliens began to pound on the force field woefully, as if depressed. Many

206

sank to the ground and began to play with the flowers they held.

"What're they doing?" Eddie asked.

"They look like they're sulking," Ariel offered.

"I think a few of them are-are crying," Joanie advised.

"This is crazy," Eddie added.

"I don't care what it is. I want to know where our people are," Mark roared, bringing everyone back into focus. "That's the only thing that matters. Also we need to find that tractor beam emitter so we can get the hell off of this planet. Brevard, where is that ship that Red and the others are trapped in?"

"Several miles from here, but we can't take off until that tractor beam is taken care of, right?" Joanie replied.

"Don't you worry about that, Brevard; I have a plan," Mark replied tersely.

"Don't you always?" Ariel quipped.

"Damned straight, Ari, and I intend to get us all out of here, no matter what it takes."

"There is great evil here," a momentarily forgotten voice intruded from behind them all. Mark turned to face Delrin, who was pressed against the bulkhead of the ship, almost cowering.

"What's the matter, Delrin?" Ariel asked.

"This place, it is not what it seems. It reeks of death somehow." He closed his great black eyes as if in concentration and then slowly opened them, as if seeing the crew who were all staring at him for the first time.

Delrin shook his head slowly side to side and said, "This place is a planet of great evil. Tread carefully here. You must. We must find your friends and leave this place, and quickly."

"Ari," Mark spoke hesitantly, "are you sensing anything?"

"I'm sensing…I-I don't know. I think Delrin must be empathic more than psychic. Do you want me to reach out and touch one of their minds?" she nodded at the youthful looking aliens surrounding the nose of the *Cagliostro*.

"No, after what happened on Chakix I'm never going to put you through that again," Mark replied.

"Are you sure?" she asked quietly.

"Positive, love," Mark replied.

"I hate ta break up this love-fest, but what're we gonna do about these guys outside the ship?" Dan asked.

"We'll wait until nightfall. Do we have an estimate when that is here?" Mark asked.

Joanie Brevard looked at him and replied, "From what I see, about eight hours longer."

"Okay, eight hours it is. When it gets pitch black here we make our move. In the meantime we keep the shields up and them out," Mark ordered.

"You got a plan, boss man?" Eddie questioned, "Leaving Red and crew captive for eight more hours is a long time."

"I know, Eddie, but it can't be helped right now. We have to slip away quietly. Plus, I have to think that they're not going to harm our people while we're still a threat to them." Mark replied.

"What if you're wrong?" Ariel asked, solemnly.

"I can't be, Ari, not this time," Mark answered.

"What about the camouflage field? Would that help us right now get outta here earlier and find Red an' the rest?" Dan interjected.

"Can you guarantee that if we use it their power draining tractor beam won't shut it down?" Mark asked.

"I'll let ya know in ten minutes," the big Jovian pilot/engineer replied. Dan got up and dashed off to the maglovator. The doors slid shut behind him and he was gone.

"What do you think he's up to?" Eddie asked.

"We'll find out soon enough I'd wager," Mark answered.

***

Dan trotted out of the maglovator to the engineering section. He entered his office there, passing the surprised engineering staff without a word, and immediately slid in behind his desk.

"Now, let's see what we've got," Dan muttered aloud.

He brought up a virtual interface and then a display image of first the hidden world and its sun, then the world itself. He zoomed in and showed just the planet, using the information the *Cagliostro's* powerful sensors had already downloaded.

Dan punched buttons and extrapolated numbers nodding and then alternately shaking his head in annoyance.

Finally seven minutes later he stood up and ran back out of the engineering center to the maglovator. Thirty seconds later he was running back onto the command deck.

"We can do it now. We don't need ta wait eight hours, but we gotta do it small," he blurted out as he entered the command deck.

"Small? How small?" Mark asked.

"Get a team o' fifty men together, no more, an' have 'em meet me on the hanger deck. We're goin' huntin," Dan answered.

Mark looked at Eddie and furrowed his brow, then rose from his seat. "Ariel, call the secondary crew in, then you and Eddie as well as Brevard will meet me on the hangar deck. Joanie, put together a team of the fifty best Rangers on the ship, and have everyone wearing stealth capable tech

209

suits. I think we have to travel small and light. Isn't that correct Mr. Sledge?"

Dan nodded and grinned wolfishly. "You got it, boss. Let's go teach these guys a lesson."

Chapter 28

"Okay, Danny, what's the plan?" Mark asked.

Fifty heavily armed Rangers along with Dan, Mark, Eddie, Ariel, and Joanie Brevard stood in the hanger deck on the *Cagliostro*.

"I'll show ya in a second, Mark," Dan replied with a grin.

Even before he was done speaking several technicians appeared and what they were leading out made everyone in the command crew smile.

"The sky cycles," Ariel grinned from ear to ear.

"Yep. It's been awhile since we used 'em an' I know we got about a hundred of 'em stored down below. So fifty is no problem ta pull up. They're small enough that with the camouflage units runnin' on 'em we won't be noticed at all flyin' outta here, an' with the telemetry Joanie got us we can find Red an' the guys, an' do it now," Dan concluded.

"What about getting us off the ground once we get back here? That tractor beam'll be on us as soon as we try to take off," Eddie asked.

"You leave that to Danny and me," Mark replied, "We'll take care of that once we get our crewmen back."

Eddie nodded and said, "You got it, Mark. Lead on boss man."

"Then let's go get our crew back," Mark ordered.

The gathered crew each sat on a sky cycle and activated them. The silent cycles crept upward and hovered a foot off the ground in anticipation.

Everyone was wearing a helmet that covered their heads completely. On each helmet's face shield a heads up display or 'HUD' relayed vital information to them.

Mark touched the left side handlebar grip and said, "Johnson to *Cagliostro*, do you copy?"

Lori Westin's voice replied almost immediately, "*Cagliostro* here, Captain, I copy you."

"Very good, Lori, we're about to get underway." Mark advised.

"Well keep watch over you all, sir, through your tech suits' transponders," Lori confirmed.

"We'll be in touch soon, Lori. For now keep the channel clear and open. We'll be running silent until communication is needed," Mark ordered.

"Very well, Mark," Lori replied.

Mark looked at his crew seated on their own sky cycles and said, "Let's go get our people back."

The sky cycles rose into the air and sped out of the force field barrier at the end of the docking bay and away from the *Cagliostro*. Once they were all clear the docking bay doors closed again behind them.

'Ariel, do you 'hear' me?' Mark thought.

'I do my love,' Ariel replied.

'I wish you wouldn't do that when we're in a serious situation,' Mark admonished her with a grimace.

'Okay, boss, whatever you say, sir,' she replied stiffly.

'Where to?' Dan Sledge interrupted.

'There are about forty miles between us and the spot the alien ship landed at. We'll be there in a few minutes. Ariel, can you link everyone's mind here?' Mark asked.

'I can,' she replied.

'Stay tight, assault team. Don't wander or get spread apart. This is an alien world and we have no idea what we're going into except that they are definitely hostile. We have to treat this situation as if we are at war with whoever this is. Prepare for the worst and either be surprised when

it isn't that bad, or be ready to deal hell when it turns out exactly as we envisioned it to be,' Mark said.

'Hey! I'm pickin' somethin' up,' Dan interrupted. *'It's the crew's tech suits' signals. We're gettin' close.'*

'Everyone get ready for whatever lies over that hill,' Mark ordered.

The sky cycles crested a low hill and beheld a valley below. Planted in the middle of the valley was the ship that had taken off with Red and the rest of the crew. It smoked from its engines and looked as if it had landed there only moments ago.

'There ain't no one around it,' Dan observed.

'No, it almost looks abandoned,' Eddie replied.

'It's not though. I'm picking up Red's and the others' life signs through their tech suits. They're all inside that thing,' Ariel confirmed.

'How are we gonna get in that thing?' Eddie asked.

'The same way our crew did. We're going to walk right in the front door,' Mark answered.

'You know this is a trap, right?' Brevard asked.

'Joanie, of course I do. But these beings-whoever they are- have no idea what they are dealing with. Do they Mr. Sledge?' Mark replied.

Dan Sledge just grinned silently as he dipped his sky cycle toward the eerily silent ship. His cycle touched down and he immediately hopped off. Dan walked confidently toward the hatchway that the *Cagliostro* had been tethered to.

Behind him most of the sky cycles landed save for ten that were being ridden by Rangers, who held their weapons at the ready for any surprise attack that might come.

Dan looked back at Mark.

'We're all set, Danny, go to it,' Mark ordered.

'You got it, boss,' Dan replied.

Dan Sledge pulled his massive right fist back and let fly. His powerful Jovian muscles rammed his rock hard fist through the steel door like it was paper. Then, grabbing it, Dan ripped it from the ship and hurled it aside out onto the ground next to it. The Rangers, led by Joanie Brevard, entered the ship ahead of everyone else. Mark, Dan, Ariel, and Eddie were in the middle of the pack. Outside the ten Rangers who were still astride their sky cycles remained there, scanning for trouble.

'Look at the size of this place,' Eddie thought through the telepathic link.

'Yes,' replied Mark, *'twenty five foot ceilings, thirty foot wide corridor. I wonder why it was designed so large?'*

'I'm sure we'll find out, hotshot,' Dan rumbled in reply.

'Do you 'hear' anything, Ariel?' Brevard asked.

'No, Joanie, I don't hear their thoughts at all,' Ariel replied.

'I've got them. I have readings on their tech suits. This way,' Mark commanded.

He pushed his way past the security crew with Dan, Eddie, and Ariel at his side.

'Ari, stay back with the Rangers, we have this,' Mark ordered.

'Like hell," Ariel cut him off. *"I'm not going to be left behind every time we get into a dangerous situation. You better get used to that again, mister.'*

Mark almost replied and then held his thoughts to himself, but the look on his face spoke volumes.

'Which way?' Eddie asked, breaking the awkward telepathic silence.

'Follow me,' Mark replied coldly.

The group continued into the steely ship. Its metallic walls seemed to hum with power. As they had with Red and his crew, the floor lights came on with each step forward that they took and dimmed behind them.

'Interestin' set up these creeps got here,' Dan commented.

'Must be a power saving thing,' Mark answered.

'Yeah I gotta agree; but that means this whole ship is basically shut down all the time an' runnin' on minimal power,' Dan conjectured.

'That makes sense, Dan, especially if it's nothing more than a lure to trap ships here,' Mark confirmed.

The group continued to walk, Mark's scanner built into his tech suits sleeve leading them unerringly toward what they hoped were their crewmen.

The group turned the last corner and came upon a blank two doors set into a wall. They were the sliding variety, as in the *Cagliostro* itself.

Mark touched them and the points around the wall looking for some sort of recessed door control. This was after scanning it with his tech suit's built in sensing array, all to no avail.

'Nothin'?' asked Dan Sledge.

'Not a thing. You're up, Danny,' Mark replied.

Dan wordlessly walked forward, balled up both his fists and brought them up above his head, and then slammed them both down toward the door from above with devastating force. The doors crumpled like soft tin before his fists' powerful impact. With one final kick he scattered the remains into the room before them.

Then Dan bowed at the waist and swept his right hand ahead of himself. *'After you,'* he said with a smile.

Ariel returned the smile and telepathically replied, *'Showoff.'*

When the group entered the unlit room, they stopped in their tracks. Before them the lights within the room now exploded into blinding brightness.

Mark stared wordlessly at the scene before them and then shook his head in disbelief before saying aloud, "What the hell?"

Before them lay the gear and the heavy battle suits of their crewmen in a pile upon the floor. All of it was heavily scarred and battle damaged.

But what gave Mark and the rest of the rescue team pause was what stood against the walls across from them: Glass cylinders which were iced over; as if devastatingly cold.

Mark walked over and rubbed the frosted over cylinder with his hand, immediately withdrawing it from the cold.

"Are you all right?" Ariel asked.

He nodded in the affirmative as he rubbed his hand. "That cylinder is frozen solid. I feel like I've got frostbite from touching it."

One of the Rangers walked forward and rubbed the surface with his glove, and instantly stumbled backward in shock. "Sir! You better take a look at this," Reynolds, the Ranger in question said.

Mark walked forward and peered into the cylinder, then recoiled in surprise. "We have to get these tubes open. That's Red in there!"

Chapter 29

Mark and Dan began scanning the frozen tubes they had discovered the crewmen in. "Can your tech suit interface with it?" Dan asked.

"I don't know. I'm trying right now, but so far no luck. I think it's going to take a while for the tech suits' processors to crack this device's code," Mark answered.

"I don't think we got a lotta time," Dan countered.

"Do you hear that too?" Joanie Brevard asked.

"Yeah, yeah I do," Dan confirmed.

In the distance, back the way they had come within the ship, there was a groaning and rending sound, as if steel were being torn or rent apart. That was followed by a rhythmic thumping sound.

"What the hell is that?" Eddie questioned.

"There's only one way to find out," Dan replied.

He began to head toward the doorway he had shattered, but Mark put a restraining hand on his shoulder. "Hold it, Danny. I need you here with me for this one. We have to get our crew out of these stasis pods. Let the security crew take care of this."

Dan looked hesitantly toward the devastated doorway and then back at Mark before replying, "Are you sure?"

"Yes. I need your big brains here with mine right now, not your big muscles. Let the Rangers earn their keep."

Mark looked toward Joanie and said, "Go take your people out there and see what's heading this way. If you have to engage it, then do so. I don't have to tell you the stakes of all of this. Use whatever force you have to."

"You've got it, Captain," the female security officer replied.

She turned and ran toward the hallway shouting behind her, "Move it out, Rangers; let's show these things, whatever they are, what they've run up against, and why they should be afraid."

***

Matt Marek stared at the green skinned and antennaed teenagers lounging languidly outside the force field protecting the ship. Professor Cirillo, the scientist who had earlier been on the command deck, had returned and was watching the strange aliens.

"What an odd bunch," he muttered to Marek.

"Yes, they most certainly are, Professor. What do you make of this? I know you have various degrees in different sciences. Do they cover anything like this?"

"Sadly, I'm not a xenobiologist by trade, but that doesn't mean I don't have an opinion," he offered.

"Care to share it?"

"Surely, Matt, but from what I can see, these aliens are either extremely disinterested, or are trying to keep our attention riveted to them and not on anything else happening here. The other thing they might be doing is trying to lull us into a false sense of security," the professor said.

"Security? How? They kidnapped a large contingent of our crew and then pulled us down here with a tractor beam. Did they really think we would consider them friendly?" Matt remarked.

The older, balding scientist turned toward the younger military man and replied, "Matthew, it is very possible that some races out here in the great beyond, of which we know next to nothing of, could actually be fooled by such an act. Remember, as a race we are not so gullible as others might be. We truly do not know what goes on out here."

Matt nodded thoughtfully and then replied, "You're right, Professor. These creatures, whatever they are, could be far more dangerous than they appear, and only our own distrusting nature may be what is keeping us alive. Someone else, hell, even some other Earthmen could be taken in by this," Matt waved his hand at the image on the monitor, "but not this crew. In two years we've seen enough to make sure we distrust everything out there until we're satisfied it's all safe."

The maglovator doors slid open with a hiss and Delrin along with Dr. Troiano walked back onto the command deck.

"Delrin wished to speak with you, Matt," Troiano began.

"What is it, Delrin?" Matt asked. He turned his gaze from the professor to the two newcomers.

"Something-something bad is happening to the crew. I-I can feel it," Delrin stammered.

"From here?" Marek replied incredulously. "We're something like forty miles away from them. How can you know?"

Delrin pointed at the monitor and answered, "From them. I feel something has changed and they know it. Look, even now they leave."

Matt turned toward the monitor and was surprised to see the strange green skinned and robed aliens getting up and silently leaving, walking away over the nearby hill, toward the direction the sky cycles had taken.

"Well I'll be damned. What do you make of that, Professor?" Matt asked.

"Your guess is as good as mine, Matthew, but whatever it is it cannot be good."

"In that we're in agreement." Marek turned back toward Delrin and asked him, "How'd you know that was about to happen?"

"I felt a change within them. Something alerted them to a development in the situation where our people are," Delrin replied.

"We should try to fly to them," Barton Samuels said. He was seated at the pilot's seat normally occupied by Dan.

"We probably won't get far with that tractor beam and its energy nullifying component," Matt replied.

"There's only one way to find out," Samuels replied with a grin.

"Agreed, Mr. Samuels," Matt said, "Let's see if we can aid our crew, because it sounds like they may be in need of it."

***

Onboard and deep within the alien ship the sounds of battle were reaching Mark and Dan's ears.

"I gotta go help them, Mark. They're in trouble," Dan growled.

"We have to get our people free first, Danny."

"Even if it means we lose more o' our people ta get these guys free? Have you lost yer mind?" Dan shouted.

"I hope not," was Mark's only reply.

Dan looked at him and grimaced, then continued to aid Mark, using the interface hovering above his own tech suit's sleeve.

Wordlessly the two men worked together as sounds of frenzied blaster fire and that strange heavy thumping grew closer and closer.

"What is that?" Eddie asked Ariel. Both of them were standing closer to the doorway, Eddie with his own blaster drawn and aimed that way and Ariel just standing nearby warily, staring at the shattered doorway.

"I'll contact Joanie and see what she says," Ariel stated.

The beautiful telepath reached out with her mind. Psychic fingers reached and touched Joanie Brevard's mind and with a sharp intake of breath Ariel recoiled and stumbled backward.

Eddie quickly caught and steadied her before she could fall and injure herself.

"What is it, Ari? Are you all right?" Eddie asked breathlessly.

She spun from his grip and ran back toward Mark and Dan, Eddie a step behind her.

"Mark!" she shouted. "Hurry up! We have to get out of here, now!"

Mark continued to look at his control panel on his wrist device. "What is it, Ari? We're almost through this encryption. We only need a few more minutes."

"We don't have *any* more minutes!" Ariel shouted. In one smooth motion she drew her pistol and shot the top of each of the closest canisters. Instantly those cylinders cracked and spilled their liquid contents along the floor. Gallons of near frozen liquid spilled out, covering everything. Hastily Dan, Mark, Ariel, and Eddie all backpedaled away from the flood of chemicals that immediately began to run down drains placed in the floor of the room.

"Are you crazy? You may have just killed them!" Mark shouted at her.

"No, they're all okay. I can hear their thoughts. They were begging you to get them out of there! They saw what was going on. Trust me, Mark, we don't have time left to play games here," Ariel concluded.

"Why? What did you see?" He gripped her by both of her arms and stared into her eyes.

Outside the shattered doorway a loud crash resounded, shaking the room itself. Security people came running toward them, followed closely by that terrible pounding sound.

All heads turned toward the doorway when Red's choking and gagging voice filled the room with a warning from behind them.

"T-they came out of the walls, the walls themselves. This whole place is a trap."

Eddie and Mark ran toward Red, who was on all fours on the floor where he had fallen out of one of the shattered tubes. He was stripped to the waist and was choking and gagging constantly, trying to get the words he wanted to convey out.

Mark turned to Ariel and shouted, "What's going on here? What is chasing our people?"

"Robots!" she shouted in reply. "Dozens of robots that are coming out of the walls in that hallway."

Mark turned toward the hallway in disbelief as a gleaming metallic leg slammed down onto the floor. It was round with a larger round disc attached to the base of the leg and used as a foot.

The mechanized creature followed the still shooting Rangers into the room and stood wholly in view. Its body was cylindrical and its arms were more akin to steel tubing than anything else. Three appendages that could only be described as fingers were at the end of each arm. The arms waved about maddeningly. The gleaming metallic monstrosity stood twelve feet tall. But worst of all it was followed by more and more identical robots streaming into the room.

"We're in trouble," Dan grumbled.

"No kidding," Eddie replied. He had already joined the security team in shooting at the metallic titans, but the blaster beams just bounced off their shining surface.

"It's some kind of refractory coating," Mark observed.

"Less talk an' more action, boss," Dan replied. He was running across the floor of the cavernous room and toward the nearest robot. With a roar he leaped toward it, his powerful fist cocked back and ready to explode forward into action.

Ralph L. Angelo Jr.

Chapter 30

Mark and Ariel helped Red to his feet when a clatter assailed their ears from across the room. They all turned to see Dan toppling one of the towering robots with a mighty right punch.

Ariel looked at Mark and said, "Sometimes I don't know how we'd survive without him."

"I agree. In these larger than life situations he's our best asset," Mark concurred.

"Where are my heavy suit and my blast cannon?" Red asked. His eyes scanned the room until he saw the pile of equipment near some of the other tubes.

"We've got to free the others," Mark ordered.

"I'm on it," Red replied. He pulled free of their steadying hands and ran toward the equipment scattered about. Other people from the first team that were captured also began to stagger toward their equipment and clothing, hastily donning their heavy suits and grabbing their weapons.

"Get the rest of our people free," Mark shouted to Red, who nodded his confirmation.

"Let's go," Mark said to Ariel. "We have to figure out how to get out of here once everyone is together."

Joanie Brevard was firing her rifle repeatedly into an advancing robot, while its round, cable-like arms whirled over its head menacingly.

The gleaming mechanoid advanced on Brevard. Two glowing orbs approximating eyes stared at her soullessly as it drew closer. Her blaster shots ricocheted off the barrel chested monstrosity again and again.

Mark moved up alongside of her. He shoved Brevard out of the way, while he hurled a solar grenade at the robot's feet. The explosion crippled the mechanical brute's legs, dropping it to the floor.

"The legs. Use your grenades on them. They're resistant to blaster fire," Mark ordered.

"Yeah we kinda knew that," Eddie replied. He hurled a grenade before he was finished speaking and it exploded beneath another robot, shattering its coil-like legs instantly.

"Let me at them. I need a round two with these things," an enraged Red Robinski roared as he ran past in his heavy suit.

The tide was beginning to turn, finally. Dan and the heavy suit wearing troopers were grappling and fighting the towering robots hand to hand while other members of the combined Rangers teams used grenades and then began firing their blasters into the exposed electronics and mechanisms of the robots' devastated legs.

But there were still many powerful robots trying to stop far less people from the *Cagliostro*.

"We have to get out of here," Ariel said to Mark.

"I know. We have to move this battle into the hallway, I have an idea," he replied. "Patch me through to everyone; blanket the room if you can."

"Will do," Ariel replied.

'Dan, Red, get us out of this room and back into the hallway. We have to get out of this place,' Mark commanded.

'Easier said than, uhhrr, done, boss,' Dan answered between grunting blows.

'We have to get out of here and blow up as much of the inside of this ship as possible. Start destroying the wall units the robots came out of. Chances are they're not blaster resistant and definitely not solar grenade-proof,' Mark said.

'All right, we're on it,' Red replied.

Red was standing next to Dan using the heavy suit's great strength amplification abilities to batter the nearest of the shining robots. While the suit did not make him Dan's equal in pure brute force, it was a huge step up in power from pure human strength.

Slowly the team forced the silent robots into the hallway, step by step working their way toward the entryway to the ship.

"Keep up the pressure. We have to get out of here ASAP. There's no telling when this ship could become airborne again," Mark advised.

The walls of the ship's hallway reverberated with explosions and bright blaster fire.

A bedraggled figure staggered up behind Mark, Ariel, and the rest. It grabbed Mark's arm in desperation. Mark broke the grip immediately by turning sideways, and his eyes went wide in recognition. "Dr. Rothstein. Where were you? You weren't with the others. We feared you were gone-killed by these things."

"N-no, they had me in a separate room. I-I was hooked up to machines...T-they were reading my brain, trying to gather knowledge about us," the older man stammered.

"How'd you get free?" Ariel asked.

"When the explosions started, the ship just let me go, as if it had to concentrate on fighting you, instead of being concerned with me. I escaped while that happened and ran toward the sounds of all this fighting," Dr. Rothstein concluded.

"Rothstein," Mark queried, "what do they want? Why did they take you captive and lure us all here?"

The older man looked up at Mark and shakily replied above the din of battle all around them. "They want human hosts. They are parasites in almost a vampiric way. But they do not drain blood. The denizens of this world drain life force, the energy that powers the human body itself. That's why they lured us all here. They leave this ship out in space as a snare, a lure, and draw hapless travelers back to this hidden world where they can do their evil to those they capture. I discovered all of this while they tried to drain my own life from my body."

For the first time since he reappeared, Mark looked at the man before him and noted how weak and tired he looked. His cheeks were sunken in and his skin color was sallow.

"We have to get him back to the *Cagliostro*." Ariel said aloud.

Mark realized what Ariel was saying. Rothstein looked like he was dead on his feet. "Hang on, Doc. We'll get you home safely. You'll be fine."

"Thank you, Captain, but to be honest I don't feel as confident as you sound," the older man replied.

A deafening new round of blaster fire screamed through the hallway on the massive ship making everyone turn toward the source of the deafening roar.

"I have to get up there and help them," Mark said.

"I know," Ariel replied, "but I'm going with you." She turned back to Rothstein. "Stay with us Doctor, please."

Rothstein nodded and smiled weakly. "O-okay Ariel, I-I'll try."

"Move it you two," Mark chastised.

The small group of three ran forward through the wide, smoke filled hallway.

'Which way?' Mark asked.

'I'm following the battle with my telepathy. This way,' Ariel answered.

Mark half dragged the Doctor behind him as they rounded a corner and caught up to the main fight.

228

Blaster fire and explosions filled the corridor. The smoke was so thick it was akin to a heavy fog.

Mark ran forward, his blaster drawn. Then he shouted, "Danny, Red, where are you?"

Then, with the sound of his voice barely louder than the noisy battle filled corridor, Red roared, "This way, Mark!"

Mark ran, pulling the doctor between him and Ariel and rejoined their companions.

Red kneeled down and said, "We've been blowing up the wall sections these monsters came out of like you suggested, but so far it's been a limited success."

"We don't have a choice. We have to keep going toward the exit. Right now this may take a while but it's our best hope," Mark replied.

A loud boom cut through smoke choked hallway.

"What the hell was that?" Red yelled. He stood up and stared toward the sound. A second later a heavy thudding sound drew closer.

"That sounds like those things walking but this one sounds different, bigger somehow," Mark speculated.

Red brought up his shoulder cannon while Mark pushed Ariel and the doctor behind them both.

Walking out of the smoke like some modern age colossus appeared a metallic creature out of nightmare. Not the rounded symmetrical robots they had been fighting right along, but an angular, larger squared behemoth bristling with smoking weapons' barrels. In one tremendous clawed hand it held the unmoving form of Dan Sledge.

229

Chapter 31

"What are we going to do?" Dr. Rothstein asked nervously.

Red didn't answer, and before anyone else could, he slung his hand held cannon around and fired, slamming the robot square in the chest with an explosive energy blast that shoved it backward.

Still the metallic titan maintained its footing and began walking forward again.

Eddie and Mark looked at each other and brought their weapons up almost simultaneously. They fired together and tagged the plodding behemoth again in the chest.

"Avoid hitting Danny," Mark ordered. "Aim for its joints if you can; the knees, the shoulders, and neck."

"What?" Eddie yelled. "You want precision shooting now?"

"From you, yes I do," Mark replied.

All around them the battle raged. Almost a hundred of the Rangers was engaged in battle with the robots that had come out of the walls, while the command crew was desperately trying to take down the largest robot of them all.

Energy beams cut the air in sizzling paths of destruction all throughout the end of the hallway. The battle had shifted now, returning to the place the *Cagliostro's* crew had entered the strange vessel.

But the towering robot still blocked their path and held Dan in one mechanical claw.

"We're not getting anywhere fast," Eddie said.

"Any other brilliant observations, Captain Obvious?" Red replied between blasts of his energy cannon.

"We've got to break out of here. We're almost at the entrance Dan punched a hole in," Mark said.

Suddenly a coarse rumble filled the floor beneath their feet.

"What the hell is *that* now?" Carl Rayborn, the Ranger who had accompanied Red to the ship shouted.

"I don't know, Rayborn, but I know it can't be good," Red answered.

"That's this ship's engines!" Mark roared. "We have to get out of here before it takes off. If we don't and it gets into space, we're all dead!"

The powerful robot that still held onto Dan began advancing on the group again; effectively blocking the shattered door they had entered the ship from.

"This is getting ridiculous," Eddie exclaimed.

"We have to get out of here or we're dead," Mark reiterated.

"I'm on this," Red acknowledged. "Rayborn, you're with me; you too, squirt," Red called to Eddie.

Eddie bristled for an instant at his nickname, but then ran to Red's side.

All about them blaster fire singed the air repeatedly. Some men were half carrying others to spots away from the danger. Still, essentially seventy Rangers stood shoulder to shoulder and fired repeatedly into the gleaming metal monsters.

"Why hasn't this ship taken off yet?" Ariel asked above the whine of the engines picking up speed.

"I have no idea, other than they may not work like the *Cagliostro's* magno disks do," Mark replied. It may take them a while to get to lift-off speed."

"Ooohhh," a familiar voice moaned above the din of battle. Everyone turned and saw Dan suddenly awakening in the robot's hand.

The robot seemed to look down at Dan and opened the palm of its other hand, aiming it at the hapless powerhouse.

"In its palm, those are gas nozzles of some kind. That thing is aiming them at Dan!" Mark shouted.

"I ain't lettin' that happen," Eddie replied.

He aimed and fired his blaster rifle in a blur, repeatedly slicing into the exposed palm of the robot. A heartbeat later the hand exploded. The robot stumbled backward. With a roar Dan tore the hand that held him apart, breaking the glistening fingers as he forced himself free.

He leaped to the floor and backed away, seeking to catch his breath.

"He's free!" Red yelled. "Now waste that thing!"

Following Red's lead a score of men fired at the robot, with Red's cannon scoring direct hits upon its chest.

"Keep up the pressure! The rest of you keep what's left of those other robots back," Mark ordered.

He turned and joined the assault on the towering robot that blocked their escape.

The mechanical monster's legs were badly damaged and its chest was deformed from the constant battering it had received. Both its arms swung about wildly as it tried to smash the attacking Rangers, but its hands were both gone, leaving only flailing mechanical stumps.

"Everybody out!" Dan shouted. He was back on his feet and was running back toward the robot. He tackled it with one impressive leap, and smashed it against a wall.

"Danny, what are you doing?" Mark roared.

"Buyin' you some time. Now get everyone outta here. Don't worry; I got no plans on sacrificin' myself anytime soon. I'll be right behind ya," Dan assured his crewmates.

"You heard the man, now go!" Mark shouted.

The alien ship's engines were whining loudly now. The security team ran for the shattered doorway and filed through quickly with Mark, Red, Eddie, and Ariel staying behind to make sure everyone got out first.

"I'd order you to go, but I know better," Mark grunted to Ariel.

"Don't worry, lover, I have no interest in overstaying my welcome," Ariel replied.

Behind them, Dan was grappling with the towering robot, and then he shouted, "Get outta here, all of you!"

"Go!" Mark ordered. He turned back to look at Dan.

The powerful Jovian grabbed one of the robot's damaged arms and tore it from the body. Then, swinging it around, he smashed it into the robot's head, slamming it back through the wall it was pressed against.

Dan added one last punch for good measure, collapsing its midsection and leaving a shower of sparks in his wake. Then he turned and ran for the exit. He grabbed Mark in one arm and leaped out the door.

The ship had just taken to the air and was already thirty feet off the ground when Dan cleared the devastated entryway. He slammed to the ground hard, holding Mark above his head and absorbing the impact himself.

"I thought I told you to get outta there?" Dan rumbled at Mark.

"Who's in charge here? Me or you?" Mark replied with a grin.

"Boss, we're not outta trouble yet," Eddie called to Mark.

Mark turned toward the sound of Eddie's voice and his eyes went wide in recognition. Before them and closing fast was a veritable army of the green skinned, white robed aliens, and now they did not look friendly at all.

Chapter 32

The command crew of the *Cagliostro* stared in disbelief at the wave of green skinned, golden haired and white robed aliens that poured toward them over the nearby low hills. Their twin antenna shook as they ran. Their teeth gnashed together menacingly and they seemed to growl as they charged.

"Let's get outta here," Dan advised.

"Danny's right," Red agreed. "Charges are low on all the rifles and we're long out of grenades. Our only shot is the sky cycles."

"You're right," Mark concurred. "We've done enough fighting for one day. Let's get the hell out of here."

The group turned and ran toward the waiting sky cycles and the ten men who still stood guard with them. Each man who landed with the second team touched his tech suit's right wrist and activated a display. After these men touched a few buttons the remaining sky cycles shimmered into view.

"The camouflage works great," Eddie exclaimed.

Mark nodded and said, "It does, you're right. Now let's get out of here. Those aliens are so close I can smell them."

He looked around and then added, "Everyone rides two up. Ariel, you're with me. Let's go!"

The sky cycles hummed to life and began to fly upward, each one going back to camouflage mode as they left the ground. The green skinned aliens were now upon them just as the cycles rose into the sky. Leaping and growling, the strange creatures bellowed their displeasure as they gave chase on foot.

Ariel reconnected her telepathic link and said,

'I can't believe how many of these creatures there are.'

'It's an almost endless sea of them,' Mark concurred.

'We've left the last of them behind, finally,' Red added.

'It's about time. I thought I was gonna have ta get off an' clobber 'em,' Dan replied.

'We don't have time for that. We have to get the Cagliostro out of here and get away from this crazy planet,' Mark stated flatly.

A heartbeat later they flew over a rise and saw the *Cagliostro* sitting where they had left it, now devoid of aliens surrounding it.

"Mark Johnson to the *Cagliostro*, do you copy?" Mark spoke into his suit's cowl microphone.

"I read you, Captain," Lilly Wallflower's voice replied.

"Have the landing deck cleared, we're coming in hot. Prep the crew for immediate take off once we're onboard," Mark commanded.

"Will do, Mark, the *Cagliostro* is ready for action," Lilly confirmed.

"Acknowledged," Mark replied. He settled his sky cycle down in the landing bay and both he and Ariel hopped off instantly. Tech crews ran forward to take control of the sky cycles. They immediately sprayed them down with an anti-fungal/anti-foreign body formula and hovered them back toward their storage pods.

"Command crew with me, on the double," Mark ordered.

Dan, Red, and Eddie joined Mark and Ariel and sprinted for the nearest maglovator.

Mark tapped his right sleeve, opened a line, and then said, "Mr. Marek, do you copy?"

"I do, Captain," Marek replied.

"We're on the maglovator and heading toward the command deck. Get us out of here, Mr. Marek. I trust you did something about that tractor beam?" Mark asked.

"Yes sir. All taken care of," Marek answered.

"Then get us out of here now!" Mark roared.

The *Cagliostro* hovered upward, and then turned on end, its side perpendicular to the planets surface, and shot away from the dangerous world in a blindingly fast flash.

An instant later it escaped the atmosphere and entered space.

The command crew exited the maglovator and replaced the secondary crew like a well-oiled machine.

"Matt, stay here please," Mark requested.

Matt Marek nodded and stopped short of entering the maglovator with the rest of the secondary crew.

"What are we going to do about that world?" Red asked.

"We're going to make sure no other simple travelers get caught in its snare ever again," Mark replied, "God only knows how many innocent people from other worlds lost their lives there. Danny, ready one of the singularity devices, like we last used over Mars."

"Mark, are you certain? Do you really want to be judge, jury and executioner for an entire race?" Ariel asked.

"How many people have these monsters killed? I'm betting the number is practically infinite," Mark replied.

"But what gives us the right to wipe them out? Are you sure you can live with yourself after you do this? Ariel continued.

Mark answered, "After what we discovered on that world, I'll sleep just fine. Danny?"

Dan nodded and a moment later said, "All set and ready to be deployed, boss."

"Wait Mark," A just arrived Dr. Troiano said. She stepped out of the open maglovator doors and walked to his side.

"What are you doing here, Anne?" Mark asked.

"Ariel was telepathically keeping me up to date on what you were about to do. This is wrong. You can't wipe out and entire planet, you don't have the right."

"Anne, everyone, I mean *everyone* on that world is a mindless monster that lives to do nothing but feed on the life force of any creature that gets in their path. They've done it for centuries. How many more innocent travelers have to die for your and Ariel's sense of moral rage to be satisfied?"

"What about just marking the area with camouflaged warning buoys broadcasting a warning in all known languages to avoid this area along with a history of what's happened here?" Ariel asked.

Mark hesitated, and turned to Dan, "Danny, what do you think?"

Dan shrugged and said, "It'd work, we could monitor the planet that way too. If we hadda come back an' finish the job we could then. But if we warn off other travelers, that might not be a bad solution to somethin' that might give ya nightmares down the road."

Mark slouched into his command chair and thought for a second.

"Do it," Mark ordered.

"I'll start configurin' the buoys now," Dan said.

Ariel looked at Mark and smiled, *'Thank you,'* she said telepathically. He nodded in reply.

"Dr. Troiano you may return to the medical deck," Mark ordered.

"Yes sir," she replied. Dr. Troiano turned and exited the command deck.

A moment later the stealthed buoys streaked away from the Cagliostro and arced down to take their places about the planet below. "Dan, get us away from here," Mark ordered.

"I'm on it, boss," Dan replied.

The *Cagliostro* streaked away toward the cloaked portion of space they originally found the trap ship in.

"Secondary buoys are away," Dan advised.

"Good get us out of here. Eddie, destroy those cloaking generators as we move past them," Mark commanded.

Eddie nodded and said, "You got it, boss."

Pinpoint blasts of energy stabbed outward from the *Cagliostro's* rear tail mounted guns, exploding the cloaking generators spectacularly.

As they cleared the cloaking field the *Cagliostro* suddenly rocked explosively.

"What the hell?" Red exclaimed.

"That came from the starboard," Dan advised.

"It's that damned ship we just escaped from," Red advised. He turned and looked at Mark with surprise written all over his face. "It's back in position outside the area of the cloaking field. It was waiting for us, and it's firing again."

"Shields double front," Mark commanded. "Eddie, destroy that thing."

"I'm on it, Mark," Eddie DiGenovese replied.

A brace of Star Core missiles shot free of the *Cagliostro's* bow, followed by repeated blasts of the solar cannons.

"It's turning about!" Red shouted. "We damaged its forward shields."

"Stay on it, Dan! Don't let it guard its weakened shield area," Mark ordered.

"I'm workin' on it," Dan Sledge grunted in reply.

"It's returning fire!" Red yelled.

Again and again the *Cagliostro* was rocked by blasts from the other vessel's energy weapons.

"Fire at will, Eddie," Mark reaffirmed.

Eddie nodded and continued to unleash the full fury of the *Cagliostro* upon the alien craft. Repeatedly the enemy ship rocked with each blast of the *Cagliostro's* cannons.

"It's banking again," Red advised.

"I got it," Dan rumbled as he matched the *Cagliostro's* angle to the enemy ships.

"Drop us in underneath it, Danny. Eddie, all four forward guns across its belly, followed by the three tail guns. I want pinpoint accuracy all directed at the same spot. Slash its stomach open and then feed it four more star core missiles," Mark directed.

"Movin' in," Dan warned. "Hang onto somethin'. This is gonna get rough."

Everyone on the command deck gripped their consoles or seat arms in a nervous white knuckled preparation. Matt Marek moved into an auxiliary seat along the wall and strapped himself in.

The *Cagliostro* streaked forward and then suddenly changed direction, slicing across the alien craft's lower section. The enemy ships guns fired repeatedly, splattering energy powerfully across the *Cagliostro's* shields, making them glow red hot in spots.

Eddie returned fire. The *Cagliostro's* mighty solar cannons finally punched through the lower shields of the enemy craft, searing the hull of the ship. The rear cannons continued their attack as the *Cagliostro* passed beneath it and away, tearing a trench through the alien steel hull of the vessel.

Now the two ships separated and arced in opposite directions away from one another. Eddie stabbed the fire control one last time, releasing four gleaming Star Core missiles.

The enemy ship fired upon the Star Core missiles and missed repeatedly. The missiles impacted upon the trench the solar cannons had dug and the strange enemy ship exploded spectacularly, lighting up immediate space brightly. An instant later all that remained was floating debris.

"What the hell did we just go through?" Eddie asked no one in particular.

"As near as I can tell, that was an automated ship that may have been in place for centuries," Mark conjectured. "Its mission was to draw other unsuspecting ships back to that world of psionic parasites where they could drain the life force from unsuspecting travelers."

"That is correct, Captain Johnson," Dr. Rothstein's voice confirmed from the comm units on each console. His face filled the main monitor from the medical deck where he was receiving treatment and monitoring the situation on the command deck. After a pause he continued, "When they had me attached to their horrible machines I was able to glean what they wanted and what they were actually doing. They intended to drain me dry of my very life force, as they intended for all of us to be drained. That automated ship was put there by their ancestors many centuries ago. So long ago in fact that they, as a race, had forgotten all about it and considered the ship some sort of god that provided for them."

"You learned all of this from the ship itself? From its computers?" Mark asked.

"I did, sir," Rothstein confirmed. "That ship was in place for at least eleven centuries killing innocent space travelers and providing sustenance for those who forgot their ancestors had created it. That entire world was a trap for the unwary."

"What kind of universe is this where monsters like those and the Tahir Ga'Warum hide around every corner?" Ariel asked.

"There has to be good out here, Ariel. It cannot all be like this with races like the Agalum calling the shots," Mark replied.

"I hope you're right, Mark," she answered. "I'm beginning to question why we ever left the Earth at this point."

"Sometimes I'm asking myself the same question, Ari," Mark answered.

He turned his seat toward Matt Marek and asked, "How did you do away with the tractor beam?"

Marek grinned slightly and replied, "After you all took off on your mission I had a team of Rangers pinpoint the tractor beam's exact whereabouts and then I sent fifty of them out with enough solar grenades to shatter a moon. They did their job and every one of them returned. They met very little resistance in the form of a few maintenance robots left on repair duty. They were in and out quickly and back on board hours before you returned. We monitored what we could from here, making sure the tractor beam was definitely destroyed. If you needed help we would have been there in a flash, but we assumed it would be better to lay low until the last possible minute before our escape from that hell hole."

Mark nodded and said, "Good work, Matt."

Mark swiveled toward Dan and said, "Time to head toward Chakix. Take us there at maximum speed, Danny."

"Okay, boss, whatever you say," the big Jovian replied.

The Cagliostro leaped into hyperwarp and disappeared.

242

"Ariel," Mark began, "get in touch with Captain Nagata and request an update."

"Yes Captain," Ariel replied.

An instant later she turned toward him and said, "Mark, Nagata is requesting our immediate help on Chakix. He says they are at war with the planet itself!"

Ralph L. Angelo Jr.

Chapter 33

"We're finally here," Dan announced. "Chakix. Three days at full hyperwarp but we finally made it and none the worse for wear."

Mark nodded grimly, then replied, "Where's the *Coronado*, Red?"

"I'm scanning near space now, Mark, and no sign of her so far."

"How can that be? That's one hell of a big ship. It can't just disappear on its own," Eddie said.

"I don't think it did," Red answered quietly.

Mark stood up and quickly walked to Red's side.

"What have you got, Red?" Mark asked.

"Debris," Red replied.

Red pointed at the debris field across a section of the planet's surface.

"Are we sure it's the *Coronado*?" Mark asked.

"It is," Ariel confirmed. "I'm receiving telemetry from its transponder device."

"All right; pull us away from the planet's atmosphere and gravity well, Dan, just in case."

"What? Do ya think the planet did this?" Dan turned toward Mark and asked.

"I do; it is Chakix after all. Remember what it did to us last time we were here?" Mark reminded them all.

"I don't need any repeating it's something I'll never forget," Ariel replied with a shiver.

Over six months ago, the first time the crew of the *Cagliostro* encountered the sentient world known as Chakix, they went through hell until finally overcoming both the living breathing entity who claimed to be the personification of the planet as well as conquering and capturing the hidden Agalum base on its surface that was within a day's striking distance of Earth. The creature calling itself 'Chakix' seemingly perished in that battle, but there was no confirmation of that, and any creature that could slip from body to body would be very hard to kill.

"How do you want to play this?" Red asked Mark.

"Cautiously. Ariel, any signs of survivors near the wreckage?" Mark inquired.

She tilted her head as if listening to something and then faced Mark. "I'm not receiving anything from the crew's transponders. Either they all perished or they're all shut off."

"Or they're being blocked somehow," Mark hypothesized.

"That's probably the case," she agreed, "because I'm not picking up any human remains around the crash site. There's nothing I can confirm as alive there, but I'm really not picking up anything at all; no signs there were ever any people aboard what's left of the *Coronado*."

"What about the base? Has there been any communications from there?" Mark asked.

"No, and they're not replying to my looped requests for confirmation either," Ariel acknowledged.

"So more dead space," Dan pondered aloud.

"We have to investigate both the crash site of the *Coronado* and that base," Mark said.

"So do we split up again?" Red asked.

"I think that's our best option at this point. If what I'm afraid happened really did come to pass, we may have to get out of here as fast as possible."

Dan shrugged and said, "Hey whatever, boss. As long as the paychecks keep comin', I'm good."

Eddie looked at him and smirked, and then said, "Danny, I never thought you were so mercenary."

"Naaah, I'm not, pipsqueak. You know better'n that," Dan replied. "I'm just talkin'."

Mark ignored them both and said, "Command crew with me, in the *Stargrazer,* that includes you, Red, and ten Rangers. Red, you send a Ranger squad to the base in one of the shuttles. I'd recommend Carl as lead there, with Joanie in charge of security aboard the *Cag* until we all return."

Red nodded his head in agreement. "Whatever you say, Boss. I agree with your recommendations."

"That's all they are, Red, recommendations," Mark replied.

Red grinned slightly and said, "Works for me, Chief."

"Let's move out. Team two will meet us in the landing deck and we'll give them their orders from there. Arm them heavily, Red."

"How many wearing heavy suits?" Red asked.

"That's up to you," Mark answered.

"Okay sounds good. I think five should suffice," Red nodded once and turned to enter the maglovator.

The doors slid open and Matt Marek entered with his secondary crew as Red and the others streamed out. Mark stopped Matt as they were about to pass each other to give him his orders. "Matt, don't play the hero here. If anything gets into this star system that could harm the *Cagliostro* or offer any potential threat-Agalum or Tahir Ga'Warum-get my ship out of here, is that understood?"

"You want me to leave you all here?" Matt asked with his eyes widened in surprise.

"That's *exactly* what I want. Are we clear?"

"As crystal, boss. It's your name out there under the 'owned by' plaque," Matt answered slowly.

"Good. Hopefully we'll all be back aboard in a few hours. Make sure my ship stays safe, as well as everyone aboard her."

"You got it, Mark," Matt replied.

"See you soon," Mark reiterated and entered the maglovator.

Matt Marek watched the doors hiss silently closed and then said, "Why am I suddenly getting a bad feeling about all of this?"

Joanie Brevard was seated at the security station and said, "You're not the only one."

Barton Samuels was at the pilot's station, where Dan normally sat, and uttered a muted "Me too."

The three people looked to one another and a cold chill of dread seemed to pass between them all.

Marek walked over to the command chair and sat down heavily in it, his thoughts now his own.

***

In the landing deck the two teams began to congregate between the *Stargrazer* and the shuttle that was going to be used. Mark stood at the center while both crews circled around him awaiting his final orders.

"The Command crew and ten Rangers will go to the *Coronado's* crash site. Hopefully we can aid survivors and begin transporting them back to the *Cagliostro*. Team two will head to the base we commandeered last year. Your mission is to secure the base. No one is answering our hails there. I doubt it's an equipment malfunction. More than likely the base has been compromised by whatever took out the *Coronado,*" Mark said.

"What do you think that is? That Chakix creature again?" Rayborn asked.

Mark nodded affirmatively. "I do. That, at least, is a possibility, and one you should be prepared for. Stay

248

camouflaged at all times, including your shuttle. Survey the area and look for obvious signs; don't just dive in head first into danger. Make sure you assess the dangers prior to getting in over your heads. If it looks bad, back out and return to the *Cagliostro.* Am I clear?"

"As crystal, Captain," Rayborn replied.

"Good. Good luck, and keep us updated," Mark finished.

Both teams separated and began filing into their respective ships.

"We're ready for take-off," Dan announced.

"Everyone here settled in?" Mark asked.

The crew all answered affirmatively.

"All right, Danny, take us to the *Coronado,*" Mark ordered.

"We're on our way, boss," Dan Sledge replied.

The *Stargrazer's* magno-disk engines began to whir and the craft lifted upward, then slowly spun about to face the opening at the end of the landing deck. Dan eased the throttle forward and the ship exited the *Cagliostro* flying away into bright sunshine.

"Don't forget the camouflage," Mark advised.

"I engaged it before we left the *Cag,*" Dan replied.

"The *Coronado* looked bad, almost like it was ripped in two," Red commented.

"I know. I'm hoping there are survivors," Mark replied.

"What could have done that? A Tahir Ga'Warum cruiser? Maybe two of them?" Eddie asked.

"Anything's possible, Eddie, but my bet is something from the planet pulled that ship down," Mark answered.

"Pulled it down? What could grab a ship and pull it to a planet?" Ariel asked.

Mark shrugged and then said, "That just happened to us above that world of savages only a few days ago. They had that powerful tractor beam that downed us, remember?"

Ariel nodded sheepishly and said, "True. I wasn't thinking straight I guess."

"Is that what you think downed the *Coronado*?" Eddie asked.

"I'm thinking it was something more…natural," Mark answered.

"What do you mean, 'natural'? Like nature made?" Dan asked.

"That's exactly what I mean, Danny," Mark replied.

"So you really are thinking that Chakix is back and is attacking our people here," Ariel asked.

"I am, Ari. It just makes sense. She stayed hidden and licked her wounds for half a year and when she regained strength she struck out at whatever earth men she saw," Mark answered.

"Heads up people, we're here," Dan announced.

The *Stargrazer* hovered above the wreckage of the *Coronado*, a once proud and mighty part of the EPIC fleet now reduced to scrap metal. The great ship was literally torn in two where it lay.

"Take us down, Danny," Mark almost whispered.

"I'm on it, boss," the Jovian pilot replied.

Gently the *Stargrazer* settled down next to the ruins of the *Coronado*.

"Everyone switch your tech suits to hazmat protocols. That should protect us from any airborne contaminants in the area," Mark ordered.

"I ain't seein' any bodies," Dan observed.

"Me neither," added Red.

"Let's move out. Security Rangers set up a perimeter," Red ordered.

Mark nodded his approval, and then said, "The rest of you follow me. Hopefully the lack of bodies strewn about is a good thing."

The door on the *Stargrazer* slid to the right, opening up for them, and they all exited cautiously.

"What happened here?" Ariel asked.

"We're going to find out, Ari," Mark replied.

The command crew approached the smoldering husk of a ship, tremendous in size, yet broken like a child's toy in an overpowering grip.

"It's like some huge hand reached out inta space and grabbed this ship, then pulled it down to the surface," Dan said.

"That's probably closer to the truth than any of us want to believe," Mark replied.

"Are you thinkin' Chakix did this with gravity fields?" Dan asked.

"Why not? She held the *Cagliostro* in place on the surface half a year ago doing much the same thing," Mark said.

"That makes sense to me," Red agreed. "If she could do it to us on the surface why not reach into space, even if it was just orbital distance and pull a ship in? Is this why you left the *Cag* out of range and had us fly the *'Grazer'* in?"

"Yes. To be honest I didn't know what to expect here. All I did know was that I never truly believed she was dead. That was just too convenient and too pat," Mark answered.

"We still don't know that she's back. You're just supposing she is," Ariel interjected.

"You're right, Ari, but everything here is pointing to Chakix's return. But right now we have to find the crew of the *Coronado*, including Captain Nagata," Mark concluded.

"If he's still alive," Red added.

Mark turned toward Red and nodded in agreement, then said "Yes, if he's still alive. I'm hoping they all are, but with this much damage…" Mark trailed off and shook his head.

"How come Chakix doesn't know we're here? The tech suits?" Eddie asked.

"Yes, we're camouflaged. In fact we shouldn't even be talking, but I can't risk Ari using her telepathy on this world. I'm not going to take a chance on her being hurt by Chakix again," Mark said.

"Mark, I'm okay. If you need me to telepathically search for Chakix' presence, I will. I'm not afraid," Ariel assured.

"Ari, I'm the one that's afraid, for your safety. I thought you were dead the last time we were on this world. I'm not going to put you through that again," Mark announced.

"You're the boss," she replied with a shrug.

"How are we going to find the *Coronado's* crew, if they're still alive that is?" Eddie inquired.

"Good question. None of 'em are wearin' tech suits like we do with trackin' devices built into 'em," Dan said.

"We'll have to do it the old fashioned way, with our suits' built in scanners," Mark replied, then touched the controls on his right sleeve. Instantly a holographic screen popped up above his right forearm. He pointed his arm across the landscape, moving from left to right and then back again. The display showed the ground before them in an orange glow. After several minutes of this, he began to walk silently forward.

"Do you see something?" Red asked.

"Yes, I see a trail, as if people were dragged away from here. But it's very faint as if it was from several days ago,

252

and judging by what we see in this wreckage that would be about right," Mark answered.

"Somethin' else is botherin' me though," Dan announced. "How come we're the only ship that responded to this? I mean Earth is only a day away from here at full hyperwarp. An' not only that, but when we were last here a few weeks back there was a whole fleet in place around this world, an' now they're all gone without a trace? What's up with that?"

"I've been thinking the same thing, Danny, and to be honest, I'm worried about that," Mark replied.

"The base here should have easily been able to contact EPIC if they needed help. Why didn't they?" Ariel asked.

"We'll find out when the other team reports in," Mark answered.

"Everyone make sure your stealth units are all on," Red reminded the crew.

"Good point, Red. Let's go," Mark ordered.

As a unit, the command crew and the Rangers team with them moved away from the tremendous wreckage of the *Coronado*.

"I wonder how team two is doing?" Eddie asked.

"I'll give them another fifteen minutes and then contact them," Mark replied.

The group continued to walk, cloaked and in silence now, following a dim trail through electronic means in their tech suits.

***

Miles away, at the site of the base, Carl Rayborn and his crew entered the seemingly empty structure.

"Eyes front and wide open people. I don't want any surprises," he spoke into his tech suit's cowl. He had a skin tight face mask pulled over his head as did everyone else with him not wearing a heavy suit. A microphone was hidden inside, as well as a small heads up display on the lenses that covered his eyes.

"Nothing moving in here so far, Carl," came the voice of Bob Warrens, a Ranger in the lead heavy suit.

"All right, Bob. Make sure you're scanning on all wavelengths. We want to be doing the surprising here, not the other way around," Carl advised.

"Yeah, I hear ya, chief," Warrens replied.

They entered the facility in a wedge pattern. Two heavy suits up front, followed behind them by ten tech suit wearing Rangers followed by three more heavy suit adorned Rangers in the rear.

"So far no signs of life," Warrens confirmed.

"That's what I was afraid of," Carl replied.

"Did ya notice, though," a Ranger named Toby Lee added, "that there's no signs of a struggle here? There's no blaster burn spots anywhere in the facility. It's like they all just got up and left."

Rayborn nodded in agreement. "You're right, Lee. Good observation." Then after a few more steps forward Carl added, "Head to the command center. Let's view the security footage once we get there. We'll contact the other team from there, once we secure the place. From here on out we use spectroscopic scans to see where we're going. Both the heavy suits and the tech suit hoods and goggles allow that. Turn 'em on, people. We don't know what we're walking into."

The group continued forward, moving deeper into the dark facility.

"How far do we have to go before we reach the command center?" Robin Bikowski asked from inside a heavy suit.

Rayborn answered, "Moving as carefully as we are, about twenty minutes more, Bikowski." Rayborn paused a moment and looked at her, then continued, "You've been here before, Bikowski, on this world I mean. What can we expect here?"

Robin shook her head full of blonde hair within the heavy suit's armored confines. "The unexpected. This planet was beautiful and horrible when we were here last. There were flying monsters and an out of control woman who claimed to be the planet's 'Goddess.' There were surprises around every corner. We all almost died here fighting the Agalum. I can't believe that was only half a year ago." She shook her head in thought, then turned and faced Carl Rayborn. "This is a terrible place. Death can overtake you here in the blink of an eye."

Rayborn slowly and grimly nodded his head, not breaking eye contact. "I'll keep it in mind."

Slowly and silently the squad of Rangers moved deeper into the underground facility, itself cut into a dormant capped and redirected volcano.

A moment before entering the command center, Toby Lee announced, "I'm getting something."

"What is it?" Rayborn asked, as he gripped his rifle tighter.

"I-I'm not sure. It's in the command center, but its readings are all jumbled," Lee replied.

"Extreme caution from here on out, people. We've lost enough friends on this mission already," Carl ordered.

Cautiously they moved forward, toward the entrance to the command center, a wide open entryway eight feet across.

Lee was the first to the entryway when, like a flash of light, tentacles stretched out and wrapped around his heavy suit, lifting him off his feet and dragging him into the control room, as if he was a child's toy.

The rest of the Ranger squad sprinted forward into the room, all protocol forgotten, with weapons drawn.

In the middle of the room stood a horror out of a madman's deepest nightmare; a towering octopus-like creature with one eye in the center of its blue mass. Its seemingly countless appendages spun about maddeningly with Lee's screaming form held fast by two of them.

Chapter 34

Mark Johnson led his team further into the dense forest, following the faint trail left behind.

No one spoke for quite a while. They were all using the camouflage mode of their tech suits and continued on silently through the dense foliage.

After many minutes of this they came to a clearing. As always the burly security chief was in the lead, his hand held cannon strapped across his chest and ready to fire.

"What do you make of this?" Mark hissed. He was standing next to Red now, both peering out invisibly from behind cover of the forest.

Before them stood a village made of thatch huts. Cooking fires were dotted about the villages, but these were all unattended.

"This place looks empty," Eddie said.

"Yeah it does, squirt. Good observation," Red jabbed him.

"This is not right," Mark added. "Ariel, can you do a mental scan of the area? Something light and unobtrusive? Perhaps just listen in to any stray thoughts?"

"I've been trying just that, Mark, and I'm getting nothing. No one's here."

Mark nodded silently, then replied, "All right, let's move in. We're stealthed anyway. Just keep your voices down. The tech suit's stealth or camo mode will naturally mask our voices to begin with. Let's not push our luck though."

"I got lead," Red ordered. "Sledge, you follow me up with DiGenovese and Mark, you come in after them. Rangers keep Mark and Ariel as safe as you can, especially those of you wearing heavy suits."

257

Everyone nodded except Mark, who furrowed his brow in annoyance.

"What?" Red asked.

"You know what. This is my mission, I should be up front with you," Mark testily answered.

"You gave me field command. Those are my orders, until you fire me this is how it's going to be. I want you safe so you can come up with some of your usual magic to save our asses if need be."

Mark nodded silently and fell in line, still obviously unhappy with Red's decision.

As one, the entire group moved forward into the small village, warily moving from thatched hut to thatched hut, pulling aside skins that covered the doorways and peering inside surreptitiously.

"They're all empty," Mark concluded aloud. "No one is here, but it seems as if they left suddenly, with their cooking fires still up and running."

"So it wasn't that long ago that they left," Eddie said.

"It couldn't have been. The fires are still hot, though not raging," Mark noted.

They swept the village from end to end, the security Rangers now taking the lead going through huts.

Several minutes later they all met at the center of the village around the village fire pit.

"This village is completely empty," Mark concluded.

"Now what?" Eddie asked.

"Now we use our suits' scanners and continue to follow the trail they left behind, though this trail should be a lot hotter than the one we followed here." Mark replied.

Mark tapped his right sleeve and a holographic reticule appeared above it. He tapped a few controls and adjusted colors on the display, leaving the background on his sleeve a bright blue. Within that blue field a glowing red line of footprints appeared before him.

"This way," he said before turning to Red and adding, "I have lead."

Robinski nodded silently with a mark of annoyance playing across his face and fell in beside Mark.

The group moved out, cautiously heading back into the forest, but on the opposite end of the village.

"How long ago do you think they left this place?" Red asked.

"An hour or two at most, judging by the thermal signature, and there were a lot of feet making the trip."

"Hey boss, are you seein' any particularly big feet?" Dan Sledge asked.

"I get your meaning, Danny, and no, not yet. No giant ape feet," Mark answered.

"Okay, just let me know if you see anything resembling that reject from a King Kong flick returnin'," Dan acknowledged.

"Believe me, Danny, you and Red will be the first to know," Mark said.

Red nodded grimly and gripped his cannon tighter.

"I see another clearing up ahead at the end of this trail, and the trail itself is getting 'hotter' the closer we get to it," Mark advised. He turned toward Ariel then and asked, "Are you getting anything? Any stray thoughts?"

"No, not a thing," she answered.

"I don't like that. That alone is suspicious," Red commented.

"You're right, it is," Mark acknowledged.

They crept forward silently for several moments.

But a sudden frenzied communication burst through their tech suits' comm array, shocking everyone but Red with its urgency.

259

"*Cagliostro* to Johnson," came Matt Marek's frenzied call.

Mark replied instantly, "What is it, Mr. Marek?"

"I've got three Tahir Ga'Warum ships entering this system and on a heading to this world. What are your orders?" Marek asked.

"The same as I gave you when we left the *Cagliostro*. Get out of there now. Don't worry about us. Just get the ship to safety. We'll rendezvous later. Move it, Marek. Keep my people and my ship safe. Johnson out," Mark closed off the communication without another word.

"Great, now we're cut off," Eddie quipped.

"We'll be fine, DiGenovese. We've got the *Stargrazer*," Dan replied.

The group entered the new clearing before them and were momentarily stunned by what they saw. "Captain Nagata!" Ariel exclaimed.

Before them, tied to posts driven into the ground were Nagata and five of his crew. Another dozen were haphazardly strewn about the clearing. Interspersed with them were some of the red skinned natives.

"Are they dead?" Dan asked.

Mark scanned them with his tech suit's sensors and then replied, "Some are. There was some kind of fight here less than an hour ago. And Danny, *now* I'm seeing remnants of a fight with the giant red ape. I see footprints and some of its singed fur."

"Surrender now, MarkJohnson, and you will die painlessly and quickly," a terrible voice boomed about them all.

Everyone looked about the clearing with weapons drawn.

An instant later the foliage about them crashed inward as hundreds of the red skinned savage warriors thundered out of the forest, led by the giant red furred ape itself, who had battled them on their last mission to this world.

But this time something was different about the ape. It stared at them cruelly, maliciously, intelligently, and then it seemed to sneer.

Mark's left lip quivered in anger and he spit out one word, one name. "Chakix."

"Yes, MarkJohnson, I am Chakix. You have returned to my world, to my people, in time for one thing, and that is to die here for your crimes against me. Your judgment has been written many months ago by me, and now your sentence will be carried out. Kill them all!"

At her command the army of red skinned savages surged toward the embattled crew en masse.

Ralph L. Angelo Jr.

Chapter 35

The *Cagliostro* turned and accelerated away from the planet Chakix, disappearing into deep space almost instantly.

"Are we camouflaged?" Matt Marek asked Joanie Brevard.

"We are," she replied.

"What are you doing?" A new voice intruded from the maglovator doorway.

Marek and Brevard, along with Barton Samuels, who was piloting the *Cagliostro,* all turned toward the sound of that voice and saw Dr. Anne Troiano angrily storming onto the command deck.

"What are you doing?" she reiterated. "You can't leave them all there. They'll be trapped on that mad world. You have to go back for them, now."

"I can't, Doc," Marek replied. "There are three Tahir Ga'Warum ships entering this system and heading directly for that world. If we don't put some distance between it and us, we could be wiped out by those monsters. That wouldn't do Mark and the crew any good, would it, Doc?"

Troiano's eyes squinted angrily behind her glasses, until after a few seconds she finally seemed to decompress. "Y-you're right Matt. I-I'm sorry. I just feel helpless right now with them trapped there."

"So do I, Doc, so do I." Marek turned toward Joanie Brevard and said, "Joanie, send out several of the probes, maybe a dozen, and hide them anywhere you can between us and that world. I want to be able to watch that place from afar so we know what our people are facing down there. If things go bad for them, no matter what Mark said, I'm going to head in solar cannons blazing to save them.

263

But for now I'll play it by his rules. Lilly, keep scanning all our usual frequencies but also the suspected Tahir Ga'Warum and Agalum frequencies as well. Let's see if we can pick up any chatter." Marek slid back into the command chair and gripped his chin pensively.

Lilly Wallflower nodded and began the job of scanning one frequency after another in a loop.

"Where should I take us?" Samuels asked.

"Just away from here, directly opposite where those ships are coming from. I wouldn't be concerned with taking on one of them or even two, but three is suicide," Marek concluded.

"You got it, boss," Samuels replied as he vectored the *Cagliostro* away.

"I'm not the boss, Bart. Mark Johnson is. Let's leave it at that," Marek said.

Barton Samuels nodded his light brown head of hair and returned his gaze to his flight controls and the holographic flight display before him.

"I don't like this," Anne Troiano whispered. She was standing next to the command chair and only speaking loud enough for Matt to hear.

"Neither do I, Anne, but it's how it has to be, at least for now," Marek replied. He nervously ran his fingers through his own close cut tawny hair.

"Those ships that entered the system are heading directly to Chakix," Brevard announced.

"Let's see what they look like," Marek ordered.

The main monitor lit up with images of three of the almost blood red organic looking ships determinedly crossing the solar system toward Chakix.

"They're in a tight formation," Brevard observed.

"Yeah, they are. They're expecting to be attacked and are holding close together for defensive purposes," Matt replied.

"Wonderful, so they know we're here then, but just haven't found us yet," Samuels muttered.

"Not necessarily, Barton. You forget, they're really at war right now with the Agalum, and not us, not yet at least. They may be expecting them to show up and attack," Matt answered.

As if on cue Joanie announced, "We have incoming."

"Where?" Marek asked.

"Three o'clock position," Brevard replied.

"Magnify that location," Matt ordered.

Brevard did as she was commanded and the monitor magnified showing two smaller Agalum vessels with a third large ship between them bee lining toward the much larger Tahir Ga'Warum ships.

"I don't get it. They have those planet crusher monsters they used against our fleet over Chakix. Why aren't they using them against the Tahir Ga'Warum?" Barton asked.

"Maybe they've all been destroyed," Dr. Troiano offered.

The maglovator door opened behind her and Delrin re-entered the command deck. "I sense much anxiety here, as well as out there." He nodded toward the scene being played out on the monitor.

"Are they really going to attack those Tahir Ga'Warum ships?" Lilly Wallflower asked. "And the two smaller ships, what Eddie called 'Predator' class ships, seem like they are protecting the larger ship between them. They look like two very beaten ships to be attacking anything, let alone behemoths like the Tahir Ga'Warum use."

Marek stared sternly at the view screen and then said, "Joanie, that larger ship is familiar. I think we've seen it before. Pull up ship recognition files. I have a strange feeling about this."

The screen flared brighter before their eyes as blast beams exploded from the bows of the sharply angular Agalum ships to impale the sides of the larger Tahir Ga'Warum ships.

Instantly the Tahir Ga'Warum returned fire, heavier bolts of a dark orange hue repeatedly pounding the Agalum ships. An instant later one of them exploded brightly.

"They're outmatched and outgunned," Joanie Brevard said. Then she paused and her eyes widened slightly as if in surprise. "Matt, I know what that ship is! We *have* seen it before. That's the Agalum leader's ship. We saw it over Chakix earlier this year."

Marek sighed. "I knew it looked familiar, and they're about to be destroyed. Samuels prepare to take us in. Joanie, call battle stations. I'm about to do something really, really stupid. Mark is going to kill me."

Chapter 36

Carl Rayborn raised his blast rifle quickly and fired. The beam of energy slashed through the air and cleanly cut through the tentacle holding Toby Lee. Lee and the still twisting tentacle flew across the room and slammed into the wall.

"Are you okay?" Robin Bikowski asked Lee.

The Ranger was slowly crawling to his feet, shaking his head within his heavy suit, which was now dented and damaged.

"I'm hurting, Bikowski, but I ain't dead," Lee replied.

With a grunt he made his way to his feet and grabbed a section of wall at the doorway.

"These suits, they make us strong and tough. If I wasn't wearing this armored thing I'd be dead right now. They don't put us in Sledge's class of strong, but we ain't that far behind," Lee continued.

Nearby the Rangers peppered the grotesque creature with blast beams, slicing into it repeatedly. Those wounds healed almost instantly as the jellied surface of the creature seemed to simply flow back together at the point of each wound.

"Back up, all of you," Rayborn ordered.

He pulled a grenade from his suit and hurled it at the horrible creature. The grenade ruptured upon contact with the monster's surface. Instead of exploding the monster froze instantly.

"That thing ain't getting out of that block of ice," roared Lee. He heaved powerfully and tore a section of wall off in his heavy suited hands. Then, turning in one smooth motion, he hurled the section of wall at the frozen horror, shattering it into a million pieces.

"What was that thing?" Bikowski asked.

267

"I have no idea, Robin," Rayborn answered.

"Do you think it killed everyone here?" Toby Lee asked.

"I doubt it, Lee. I think it was left to kill anyone who showed up afterward," Carl Rayborn replied.

"Like us," Robin stated.

"Yes, just like us," Rayborn agreed.

"We should contact Mark and the others, let them know what we found here," Lee offered.

Rayborn nodded and then said, "You're right. Let's take care of that right away."

Rayborn brought up his holographic control panel on his right sleeve and spoke into it, "Rayborn to Johnson, Do you read, Mark?"

A moment passed and then two with no answer save uncharacteristic static.

"That's odd. I've never heard static on any of Mark's comm units," Bikowski said.

"You're right, Robin, I haven't either," Rayborn noted.

"We're being jammed," Marcus Blum, another Ranger in a heavy suit said.

"Yeah, I kind of thought that too, Blum," Rayborn responded. "Let's clear the rest of this base and then get out of here. According to the schematics I pulled up the administrator's office is this way. Follow me and stay tight and frosty. We have no idea when we might run into this things bigger, nastier brother."

The group moved out of the command center following Carl Rayborn's lead into the depths of the dark and powerless base.

"First thing we should do is get some power restored in this place so we can see what we're doing," Lee commented.

"No," replied Rayborn. "We have no idea if this place is rigged in any way. For now we use spectroscopics to see. We already met one surprise in this place, no reason to doubt that there'll be anymore."

"You think it might be set to explode?" Bikowski asked.

Rayborn shrugged. "Why not? Anything's possible here."

Grudgingly Robin Bikowski agreed. "I guess you're right. Damn, this is like walking through a mine field."

"Pretty solid analogy. We have to move cautiously and use all the gizmos that the boss gave us in these suits. Tech suits should be scanning in all directions and heavy suits should be leading us, clearing the way if need be. Let's go people, times a wasting," Rayborn concluded.

Three heavy suit wearing Rangers took the lead, followed by Rayborn and Bikowski with Lee following behind them with the next group.

"You know, I'm thinking this is a strange thing going on here," Lee offered.

"What is, Lee?" Rayborn replied.

"Well, we enter this base and find it empty, then we find it powerless and the only living thing we find in here is a monster. No tech is running in here of any kind. The place seems powerless and empty as if everyone got up and walked out. Why would that happen and how?"

Rayborn stopped and turned toward his fellow Ranger, his face behind his black facemask furrowed in deep thought.

"Do you think they evacuated?" Bikowski asked.

"That would explain why there's no sign of a battle, but the next question is why did they leave?" Rayborn asked.

"Maybe the power went down and they all simply left?" Lee offered.

Rayborn nodded pensively and then said, "That's all possible, I guess, but I think it's something more than that. I'm not seeing any sign of an emergency exit here. It's more like they all simply got up at once and walked out."

"But what could make them do that?" Bikowski questioned.

"Maybe mind control?" Bob Warrens replied. He was walking with Marcus Blum and Lee behind Rayborn and Bikowski and had stopped when they did.

"Mind control?" Rayborn repeated. "That would make sense actually and it would explain a hell of a lot."

"Except where did everyone go to, and why?" Robin Bikowski questioned.

In answer a heavy metal clang sounded from somewhere ahead of them all.

"What the hell was that?" Bikowski asked.

"No idea, but I'm suddenly reading life signs from that direction, and human life signs at that," Rayborn replied.

"What's down that way?" Warrens asked.

"The gym and auditorium. They did the large meetings there," Rayborn replied.

"How do you know that?" Robin asked.

"I read the base reports before we left the ship," Rayborn replied with a slight grin tugging at his lips.

"How many people were in this base?" Bikowski asked.

"Six hundred plus," Rayborn answered.

"An' how many life signs are you reading down there?" asked Lee.

Rayborn met his gaze and replied, "Six hundred plus."

Without another word the group quickly headed toward the auditorium. They rounded a corner and walked into the dark, cavernous room and every one of them pulled up short in surprise.

Before them stood all six hundred of the missing base personnel, all with blank, glassy eyed countenances. Every one of them held something in their hands. Some held pipes or wooden tree limbs; others held blast guns and curved blades. All of them looked like they had no idea where they were.

"I think we found our people," Bikowski said.

"These aren't 'your people' any longer. They are mine, now and forever, in both mind and body," every one of the six hundred replied as if of one mind.

"Chakix," Rayborn blurted out, "this is just what the natives sounded like half a year ago when she mind controlled them."

"Correct, Earther," the multitude eerily replied as one, "and I now command my new subjects to kill you all."

Like a wave crashing upon a shore, the mind controlled group surged forward toward the stunned Rangers.

Ralph L. Angelo Jr.

Chapter 37

The red skinned people of Chakix swarmed toward the command crew of the *Cagliostro*.

"This is like last time we were here all over again with Chakix mind controlling her people," Eddie shouted.

Instantly Eddie's gun was up and firing, sweeping across the crowd rushing toward them in an arc, dropping a dozen instantly.

"I'm goin' in," Dan Sledge bellowed. He leaped forward and slammed into the horde, scattering them with powerful swings of his Jovian muscled arms

"Hang back, Sledge!" Red shouted. He hurled a grenade into the midst of the savages. The concussive force of the blast threw them painfully into the air, only to land hard and insensate on the ground.

But the crew of the *Cagliostro* was only fifteen strong and the mind controlled denizens of this world numbered far more than that.

Dan swung his mighty arms left to right, sending a dozen to the ground with each swing.

Suddenly a huge shaggy red paw slammed down on Dan's head, smashing him to the ground. The paw then rose again with Dan's limp form within it to batter him relentlessly into the ground.

The great red furred ape hammered Dan into the planet's surface until it was certain he was at the very least unconscious.

"Danny!" shouted Mark.

Instantly he fired his own pistol into the hundred foot tall creature. The blaster beams hurt the creature but did little to stop it.

"Did you think that puny weapon would stop me, MarkJohnson?" the red ape roared. Chakix was driving the mindless creature like a man drove a vehicle, controlling its every move.

"Let him go, Chakix. Your beef is with me!" Mark shouted. He continued to fire his weapon, spraying the ape repeatedly. All around him his companions were firing their weapons into the crowd of red skinned, sword wielding natives. But it was akin to trying to put out a raging forest fire with a water pistol. They just kept on coming.

"No, MarkJohnson, my 'beef,' as you say, is with all of you," Chakix replied,

The red furred ape lifted Dan's limp form over its head and hurled him away, over the towering treetops and into the distance.

"Dan! No!" Ariel cried.

Red swung his heavy energy cannon around and fired in one motion, directly into the ape's chest. A gaping hole appeared there instantly and the enormous creature fell to the ground, lifeless.

Almost instantly the crowd of natives began to scatter, most not understanding what they were doing there in the first place, as if their minds were suddenly freed of some cloying mental fog. Fearfully they looked over their shoulders as they ran, traumatized at the sight of their red furred protector laid low.

"Form a perimeter," Red ordered his Rangers.

"No way is Chakix gone," Eddie blurted out.

"Agreed," Mark replied. "Is everyone okay?" He looked around them and did a quick count.

"We're all fine, Mark. Just a little worse for wear," Ariel said. "How'd they find us in the first place? I thought we were invisible?"

"I have to think it was something like weight sensing from Chakix herself. She must have sensed our footsteps," Mark answered.

"We have to get these people cut down," Ariel said. She moved to Captain Nagata's limp form that was still tied to a stake jammed into the ground.

"Right, let's see to them and hope they're still alive," Mark replied.

Silently the crew of the *Cagliostro* cut down the helpless men and women who were tied to the stakes and laid them down on the thick grass.

"I hate to break up this party, boss, but we have to look for Danny too," Eddie said.

Mark tapped his sleeve and instantly a holo display formed above it. He tapped a few controls and an orange dot formed on the display and blinked steadily.

"That's Dan. It looks like he's up and moving back this way. He's tough. I had a feeling he'd be okay," Mark advised.

"How are we looking?" Red asked. He nodded toward the crew of the *Coronado*.

Ariel brushed her long blonde hair back from her face and turned toward both Red and Mark.

"Not good. Several are already dead, from exposure more than likely and some bloody wounds. Nagata's still alive, but just barely. I wish Anne or one of the other doctors were here to tend to them."

"Noted," Mark began. "From now on a doctor accompanies every surface mission, no matter their objections. If they don't like it, they can work somewhere else."

A familiar voice intruded on them from the group's comm units, "Landing team two to landing team one, Rayborn to Johnson, do you copy, Johnson?"

Mark tapped his sleeve immediately and a holographic image of Carl Rayborn's face appeared in the air above his sleeve. "Johnson here, Carl. I have you on visual as well as audio. What's your status? I couldn't get through to you for a while. Are you and your people safe?"

Rayborn nodded and said, "We are now, boss. We were surrounded by about six hundred base workers turned mind washed zombies who were going to kill us when something happened to them. It was like a switch was thrown-"

"Or a connection broken," Ariel interjected.

Mark looked at Dan and nodded silently, then returned his gaze to Carl's image before speaking again. "That *might* have had something to do with us, Carl. We were under attack by Chakix and her hundred foot tall red furred ape that she was possessing. Red blew a hole in its chest. The natives here that were attacking us dropped out of their fog as well and ran off into the forest."

"Geeze! Are you people all right?" Rayborn asked.

"We are now," Mark replied. "We just have to find Danny. The ape hurled him away from here. We were just going to look for him when you called. What's the status of the base staff?"

"They're a little groggy and disoriented, but otherwise seem fine. What I want to know is how did Chakix mind control them?" Rayborn asked.

"I believe it was air borne pathogens that they all breathed in over the past few months," Mark answered, "When we returned home several months ago I did some testing on air and soil samples we had taken the last time around. Then I ran some computer simulations. Nothing was conclusive, but there was a common element to all the samples that defied description. I think that's the tie to Chakix herself."

"Oh that's wonderful that means we're breathing them in right now, too," Eddie commented.

"Yes, but it must take months to build up enough of a residual in a body to allow her control. But just in case, close the mask on your tech suit that we use for camouflage. It'll protect you from breathing in anything we don't want," Mark advised.

"In other words it's got a filter built in," Dan Sledge's familiar basso tones replied from behind them.

Everyone turned and saw Dan emerge from the brush behind them.

"Are you okay?" Ariel asked immediately.

"Yeah. I got some aches an' pains, but this ol' hide is tougher than any ape's ever gonna be. Now where is he? I want my round two," Dan continued, but then his gaze stopped at the huge body lying in the clearing on the opposite side of the group with the still smoldering hole in its chest.

"Heh, I guess you couldn't wait fer me to get back," Dan concluded.

"Don't worry, Danny, the next threat we face is all yours, I promise," Mark concluded.

Before anyone else could speak an alarm claxon went off from each of their suits and Mark shouted, "Teleporters!"

Immediately a group of twenty Tahir Ga'Warum appeared complete with black tendrils of smoke swirling about their pale forms. They all held weapons on the landing party from the *Cagliostro*.

"Stand down," Mark ordered his people.

"You are correct to do so, Mark Johnson," one of the monstrous aliens hissed, "for any other action would result in all your deaths. I am called Karem, and I lead this body of Tahir Ga'Warum. You are ordered to surrender and you

277

will be taken into custody for interrogation, which will begin immediately."

Chapter 38

"They're firing on the Agalum leader's ship, Matt," Joanie Brevard exclaimed.

"Are they firing back?" he snapped in reply.

"The Predator ship that was protecting them has gotten between the two larger ships and is taking a battering from that Tahir Ga'Warum cruiser," Joanie answered.

"Bring us in, Mr. Samuels, but don't drop our camouflage. I want to stay hidden as long as possible," Marek said.

Barton Samuels nodded and returned his gaze to his holographic HUD hovering above his console. "We'll be in targeting range in thirty seconds," Samuels advised.

"Kenji, lock up your sights and prepare to fire on my mark," Marek told the gunner who sat at Eddie DiGenovese's usual station.

Kenji Cho nodded and set his jaw sternly. He was in his early thirties and another former soldier who was trained as a sniper, as was Eddie himself. "I'm locked on the Tahir Ga'Warum ship, Matt. I am ready to fire at your command," Kenji said.

"Good. Brevard, status of the two Agalum ships?"

"The Predator class ship is about to lose its shields. Once it does, it's going to be blown apart by the Tahir Ga'Warum vessel," she replied.

Suddenly the main monitor flared with bright light. Instantly the monitor compensated for the increased brightness and dimmed until it could return to its former settings a heartbeat later.

"The Predator, it's gone, just like the other one," Brevard advised. "The Agalum ship is powering up its weapons. I can tell you now it's not going to be enough.

279

That ship is barely able to defend itself against a one man attack fighter, judging by the armaments and class of shields it has."

"So it's all for show. Okay, let's do something stupid and hope the Agalum don't turn on us in mid-fight. Let's take that organic looking monstrosity out," Marek commanded.

Samuels dove the *Cagliostro* toward the battle taking place before them.

"In range now," Joanie Brevard advised.

"Hit that bastard with everything we've got, Cho," Matt Marek ordered.

All three forward missile tubes spit deadly star core missiles at the sinister looking Tahir Ga'Warum ship. Its blood red hide shuddered with solid and powerful impacts upon its shields.

The *Cagliostro*, still invisible, sliced through space above the Tahir Ga'Warum ship.

"Now, fire all Solar Cannon banks," Matt ordered.

First the forward batteries unleashed their deadly solar blasts upon the other ship's shields, and then when the *Cagliostro* had flown past, its tri-tailed solar cannon array fired again and again, slashing across the Tahir Ga'Warum ship's hull.

"Bring us about, Samuels, and then let's see if our reputation has preceded us. Drop camouflage on my command," Marek told his crew.

Brevard nodded and readied herself to return the *Cagliostro* to visibility.

The *Cagliostro* spun through space and quickly reversed direction, its forward weapons aimed and locked upon the terrible Tahir Ga'Warum ship.

"They'll be able to track us from our weapons fire and exhaust trail now that they know we're here anyway. You might as well drop the camouflage and double the power to the shields," Joanie said.

"Okay. They haven't fired on us yet but they also stopped firing on the Agalum ship, which is just hanging there in space.

"Okay, drop the camo now, Brevard, and Lilly, put me through on all known frequencies. I want to make sure they hear this," Matt ordered.

Instantly the *Cagliostro* appeared above and in line with the Agalum ship.

Matt began to speak as soon as the ship de-camouflaged. "This is Major Matt Marek of the EPIC star cruiser *Cagliostro.* I am ordering the Tahir Ga'Warum vessel to de-power its weapons and stand down. You are in Earth Protectorate Interstellar Command space. Prepare to surrender and be boarded. No harm will come to you and your crew if you comply. The Agalum ship you are attacking is forthwith under our protection. You have twenty seconds to power down your weapons or be destroyed."

Marek nodded his head silently and Lilly Wallflower cut the communication.

Almost instantly a hollow, eerie voice replied, "You would protect those who are your sworn enemy?"

A chill ran through the command deck crew as the Tahir Ga'Warum's voice elicited an almost primal reaction in all of them.

Matt nodded toward Miss Wallflower and she opened the comm signal again. "We would. While we have no love for the Agalum, we have seen firsthand the destruction you have visited upon them and their worlds. You have already destroyed two Agalum ships that were escorting this vessel. This ship is no match for you. While we may be at war with the Agalum, we will not stand idly by while a superior

281

force destroys a helpless ship and its crew. Stand down now and return to your own dimension. You won't be given this opportunity again."

In reply the Tahir Ga'Warum ship immediately opened fire on the *Cagliostro*. Terrible beams of unknown energies raked the ship's shields, sending terrible tremors through the gleaming manta-ray shaped vessel's hull.

"Evasive maneuvers return fire and don't hold anything back, Cho." Matt ordered.

The *Cagliostro* leapt forward under Barton Samuels' deft control. Deadly beams of energy slashed across the *Cag*'s hull.

In reply Samuels spun the ship over and over on its starboard side, making accurate blasts mere glancing shots.

Cho fired the forward solar cannons again and again repeatedly. Glowing blasts of death and destruction streamed through space, turning the larger, slower maneuvering Tahir Ga'Warum ship's shields a bright, glowing red.

More energy poured from the Tahir Ga'Warum's weapons array, cutting through the space between the two ships, to strike a glancing blow upon the swiftly maneuvering *Cagliostro's* shields again and again.

"Shield status?" Marek asked.

"Eighty eight percent and holding," Joanie Brevard replied. She pushed a lock of her blonde hair out of the way as her hands flew across her control panel, moving shield strength from one shield array to another.

Again and again the *Cagliostro* rocked from repeated hits by their fearsome enemy's weapons.

Matt Marek ordered, "Bring us about, Samuels. Prepare for ramming."

A collective "What?" rose from every throat on the command deck.

"Don't question me. I know what I'm doing. Aim us toward the top of their hull, directly above their bridge. Cho, continue the bombardment but concentrate all your weapons fire directly on that same area," Matt ordered.

"Okay, you're the boss." Cho shrugged.

Three more Star core missiles exploded from the bow of the *Cagliostro* and streaked toward the Tahir Ga'Warum ship's upper hull, to explode brightly upon the sinister looking craft's shields. Immediately the *Cagliostro's* solar cannons fired again, lighting up the enemy ships shields once more.

"They're returning fire," Brevard advised, and a heartbeat later the *Cagliostro* rocked once more.

"Shield status?" Marek questioned.

"Sixty percent and beginning to fall," replied Brevard, some nervousness making its way into her voice.

"Begin ramming run, Samuels," Marek ordered. "Brevard shields double front, full remaining power to forward shield arrays."

Without hesitation Barton Samuels rammed the throttles to full sub-light and the great ship leapt through space, covering the miles between the two vessels instantly.

At the last possible instant, Marek shouted, "Pull up now!"

The Cagliostro swept above the slightly larger Tahir Ga'Warum ship, its shields slamming into and skidding across the shields of the enemy ship.

The command crew aboard the *Cagliostro* was thrown about. Only their quickly deployed crash restraints saved them from injury.

The space between the two ships lit up explosively in a shower of sparks.

"Shields full rear, fire all tail cannons now!" Marek commanded, even before the *Cagliostro* had cleared the hull of the enemy vessel.

The three rearward facing tail cannons on the *Cagliostro* streamed lethal energies as they careened across the bridge area on the Tahir Ga'Warum ship.

"Status?" Matt barked.

"Our shields are down to twenty five percent, theirs are even less from that stunt," Brevard replied.

"Bring us about and continue to fire on that same area of that ship," Matt ordered.

Again the *Cagliostro* danced through space, now flying vertically on end toward their enemy and closing the distance between them quickly. The forward cannons continued to stream solar energy, splashing across the larger ship's hull repeatedly as the *Cag* drew closer.

"Matt, their powering up their forward weapons again!" Joanie Brevard exclaimed.

"It's all or nothing now. Cho, take them out, or they take us out!" Marek shouted.

Without hesitation Kenji Cho fired all forward weaponry simultaneously, keeping the solar cannons locked on target and firing repeatedly at the Tahir Ga'Warum ship's bridge.

The *Cagliostro* flew through a hail of death that burst forth from the Tahir Ga'Warum ship's weapons again and again. The *Cagliostro's* shields glowed white hot under the onslaught. The command crew knew they were mere seconds away from being destroyed.

But instead the Tahir Ga'Warum vessel suddenly and spectacularly exploded brightly. The *Cagliostro* flew past and above it once more, shuddering from the explosion of gasses from within the Tahir Ga'Warum ship's now shattered hull.

A whoop of joy burst forth from the command crew. Some shook their fists in the air at the shattered and burning image on the monitor.

Matt Marek showed no emotion and quickly turned toward Miss Wallflower. "What about the Agalum? Do they have anything to say? If they power up so much as a flashlight, we might be in trouble right now."

"No, I'm getting a communique from them now. Their quoting an ancient Earth proverb. 'The enemy of my enemy is my friend.' That's all they said," Wallflower replied.

"Okay. Keep them in sight at all times. Do not forget this little truce aside we are fighting a war against them," Matt said.

"I've got them in my firing reticule, just in case, Matt," Kenji Cho confirmed.

"Good. I need a ship wide status report, ASAP," Matt ordered, "beginning with shield and weapons status."

"Shields are down to two percent but are already beginning to climb," Brevard replied. "Weapons status is the forward solar cannons are overheated and will need at least ten minutes to cool before they can be fired again. The Star Core missile tubes however, are reloaded and ready to be fired immediately."

"Bless you, Mark Johnson," Marek muttered under his breath. "What are the Agalum doing now?"

"They're powering up their engines and appear to be ready to hyperwarp away," Brevard answered.

"Keep them in view. Any move they make that can be considered hostile must be dealt with. Do you all understand me?" Marek asked.

"They're powering up to hyperwarp right now, Matt," Brevard advised.

"I'm receiving a message, Matt," Miss Wallflower interrupted, "Until we meet again, Earthmen."

On the monitor the Agalum ship leapt through space and disappeared into hyperwarp.

"Good riddance," Matt said aloud.

"What are your orders, sir?" Lilly Wallflower asked.

"Get shields back to something that can take more damage than a handful of toothpicks being thrown at them to begin with, and then return us to Chakix. I have a feeling Mark and the rest of the crew are going to need us," Marek replied.

Chapter 39

"What are we going to do? We have to do *something*! My God, did you see that?" Robin Bikowski shouted.

"Calm down, Bikowski, give me a minute. I have to think about this," Carl Rayborn answered.

"They may not have a minute, Carl. We have to get to them fast," Bob Warrens interjected.

A man wearing an official EPIC uniform walked toward them and interrupted their conversation. "I'm Mal Cummings, and I'm the acting leader of this base. I saw what just happened with your people on your hologram display. I suggest you stand down and wait for reinforcements to get here from either your ship or another. Those… things that took them captive look like they're too much for a squad that's in as bad a shape as yours is right now. Be smart about this. Getting yourselves killed is not going to help anyone."

"To hell with that!" roared Rayborn. "Rangers, with me. Move out, weapon up, and we'll figure this out as we go, Head for the shuttle. Once there reload all weapons magazines and replace any half used power units. We may only have minutes to save them from those teleporting space vampires."

The squad of Rangers brushed past the stunned administrator and headed toward the exit to the facility.

"W-where do you think you're going? I-I'm in charge here, and I order you to stand down," Cummings stammered.

Bikowski turned toward him as she walked past in her heavy suit and said, "Stuff it, Cummings. You need to read a few pages out of Mark Johnson's leadership manual so you can see how it's actually done. If you want to hide under your desk, go ahead. The *Cagliostro's* Rangers have

287

a mission to complete. Now get outta our way or get run over."

Marcus Blum and Bob Warrens both high fived her as the group ignored the administrator and headed back out into the bright sunlight.

"That was cool an' all, but what do we do now?" Blum asked.

"Yeah how are we going to find them? They could have teleported into space already with those monsters," Bikowski said.

"It doesn't matter where they are. We can track them with our tech suits," Carl Rayborn replied.

He tapped his sleeve and worked the controls. Immediately a holographic map appeared hovering above his sleeve. On it was displayed several dots clustered together.

"That's them and they haven't left the surface yet, but they're all huddled closely together somewhere about a hundred miles from here," Rayborn advised.

"They moved already. They weren't that far from here when this all went down," Warrens commented.

"Bob's right. Those suckers TPed them away already," Bikowski agreed.

"But what's a hundred miles from here?" asked Rayborn to no one in particular, "A hidden base of their own?"

"We're gonna have to find out, chief," Marcus Blum replied.

"Yeah let's get to it," Rayborn replied as he started double timing it toward the shuttle.

"I don't think we should head there straight off," Robin Bikowski said.

"Why not?" Rayborn asked as he stepped into the shuttle.

The rest of the Rangers piled in behind them and took their seats, locking into restraint harnesses and muttering amongst themselves.

"Because we have a much tougher ship than this one not too far from here," was her reply.

"The *Stargrazer*. Smart thinking, Bikowski. At this point I'll take any advantage I can," Rayborn replied and nodded his head affirmatively.

He turned and looked over his shoulder from his pilot's chair and said, "Wings up, Rangers. It's time to bring the battle to those things."

The shuttle rose straight up and then streaked off toward the *Stargrazer*.

***

The back of the powerful, pale clawed hand slashed across Mark Johnson's face. The shock of the blow nearly made him pass out, but he fought for consciousness and won.

Mark was suspended by his arms from a mechanical rack of some kind. They were aboard a Tahir Ga'Warum ship. The walls pulsed with what looked like blood coursing through large veins, and everything around them was a bloody shade of red. Mark and the alien were the only ones in this large, dark room with the pulsing, organic walls.

"You'll...have to do...better than that, you...ghoul," Mark spat out words and blood slowly.

"You are brave, Mark Johnson," the Tahir Ga'Warum named Karem said, "but that will not save your life, nor that of your crew. You will tell me of your planet's military might and any other tactical secrets I require of you. You may resist for a time, but in the end I always have my way. I am a grand inquisitor amongst my people, after all. Even amongst my own kind I am feared and given a wide berth.

289

You will learn this slowly, and very, very painfully. Do not bother to try to escape with any of your vaunted technological devices. This room is encased within a null energy field. None of your so-called 'brilliant' technology will work within it,"

"Not that I like pain, Karem, or want to die particularly, but you better stop wasting both our times and just kill me now. You're not going to get anything out of me," Mark grunted.

"We shall see, oh brave Earthman," Karem replied and slapped Mark across the jaw again, this time sending a tooth flying out of his bloodied mouth.

Mark began to chuckle. "You're really not listening too closely, ghoul. You don't scare me. You say there are people amongst your race that fear you? I have entire intergalactic realms scared spit less of me. The Agalum speak my name in awe and fear. In two years I've destabilized their control of space. I've uncovered their vast conspiracy against my people that was undermining our space programs and I've beaten them time and time again. They thought they were the undisputed rulers of the galaxy. That was until they met me. In less than three years I've caused their empire to crumble and their hold on the galaxy to weaken. The Earth's fleet has dealt them one defeat after another now, and the face they put on all of their woes is mine. So don't tell me about how dreaded you are. You're a girl scout compared to me when it comes to being feared."

The Tahir Ga'Warum interrogator fumed. His chalk white nostrils flared and the ever present black smoke that swirled about his body seemed to grow more frenzied, more furious, mirroring Karem's own anger. He lashed out again. This time his clawed fist was balled and it collided with Mark Johnson's face painfully.

Mark's head snapped back and the restraints he was held in stretched to their limits. But then he sagged forward and hung limply, blood dripping from his open mouth.

With a slight whoosh of teleportational energy another Tahir Ga'Warum suddenly appeared from the darkness amidst a swirl of black smoke. He gripped Karem's arm before the inquisitor could deliver another painful blow. "The human is of no use to us if he is dead, Karem."

Karem stared at the newcomer with wide eyed anger, but then almost immediately softened. He still pulled his arm free of his companion's grip before replying, "The Earthman called me something that I do not understand, but still it angers me. I know it was derogatory," he hissed.

"What was it? What did this weak Earther call you?"

"He said-he said I was a 'girl scout.' I do not know what that means but I do not like the sound of it, at all."

"Stay your hand, Karem. It does none of us any good if he is dead. His mind is said to be brilliant, at least amongst his kind. To plumb those depths would mean our victory would come all the sooner over the Earthers, especially now that the Agalum have all but fallen to our power."

"You are, of course, correct, Jarrell," Karem allowed. "I will await his return to consciousness."

"What of the others? Perhaps the female may be tortured before him. A bit of bloodletting may go a long way in loosening this male's tongue. He seems to have a connection to her," Jarrell wondered aloud.

"That is perhaps an avenue we may look into, when this dog reawakens from my gentle touch." Karem yanked Mark's head upward by the hair. Mark was out cold and his mouth dripped a long gob of blood to the floor.

"Such fragile creatures. One wonders how they could have become a threat to anyone," Jarrell conjectured.

"It is just another example of how weak the creatures in this dimension are, and how ripe they are for our subjugation," Karem said. "The Agalum have proven how weak they are already. They have been defeated by our forces in a relatively short amount of time."

"That is true, oh supreme inquisitor, but bear in mind that they were fighting the Earthmen at the same time they were engaging our forces," Jarrell replied.

"True, Jarrell. Perhaps they would not have fallen so quickly against our might if we had attacked them without the interference of the Earthers; but do not be fooled, the outcome would have been the same. We are the supreme conquerors in our own dimension, the supreme predators, and we will be in this one as well. Entire civilizations will become our food supply. The blood in their veins will power our own life force for unending millennia, but I believe I will start with this one. If he will never give in and supply us with his secrets what use will he be? Perhaps I can gain his knowledge by eating his heart, or at least his throat," Karem finished horrifically.

He grabbed Mark's limp hanging head and turned his throat toward his own mouth, and then he opened his jaws, which distended horribly, showing rows of deadly teeth.

He reared back and his mouth began to descend toward Mark's helpless neck when the entire ship they were within began to shudder violently.

Karem paused and looked toward his companion. "What was that?" he bellowed in surprise.

"I-I do not know," Jarrell answered.

Again the ship shook, and this time alarm klaxons went off across the length of the parked vessel.

"You fool! We are under attack!" roared Karem.

Chapter 40

The Tahir Ga'Warum ship was sitting on the surface of Chakix, out in the open. Soaring down from the heavens above came the *Stargrazer*, in full camouflage mode, its forward solar cannons blazing.

At the controls Carl Rayborn and Robin Bikowski rolled the sleek ship through the air avoiding return fire from the Tahir Ga'Warum ship.

"Concentrate fire on its engines, Bikowski. We don't want that thing getting into the air or worse yet into space," Rayborn ordered.

Bikowski nodded and spat back, "I'm on it, Carl. Where's the shuttle?" she asked.

Two blasts from the grounded enemy vessel rocked the sixty foot long ship with narrow misses.

"Shuttle is landing now and ground troops are about to disembark. They're getting close with those shots-they're targeting where we're shooting from," Rayborn replied.

"Yes, I know," the female Ranger replied.

"They're starting to power up their engines now. Target their exhaust ports. That should put them out of commission, at least for a few minutes," Rayborn advised.

"I'm on it," Bikowski repeated.

Twin blasts of solar energy leaped from the dual cannons under the *Stargrazer's* nose and sliced into the aft section of the horrible looking blood red Tahir Ga'Warum ship. It sat in an empty area the Tahir Ga'Warum had cleared of trees and vegetation with their own powerful weapons. Blackened earth spread around the ship for a quarter of a mile.

"Star Core missiles away," Bikowski said.

Two of the powerful missiles flew from the *Stargrazer's* belly as it passed overhead, directly into the engines of the downed vessel. The rear of the Tahir Ga'Warum ship bounced once into the air and then dropped heavily down to the ground, leaving a cloud of debris billowing from beneath the vessel.

"They're down," Rayborn announced, "and they're not getting back into the air anytime soon."

"I was worried about the ship exploding with our people onboard," Bikowski confided.

"I was hoping it was too big for that to happen especially since their engines were not running, at least not at first. Now it's up to Blum, Lee, Warrens, and the rest of the team to see this through," Rayborn concluded.

***

Aboard the Tahir Ga'Warum ship the decidedly frightening looking warriors began to arm themselves and teleport out of the ship. Once outside they were surprised as forty Rangers attacked from within their camouflage fields. Unseen and deadly, they fired blasters again and again at the just arriving ghoulish aliens. Some were using rifles; some were clad in heavy attack suits and were meeting Tahir Ga'Warum troopers head on, delivering powerful blows to the surprised aliens' bodies.

Marcus Blum hefted a personal cannon like Red used. He dropped to a knee and fired into the chest of an advancing Tahir Ga'Warum warrior, blasting him from his feet and into the side of the ship with a wet splat.

Now the battle was joined in earnest as both sides careened toward one another. Energy blasts seared the air from both sides of the battle and teleporting aliens were met time and again by vengeful Rangers who attacked invisibly. The Rangers were outnumbered with that equation going badly against them as more and more Tahir

Ga'Warum appeared from the ship, but they seemed to have the advantage with their camouflage.

***

Jarrell teleported in a blast of black, noxious smoke from the interrogation chamber as Karem stood angrily and shook his fist impotently at the events taking place around him. He crushed a communication device in his fist that he had just been informed of the attack upon his ship on.

"Not so good to be on the receiving end of a beating, is it, you monster?" a voice mocked from behind him.

Karem spun and his eyes went wide in recognition. Mark Johnson stood behind him, free of his bonds. In his hands he held a sword that had been hanging on the wall of the chamber in a display.

"Wh-how did you get free?" the astonished alien asked.

"Not all of my inventions are hard technology. This suit has simple vials of a powerful acid in each sleeve's epaulets. The tech suit itself is impervious to the acid, but obviously not your metal bonds you had me held in. When you closed the metal bands on my wrists you broke the tubes containing the acid within the sleeves and it went to work right away. I purposely made you angry so you'd put strain on the bonds you had me held in by hitting me repeatedly. Painful, but it worked," Mark concluded. He wiped a trickle of blood from his jaw and grinned slightly.

"I am vastly superior to you, Earthman. My strength is a hundred times yours, at least. You have no chance against my vastly superior might. I will grind your skull to paste," Karem growled.

"Come get me," Mark replied.

With a howl of rage Karem disappeared in a blast of smoke.

Instantly Mark spun the blade he was holding around behind him in a frenzied arc, to impale the surprised Karem

295

who appeared a nanosecond after he teleported away directly behind Mark, his jaws set wide to bite down on Mark's unprotected throat. The sword dripped black gore. It was embedded in the surprised Tahir Ga'Warum's own throat. Frantically he clawed at it, and Mark pushed against it, forcing the ghoulish creature to the floor.

With an angered snarl Mark snapped the blade free. Then he said, "You lose, monster. This galaxy is not you and your kind's buffet table. So much for the 'Grand Inquisitor'."

Karem stared with hate filled eyes as the puddle of ichor about his throat grew exponentially, and then those eyes dimmed and saw no more. With a final deflating sigh the alien lie still and perished where he lay.

Mark stared at the corpse at his feet for a few seconds more; making certain his enemy was truly dead. Then he sprinted for the dimly lit exit from the room amidst its dull red glow. Near the doorway was a table of sorts, organic looking and pulsing on its own, but atop the table lay Mark's blaster and weapons belt.

Quickly he checked it all and once again secured the belt about his waist. He gripped his blaster with a strong familiarity.

Setting himself, Mark burst through the doorway, kicking the door aside and stepping determinedly into the hallway of the alien vessel. Tahir Ga'Warum were all about him, running in both directions, but they ignored him as if he wasn't there.

'Of course,' he thought to himself, *'the tech suit is back online now that I'm out of that room and these things can't detect me yet.'*

Deftly he sidestepped more of the aliens who ran past in a form of controlled chaos. Again and again explosions could be heard coming from outside.

'I've got to find the others,' he thought.

Instantly a familiar female voice replied in his mind, *'Mark? Where are you? Are you all right?'*

'Ariel!' he practically shouted aloud. *'Yes, I'm fine. Where are you all?'*

'Here,' she replied and an image appeared in his mind of exactly where the others were being held.

'I'm on my way!' he mentally shouted.

Mark Johnson ran invisibly through the ship, narrowly avoiding charging Tahir Ga'Warum troops who brushed past him in groups. Others teleported in and out, moving to other parts of the ship. Once he saw several bloody and wounded dripping black ichor teleport in to what he could only assume was an infirmary of sorts. He ignored them and continued toward his destination.

Mark pulled up short before a doorway that he immediately recognized from the picture Ariel had put in his mind. Inside he saw Ariel and the rest of the crew being held in clear pods that he recognized from the last time he had been aboard a Tahir Ga'Warum ship half a year earlier. Four of the smoke encircled warriors stood in the room staring at their helpless captives.

With a roar Mark exploded into the room, shooting his blaster at the surprised aliens and killing three of them almost instantly. His blaster beams careened about the chamber, slicing through several of the pods holding his companions.

The fourth ducked, and avoided the blast meant for him. Instantly he teleported from where he was standing to in front of Mark and before Mark could react he gripped him by the throat and lifted the *Cagliostro's* captain into the air. "You did well, human, for one so weak. But your run is over. I should have let Karem kill you while he had

297

the chance. Instead I stayed his hand. I won't make that same mistake twice."

"You're Jarrell," Mark grunted between straining teeth. He held the alien's powerful arm with both hands, trying to break his grip. Jarrell stared at him bemusedly. But then he noticed Mark was no longer struggling. Instead he began to smile. Jarrell spun about to see what his supposed captive was smiling at.

The powerful fist that connected with his face snapped Jarrell's head around. He instantly dropped Mark, who landed on the floor cat-like but still gasping for air.

Mark looked up as he rubbed his throat to see a very enraged Dan Sledge raise both of his mighty Jovian fists above his head and pound them down upon Jarrell's shoulders, driving him through the suddenly shattered and splintered floor.

The shocked alien disappeared to another deck far below.

"Are you all right?" Red asked. He helped Mark to his feet.

"I am now," Mark replied. Ariel ran into his arms and kissed him quickly, but with fire.

"I'm glad to see you too," Mark said with a grin.

The ship rumbled about them once again.

"Let's get outta here," Eddie advised. "This place is under attack, probably by our own people."

"No kiddin', hotshot," Dan grunted. He threw Eddie his blaster from another organic table that held their weapons.

Everyone snapped their weapons belts in place, pulled their hoods and goggles back over their faces, and activated their camouflage units.

"Red, take point. Eddie, follow him. The rest of you Rangers back them up," Mark ordered the ten warriors who had accompanied them through this mission.

298

Liked the well-oiled machine they were, the Rangers fell into familiar roles as the group invisibly stepped into the empty hallway.

'*How do we get out of this place?*' Eddie asked within Ariel's reestablished telepathic link.

'*This way,*' she replied.

'*How do you know?*' Mark asked.

'*I was tapping into their minds when we were in those tubes. There's an airlock this way,*' Ariel answered.

Mark uneasily followed Red and the Rangers after Ariel put the airlocks location into their minds.

'*I'm a little concerned that you were poking around in these creatures minds. Did you forget what happened the last time you tried that with Chakix's red skinned people? I thought we talked about you doing this, as in never again?*' Mark said. Ariel ignored him and continued on.

'*This ship seems like it's empty,*' said Red.

'*Good. The less resistance the better,*' Mark answered.

'*Maybe fer you, but me? I just want to crush some heads at this point. These guys are even lower on the ladder than the Agalum, as far as I'm concerned,*' Danny grumbled.

They arrived at the airlock and it was open. Outside they heard the sounds of battle.

'*Uh-oh,*' Ariel thought. '*That sounds like a lot more than just forty of our Rangers in battle.*'

'*Agreed, Ari,*' Mark answered as he pushed past the others and cautiously stepped outside.

He stopped where he was invisibly standing. Above flew not just the *Stargrazer*, but their shuttle as well as several of the local base's two man attack craft. Solar blasts flew from the bows of the ships flying past, skewering the frenzied Tahir Ga'Warum where they ran. Many teleported away, but then would be fired upon when they reappeared elsewhere a moment later.

On the ground, EPIC soldiers from the base stood shoulder to shoulder with *Cagliostro* Rangers, both heavy suit wearing and regular tech suit garbed Rangers alike. A burly Tahir Ga'Warum thundered straight toward the stealthed command crew from the *Cagliostro*.

"I got this," Danny announced.

Deactivating his camouflage unit, the powerful engineer/pilot seemed to appear from nowhere within the charging Tahir Ga'Warum's path. The creature's eyes went wide at the sight of Dan, who drew his powerful fist back and unleashed it directly into the alien's face.

The powerful alien stopped as if he had run headlong into a brick wall and simply crumbled to the ground, insensate.

"That felt good," Dan said, while wiping his hands together. He was grinning from ear to ear.

"Rangers, join the rest of the EPIC forces and our people. Let's wrap this up and get out of here," Mark ordered.

"I don't think we have to, Mark," Eddie said. He was looking skyward and pointed at something shimmering into view.

A voice thundered over the battlefield. It was Major Matt Marek's. "Tahir Ga'Warum forces stand down or be obliterated. This is your only warning."

The *Cagliostro* had returned, and her acting Commander was not playing around.

***

Twenty four hours later the crew of the *Cagliostro* was back aboard her and the remaining Tahir Ga'Warum were in custody at the Chakix base.

"Take us out of here, Mr. Sledge," Mark commanded.

300

"Believe me, boss, wit' pleasure," Dan replied.

Dan slid the holographic throttle forward on his board and the ship accelerated toward space.

"Full throttle toward Earth, Dan. Ariel, scan all EPIC frequencies continuously. I want to know why we haven't heard anything from Earth since we arrived at Chakix," Mark ordered.

Dr. Ann Troiano, entered the command deck from the maglovator and said, "Our exo-biologist, Madison Monroe, is going over everything we recorded about the Tahir Ga'Warum. He thinks he might be able to get an idea on how their teleporting ability works, but he'll probably need you to confer with him," she said to Mark.

"That's fine, Ann, but after we get home. I'm more concerned with what's going on there right now," Mark replied.

"Chakix never appeared again," Ann said. It was a statement, not a question.

"Correct," Mark answered. "After Red blew a hole through the giant red ape's chest, she never appeared again. Maybe it takes time for her to regenerate her connection to the people and creatures there. Or maybe killing the ape while she was inside it, controlling it, killed her too, but I kind of doubt it."

"Mark!" Ariel shouted, "I-I just received a message from Earth."

Mark quickly stood from his command chair and crossed the distance to her console in two steps. "What is it, Ariel?" he asked.

She spun her seat toward him, her face ghostly white. She hesitated a moment and then finally stammered, "M-Mark, Earth has fallen. The Tahir Ga'Warum have taken the planet."

Ralph L. Angelo Jr.

The End, for now…

Cagliostro Chronicles III Appendix

Agalum-Race of manipulative aliens bent on controlling earth's destiny for their own sake.

Atlow- tentacled leader of the Korai Vessel the Cagliostro rescues.

Bikowski, Robin-Female Security Ranger.

Blum, Marcus-heavy suit wearing Ranger.

Brevard, Joanie-Security woman on Red's team.

Captain Nagata-Captain of the *Coronado*

Cho, Kenji-Pilot on secondary command crew.

Cirillo, Anthony-Scientist aboard the *Cagliostro*

Delrin-Last surviving Plaxian.

Dr. Alan Rothstein-secondary doctor aboard the *Cagliostro*.

Jacobs, Ben-Tertiary command crew leader.

Jarrell-Tahir Ga'Warum warrior and confidant to Karem.

Karem-Tahjir Ga'Warum Grand Inquisitor, an interrogator and torturer.

Korai- Gold skinned alien race with tentacles for hands and a stalk they stand on with small tentacles at its bottom they use as feet.

Lee, Toby-A Security Ranger

Plaxia-Ancient World of the Plaxian people who were great builders, scientists and engineers.

Rangers-what the security force aboard the *Cagliostro* is now known by.

Rayborn, Carl- Security Ranger.

Tahir Ga'Warum- Alien race that is battling the Agalum.

Samuels, Barton-Pilot on the *Cagliostro*.

Smithson-Ranger

Volgers, Cane-Ranger.
Warrens, Bob- Ranger.

If you liked this book, make sure you read the first book in the series, 'The Cagliostro Chronicles' Available at Amazon.com and other fine retailers. ISBN# 978-0692255506

Ralph L. Angelo Jr.

Be sure to read 'The Cagliostro Chronicles II: Conflagration' too. Available at Amazon.com and other fine retailers. ISBN# 978-0615854427

Ralph L. Angelo Jr.

Other books by Ralph L. Angelo Jr

- Redemption of the Sorcerer, The Crystalon Saga, Book One: A mighty sorcerer and ruler of his world is deposed and exiled to a world identical to his own, save for one difference, magic doesn't exist there. Now he must fight against seemingly insurmountable odds to regain his powers in time to save both parallel universes from utter destruction. ISBN# 0615763030
- Torahg the Warrior, Sword of Vengeance: In a land before recorded time, a world of warriors, monsters and wizards, a young prince is framed for the death of his father by his own evil brother and riven to exile. For twenty long years he wanders the world, until finally he is coaxed into returning to his homeland seeking justice for his father and bloody revenge for himself.
  ISBN# 1490516263
- The Cagliostro Chronicles: In the depths of space awaits danger for all mankind. When man's first faster than light space flight begins, it opens up a whole new universe for mankind. But it is a universe filled hostile enemies as well as a century-long conspiracy against humanity. Will mankind survive? ISBN# 0615854427
- Help! They're All Out to Get Me! The Motorcyclists Guide to Surviving the Everyday World: A Non-fiction motorcycle safety and

instructional manual for the new and returning riders. A 'Must Read' for those seeking to better their motorcycling experience. ISBN# 0615756786

- My Enemy, Myself, The Crystalon Saga, Book Two: It has been two years since Crystalon defeated the mad warlord Maceyis. Much has changed in that time. Crystalon has become his adopted world's hidden mystic guardian, protecting the Earth from those who would threaten it with evil, sorcerous intent.
  Until a visitor from his past, one he never expected to see again would appear within his very home. Now he and his companions must travel between worlds to his home dimension, a universe where he is hated and feared, to face a threat that dwarfs any challenge he has ever faced before. The challenge of an enemy who wears his very face. The challenge of 'My Enemy, Myself'. ISBN# 149950523X

- The Cagliostro Chronicles II: Conflagration
  The star cruiser Cagliostro must land on an unknown alien world to make repairs after an almost disastrous battle in space only to discover a new threat to Earth and humanity. But alone and unable to return to Earth until they can complete repairs will they be enough to stop this new threat by the Agalum empire? And what of the strange new foes they encounter upon this world of prehistoric monsters and aliens? It's more fast paced, interstellar action in the sequel to the best-

selling 'The Cagliostro Chronicles'. ISBN#
978-0692255506.

- Hyperforce
  A team of fledgling superheroes must join
  together to face a threat from the stars as a
  young alien prince crash-lands on Earth seeking
  aid against a terrible enemy. The team that will
  become known as 'Hyperforce' will face this
  and many other threats in their debut novel.
  Join Captain Power, Solaron, Dragonfly,
  Starbolt, Creature, Silver Shadow and Stryker
  as they seek their place in a strange new and
  ever evolving world. An action and adventure
  lover's paradise. If you loved silver and bronze
  age comics, you're going to love Hyperforce!
  ISBN# 978-0692302156

www.ingramcontent.com/pod-product-compliance
Lightning Source LLC
Chambersburg PA
CBHW030022180626
46810CB00001B/166